MASKS OF DEVOTION

TOGETHER WE STAND - BOOK FIVE

MAGGIE COLE

PULSE PRESS

FREE GIFT FOR YOU

Dear Romance Addicts,

A while back we had Team Week. This was in my Romance Addicts group (click to join if you aren't a member and want to have some fun or go to https://www.facebook.com/groups/maggiecole/) At the time, only four books in my All In series were published.

Team Tom and Liv took the gold! But Teams Meg and Collin, Jack and Maddie, and Blake and Laura all gave them a run for their money!

The combination of teams created these specifics for me to create a story around:

Characters: Dakota Jinx and Logan Alexander

Theme: Brother's Best Friend

Five Props: Tattoos (important to character), Journal, An important heirloom (not jewelry), Pantyhose (40's vintage style with the line up the back), Ice 🧊

Location: Montauk Point Lighthouse, Long Island New York

Click here for your freebie short story just for fun!

XOXO -

Maggie Cole

PS - Make sure you check out the Sneak Peek for Roots of Vengeance, book six, of the Together We Stand series, after the Epilogue.

To my readers,
May you fall in love with the Brooks family as much as I have.
XOXO
Maggie Cole

PROLOGUE

Kade Coral

ESPIONAGE CREATES SECRETS AND LIES SO DEEP SOMETIMES YOU have to remind yourself what side you're on and why you're doing what you're doing. It's a labyrinth of twists and turns, and, to get through it, you have to stay focused at all times.

Interpol warned me in my training the enemy will become human, likable, and at times I might become sympathetic to their cause. They made it clear my life would become as classified as my assignments, but they didn't warn me those I trust the most—the friends who have always been family to me—would feel hurt, betrayed, and sometimes question my motives.

Protocol about sleeping with the enemy to gain access to information vital to your mission is clear. But there are no rules or guidelines about how to protect your heart or the woman's you love.

Gracie Brooks has always been in my life. Her oldest brother Hudson and I met when we were four, and, the day she was born, he spent the night at my house. The next day, when his parents brought Gracie home, I remember staring at her in awe.

I'm an only child, and the Brooks children are the siblings I've never had. Gracie and Gabriella were like my little sisters. But Gracie grew up. And the moment I noticed her as a woman and not a girl created an ache in my body I hadn't felt before.

Everyone thinks I went away for college, and I did...until the CIA showed up in my dorm room during the second month of my studies. The military needed the patents I created, and they wanted me to fly around the world into military bases and teach the top leaders and teams how to tap further into the cyber world of evil.

They offered me so much money, it didn't make sense to stay in school. Plus, it sounded a lot cooler than sitting in class listening to a boring professor whose IQ was lower than mine.

One day, I was surfing the dark web and discovered information to take down several gangs. The CIA moved me into the gang unit, and I returned home to Florida. Several years passed, and Interpol showed up at my house. What they offered sounded pretty exciting and would give me more clearance to help destroy the Twisted Hearts. The gang leader grew up on the same island I did and was secretly making significant headway into international cybercrimes.

Shortly after I joined Interpol, I was at the Brooks' for a family party and Gracie strolled in. I had to remind myself she was Hudson's little sister—hell, I always thought of her as my little sister—and pry my gaze away from her while trying not to kill the loser boyfriend she had brought to the party.

I tried to stifle my feelings for her. So, I fought it for years, secretly pining for Gracie and trying to date other women to forget about her. But my desire for her only grew.

Over the years, flirting became a new normal for us—when no one else was around. When the family was present, we both acted like we always did. Hudson would kill me, not to mention

Ryland, if they discovered I had feelings for Gracie. There was bro-code in play and it was something you didn't break.

But it got harder. No matter who I dated, she was all I wanted. Numerous times, I would be out with a girl and run into Gracie. Both our dates would end up leaving early, and we would spend all night talking wherever we were. I'd take her home, drop her off at her door, and restrain myself from kissing her.

And one night, I tapped into Satan's well. We shared a kiss so riveting, I was breathless and craving more. When I got into my car, I spent over an hour talking myself out of going back to her door and asking to come in.

So I stayed away from Gracie for several weeks, obsessing over her and scolding myself for not being able to control my feelings for her. But the moment I ran into her, my desire for her won, and, without thinking about why I should leave, I made a beeline toward her.

That night, I didn't take her home. I took her to my hotel room. Several hours later, I got instructions from Interpol I needed to get on a flight to Europe for a new assignment.

And it was permanent which meant years. How long? No one could tell me. Gracie slept in my arms, and I felt like my world was crashing in around me. Not going wasn't an option—the skills I have, no one else does. The intel I had on the Twisted Hearts and all the evil they spewed into the world, I couldn't ignore. They needed to be taken down because their plans could destroy humanity as we know it.

Plus, I worked for Interpol. I'm a trained spy who has clearance to kill. You don't just get out.

When Gracie woke up, I told her I was leaving in six hours. I died that day. So did she. I saw it. Not a day has passed in three years I don't think about her, or bring up her Instagram account, or re-read text messages we spent years exchanging while flirting on the down-low.

One day, while digging into the dark net on the Twisted

Hearts, a guy who I'd seen on a lot of her Instagram photos, Fisher Corbyn, popped up. My gut instantly dropped. I had already run a background check on him because I kept seeing him on her feed. On paper, he was a wealthy businessman. I assumed I couldn't stand him because he was into Gracie.

But I was wrong. My distaste wasn't only about his interest in her. I should have listened to my gut.

For close to two years, I friended Fisher, doing "business" with him, and all the other things I needed to do to get into his trust zone. He's trying to claim Gracie, and by the time I finish with him, he's going to be behind bars for life or dead. I'll be more than happy to put the bullet in his head.

Interpol finally agreed to let me return to Florida, and I only have one mission in doing so. To win Gracie forever and keep her out of harm's way. And I'm going to have to do it without Fisher catching wind of anything. He's out to make Gracie his forever, and he'll stop at nothing to get her.

Espionage is the legal means I have to go after Fisher. But this isn't just about business anymore. This is personal. My woman is the only reason it counts.

Gracie

Three and a Half Years Ago

MUSIC POUNDS LOUD IN MY EARS, VIBRATING MY BONES. TED LEANS into my ear and screams, "I'll get us a drink. What do you want?"

"Water." I don't drink a lot. The summer heat is thick, and people are wall to wall on the rooftop bar. Alcohol is the last thing I want tonight.

Several of my friends are here with Ted and me. He's asked me out numerous times, and I finally accepted to try and get Kade off my mind.

Kade. My oldest brother's best friend. A member of our family and the guy who's been a part of my life since I was born.

And the hottest, sexiest, only man alive who burns my loins at the mere thought of him.

We've flirted for years but never crossed the line...until a few weeks ago.

As usual, we were texting about our dates, both dropping

enough hints where we would be. Sure enough, Kade showed up at the exact restaurant.

Like other times, we ended up at the same table, and both our dates eventually took the hint and excused themselves.

We talked all night. Kade escorted me to the front door of my condo, which wasn't unusual. But this time, I didn't go in. I stepped forward and tilted my head up, and everything I had assumed was proven wrong.

Like a puzzle, our bodies synced perfectly together. His arms, which bulge with muscle, wrapped around me and sent the flutters already tingling into zing mode. When his fingers slid into my hair and palmed my head, I trembled. That was before he kissed me.

Lips, tongues, and flesh created a singing fire of throbbing pulses. My insides quivered and I had to try to remember how to breathe when he released me.

"Good night, Gracie," he said with smoldering heat in his dark eyes.

"Good night," I whispered, slowly turned, went inside, and sat on the floor against my door for hours replaying our kiss.

Yep, I was wrong. Kissing Kade wasn't nice. It wasn't great. It was earth-shattering, panty-dripping, melt-in-your-mouth deliciousness I didn't know existed.

Our kiss was several weeks ago. Since then, neither Kade nor I have texted the other.

Ted hands me a bottle of water. I take a big sip, trying to cool off from the heat and thinking about Kade's lips and body against mine.

Then I see him. He steps off the elevator, and I have to blink, wondering if I'm imagining things.

I'm in St. Petersburg. It's about a half hour away from Anna Maria, the island we live on. We haven't had any contact to know the other person will be here.

Kade's taller than most guys, and I spot him first.

Butterflies take off in my stomach. My date yells something else in my ear, but I don't comprehend anything. All I can do is gawk at Kade.

He scans the bar, and the moment his eyes lock into mine, he freezes. But it's a brief pause before he shoves through the crowd. Within seconds, he's in front of me. The expression in his eyes I saw after our kiss is there, and he wraps his arm around my waist to lead me away.

Ted steps in front of us and shouts something I can't make out to Kade.

Kade shakes his head, says something in his ear, and I give Ted a "I'm sorry" look.

Ted is still not satisfied with whatever Kade said to him and gets angrier, but Kade is much stronger and bigger than him. Another one of our friends, Demitri, steps forward and yells in my ear, "Why is Kade here?"

"I need to go. Tell Ted I'm sorry, but it is never going to be."

Demitri scrunches his face in disapproval but then maneuvers Ted aside. Kade guides me to the wall in the corner of the bar. Pressed against the brick, Kade stands in front of me with his arms on each side of my frame.

"What are you doing here?" I scream through the music.

His eyes roam my face, and he licks his lips before swallowing hard. Energy hums off him, crashing into my cells, lighting me up like a blowtorch.

Before I can think any further, I cup his face and our lips and bodies mold together. The zing, the zang, the voltage of power crashes through me, and the throbbing I always feel around him intensifies.

His erection presses against my stomach, and I crave it. The scent of his skin makes my nostrils flare. His tongue, urgently slipping around mine, sends so much heat to my loins I moan. If the wall and Kade weren't holding me up, I would fall from my knees going weak.

Kade's lips move across my cheek and over to my ear. "Want to go?"

All I can do is bob my head.

He guides me through the sea of people and into the elevator. It's crowded, and he stands with his arms locked around my waist and his erection I'm dying to experience, digging into my spine.

My heart is thumping but so is Kade's. It beats into my shoulder, and I slide my hands on the sides of his thighs.

He kisses the top of my head, and the elevator opens on floor ten.

"Excuse us," he bellows.

He has a room here?

Please let it be. Please, please, please.

When we step out, he leads me down the hall, slides a key into the lock, and holds the door open for me to go in.

Every butterfly in my stomach multiplies. It's not the *what are you doing* nerves. Instead, it's *this is finally going to happen* nerves.

For the last few years, I've fantasized about Kade way too much. It's influenced my ability to have a real boyfriend. No one can measure up to Kade's dark and handsome features, or muscles I want to lick all night, or arms I imagine wrapping around me.

Kade is the smartest guy I've ever met, but there's a sense of bad boy about him, and I'm not sure why. He's never been in trouble, and his moral compass is higher than most, but something about him screams if anyone ever tried to do anything to me, he'd kill them.

I don't have any reason to worry about anyone hurting me, but it still makes him even sexier.

"What are you doing here?" I repeat.

"I've been here for work the last few days."

"Oh." My pulse races as we lock gazes.

"I've missed you."

"Why didn't you text or call?"

"Because I'm in love with you, and your brothers are going to be pissed."

He loves me?

My feelings aren't just one-sided fantasies?

"I guess since I love you, too, they'll need to get over it."

His lips turn up and he steps forward. "Did you say you love me, too?"

"Yeah."

"I'll take a few black eyes from your brothers if you want to stop playing games and make this real."

New flutters erupt. I step as close to him as I can. "Real as in us together. No more fake dates?"

"Yes. I want you and me only."

"Me, too."

His grin widens, and his massive hand firmly holds my head. He dips down, and his lips brush mine then he murmurs, "I want you so much, Gracie. You're all I think about."

"You're all I think about."

The slow burn of his kiss smolders, and the flames grow hotter and more intense as he deepens every stroke of his tongue and caress of his hand.

Our clothes come off, and warm flesh stretched across muscle embraces me and holds me tight.

All things pleasurable up to this moment in my life take a back seat. Nothing compares to the touch of his fingers, the brush of his lips, or the swipe of his tongue. And when his tongue moves to my sex, it's like the sky has opened, and I've entered the gates of heaven.

I'm trembling and gasping for air, tugging his thick hair then pushing his head against me. "Don't stop. Oh God. Kade!"

His tongue flicks faster, his mouth sucks me harder, and heat and adrenaline whip through me while dizziness overpowers me.

"Kade!"

He grips my hips tighter, holding my shaking body into his face while continuously making me climax. I don't know where one ends and the next begins. I think I might pass out. The sounds flying out of my mouth are incoherent, and my eyes keep rolling.

"You're beautiful, Gracie," he mumbles when I come down.

Bursts of tingles explode on my skin as his lips make contact. He shimmies up my torso, worshiping my stomach, the curve of my waist, the length of my cleavage. Then his tongue traces the edge of my puckered nipple before drawing it into his mouth.

He's a sex god. He has to be.

I urgently stick my tongue in his mouth, fresh from my orgasms, throbbing for his hard and dripping with pre-cum cock.

I slide my hand to him, dragging my fingering on the vein of his shaft.

His deep, throaty groans escalate my need for him to take possession of me.

"Kade, I want you in me. Please," I whisper.

He holds my head with both his hands. "I didn't come prepared for this. I don't have a condom."

What? Oh no. No, no, no, no!

"I'm clean. Are you clean?"

"Yeah."

"I have an IUD."

He closes his eyes. "Gracie—"

"Please. I'm okay with it if you are."

"You sure?"

"Yes."

A shift of his hips, a bend of my knees, and Kade slides into me, taking me to heaven.

"Oh fuck, Gracie," he growls.

"Oh God, you're so big," I pant.

"You okay?" He stills.

"Yeah. Oh God...Kade...you feel so good," I whisper and wrap my legs around him as his length and girth fills me like never before.

His lips devour mine while he thrusts inside me, slowly at first, then with more speed and force.

The hotel air conditioner goes off, but I barely hear it through our moans and sound of our flesh slapping against each other. The smell of Kade's skin and our sex flares in my nostrils, stirring more flutters in my stomach.

If pleasure could be wrapped up, I would choose this moment as I'm filled with a never-ending cyclone of endorphins.

Our skin slides from sweat, and, like a dog needing water, I lick the salty drop running down Kade's neck.

He thrusts harder, and I unravel, spasming hard on his cock in the only orgasm I've ever experienced during intercourse.

I'm oscillating in his arms and whimpering, trying to take lungfuls of air when he explodes, pumping his hot seed deep in me and stretching my walls into another intense orgasm.

We lie collapsed against each other, and I'm the happiest I've ever been, safe and loved in his arms.

"I'll never get enough of you, Gracie," he mumbles and kisses me with new fervor.

His cock never leaves me, and he hardens again. The bliss train starts all over, and for hours we stay glued to each other, making love and having one climax after another.

When we finally stop, it's early in the morning. He wraps me in his strong arms, and I fall asleep, dreaming of my future with him.

But there is no Kade and Gracie. It is only a dream.

When I wake up, Kade wears a dazed expression and stares at his phone with a clenched jaw. I trace his jawbone. "Hey. Is everything all right?"

He closes his eyes, and his face pales.

I sit up. "Kade, what is it?"

Slowly, he turns to me. "I have to leave in six hours."

"We can go now if you need to. I'm done getting my beauty rest," I tease.

He closes his eyes again and sighs then opens them and focuses on the ceiling.

My gut drops.

"I have to fly to Europe. They reassigned me."

Europe? Reassigned?

"What are you talking about? And who are they?"

"My job."

My heart races. "How long are you going to be gone?"

"I'm not sure, but it's a long-term assignment, so I'm guessing years."

Suddenly, it's hard to breathe. "Is this your way of getting rid of me?"

He cups my face. "No, Gracie. I love you."

"I don't understand what is happening."

"I didn't ever assume they would move me. I'm so sorry."

"Take me with you then."

"I can't."

"Why not? If you love me, then—"

"I can't, Gracie. It's too dangerous where I'm going. You have to stay here."

"Too dangerous? How is making patents and doing cyber stuff dangerous?"

He runs his hand through his hair and concentrates on the ceiling again.

"Kade, answer me," I desperately plead.

He blinks hard. "I can't answer your questions. I wish I could, but I can't."

"So you're going to fuck me and leave?" I hurl at him as a tear falls down my cheek.

He scoops me up and holds me on his lap. His arms tighten around me, and his hand holds my head to his chest. "I'm so sorry. This isn't what I want."

"Then quit," I demand in a shaky voice.

"I can't."

"Yes, you can."

"No, I can't," he says sternly.

He's leaving. You screwed him all night, and now he's moving in six hours?

I try to escape his hold, but he clutches me tighter.

"Let me go, Kade."

"No. Gracie, listen to me."

I stop moving, but my insides are a quivering mess of fear and sorrow.

"I didn't anticipate this. I don't want this. I want you. I'm so sorry. I love you. Don't doubt my feelings for you, please."

"You're going to go?" I whisper.

"I have to."

Anger matching how I feel about Beckett being in prison takes hold. I escape his grasp and throw on my clothes.

He jumps up and grabs my arm to stop me, but I slap him with my other hand.

Kade retreats, stunned, then inhales deeply.

I want to tell him I'm sorry for hitting him, but my anger doesn't allow it. I finish getting dressed and head toward the door.

"Gracie, where are you going?"

Holding my hand in the air, I wave as tears fall down my cheeks so quickly, I can hardly see. "Bye, Kade. Have a nice life."

"Stop, Gracie," he says, but I step out the door, and he's still naked.

When I get to the lobby, I go into the women's room and throw water on my face, sobbing, and trying to make myself presentable enough to stand outside and wait for an Uber.

Am I ever going to see him again?

Why doesn't he quit if he loves me?

He doesn't love you. He only said it to get you to sleep with him.

You're such an idiot.

I finally calm down enough to go outside to find transportation home. Kade is leaning against the brick wall. As soon as he sees me, he puts his arm around me and leads me to his car, which the valet has parked.

Not knowing what else to do and with the idea this may be the last time I ever see him on replay, I allow him to put me in his car.

He quickly gets in. The entire ride, he holds my hand and kisses it from time to time as I gaze out the window, crying.

When we arrive at my condo, neither of us gets out.

"Gracie—"

I hold my hand in the air. "Please don't."

Tears and pain fill his eyes. I must be a masochist because I reach for his head and kiss him one last time. He holds my head firmly to his and whispers, "I love you."

"But it's not enough, is it?"

"That doesn't have anything—"

"I have to go." I quickly retreat and get out of the car.

He follows, but I spin. "Don't walk me upstairs. It's over. You made your choice. I wish you lots of success and hope the money you earn will make you happy."

He furrows his brows. "You think—"

"Goodbye, Kade." I trot to the elevator, and he gets on.

I hold the open button. "I said not to come up."

"Gracie, please don't—"

"No," I scream at him. A new well of tears flow. "Please go. I'm not sure what you expect from me, but I can't do this. You say you have to go, then go."

He closes his eyes and hesitates.

"Go," I sob.

"I'm sorry. I love you." He steps out, and I hit the close button. When the doors shut, I hit my floor and hold it together until I get to my unit.

As soon as I open the door, my eyes go to the Tiffany vase Kade sent me on my birthday several months ago, along with two dozen long-stemmed roses. I pick it up and throw it at the wall, and it bursts into pieces everywhere.

In a trance, I fixate on all the shards.

Broken glass and shattered dreams are the only things left.

How could you have been so stupid?

The note he sent me is still on the table.

GRACIE,

Happy 24th birthday.

Love,

Kade

LOVE, KADE. WHAT A LIE.

If he loved me, he wouldn't be leaving.

And you slept with him. There's no way to erase it.

He used you for a final fling before leaving.

Kade isn't one of those guys.

He just proved he is.

I slide down the wall and hug my knees, sobbing, crumpling the note in my fist.

He says he has no choice. This isn't personal. He doesn't want to go.

There's always a choice.

Money is more important to him than you are.

Pain I haven't felt since Beckett went to prison engulfs me. I spend several weeks wondering what I could have done differently, missing Kade, ignoring his final *I'm sorry* message, and hurting so bad I can't contemplate how to move forward.

My friend finally makes me go out one night. Instead of my usual water, I have a drink. For the first time in weeks, I laugh. So I drink more. The pain of Kade slowly goes away, and I get so

15

drunk, I wake up in bed with someone I have no recollection of who it was or what we did. The pain of Kade rushes to the surface and escalates, so when the guy sleeping next to me opens his eyes and smiles at me, ready to go another round, I don't tell him no. I have sex with him, trying to feel how I felt with Kade. It doesn't work, but I let him buy me breakfast and mimosas after, trying to mask more thoughts of Kade and convince myself this is how people get over a broken heart.

2

Gracie
One Year Later

"Fishbowl me," I yell out, already feeling the buzz of the alcohol, while raising my hand in the air at Connor, who's bartending.

He salutes me and reaches for a new plastic bucket the fishbowls come in.

"Don't look now, but there is a guy over there staring at you," my friend Becca says.

"Where?"

She bobs her head to the right, and I follow her movement.

"And you do exactly what I said not to do!"

"Who cares. He's either into me or not." I survey the crowded bar and have to put my hand over my forehead to shield my eyes from the sun setting over the ocean.

A blond, blue-eyed guy, who might be a few years older than me, cockily holds up his drink.

Hmmm. Not bad.

Not Kade.

Forget about Kade. It's almost been a year, and he's not contacted you.

Kade never missed a birthday of yours. Even when you weren't into each other, and he was in college, he texted you "Happy Birthday."

Not this year. He's forgotten about you. Time for you to forget about him.

I don't respond and tell Becca, "He's okay."

"Okay?" she cries out. "He's eye candy dipped in chocolate with some extra sugar and needs to be licked."

"You should go tell him you want to screw him then."

Becca puts her hands over her face. "You're crazy."

Connor places another fishbowl in front of me. "Seems like Daddy Warbucks over there has the hots for you. He just told me to put your tab on his for the entire night and asked me what your name is."

I groan. "You didn't tell him, did you?"

Connor arches his eyebrow. "No. The last time I told a stranger at the bar your name, you told that annoying chick I wanted to go out with her, and she wouldn't leave me alone. I was about to file a restraining order."

"Oh please. Mimi wasn't so bad."

Connor crosses his arms. "She followed me around the island. I couldn't go anywhere without her showing up."

Okay, she was a psycho.

I wince. "Sorry."

"Gracie, he's coming over," Becca mutters excitedly.

"Don't care." I take a long sip of my drink.

The barstool next to me is empty, and he sits down, turns toward me, and says nothing. A woodsy lavender aroma hits my nostrils.

At least he smells good.

After so many minutes of ignoring him, I finally turn. He's displaying perfectly straight white teeth.

I take a sip of my drink. "Do you always gawk?"

He licks his lips. "Nope."

"Then why are you doing it now?"

"The bartender said it was your birthday. I'm trying to figure out how old you are."

Way to go, Connor. Why don't you hand him my driver's license next time?

"How old do you think I am?"

He leans into my ear. "Old enough but not old enough."

Against my desire to not give him any extra attention, I concentrate on stirring my drink but ask, "How old would that be?"

"Sorry, not playing your game." He motions to Connor.

"What game?"

"Where I guess your age and either pick too young or too old and ruin all my chances with you."

"Who said you have any chances?"

He pretends to stab his heart. "Ouch. A real ball buster, huh?"

Connor sets three purple shots in front of all of us.

I nod toward the drink. "What's this?"

"Purple haze." The man picks the tiny glass up and holds it in the air. "Happy Birthday. Cheers."

What the hell. It is my birthday. Might as well have some extra fun.

I clink the glass with his and Becca's and shoot it back.

"I'm Fisher. What's your name?"

"Gracie."

"You from here, Gracie?"

"Yep. Island born and bred."

The band plays, and the music becomes louder.

I tell Becca, "Demetri has arrived. He's by the other bar."

"Who's Demetri? Do I need to be worried?" Fisher shouts in my ear.

When I turn, his face is next to mine. I say, "You're awfully forward."

"Bet I can make sure you have the best birthday you've ever had."

Like that will be hard.

"Doubt it. My birthdays are always fabulous."

He rises and tugs me off the barstool. "Come on, then."

"Hey, where are you taking me?" I shout as he leads me through the sea of bar patrons.

We get to the outdoor patio, under the tiki hut. He wraps his arms around me.

"What are you doing?"

"This place is a bit lame, don't you think?"

"Lame?"

"Yeah. Let's liven it up." His body sways to the music, and he moves mine with his.

"This isn't a dance floor."

He shrugs. "It is now."

I try to resist, but he holds me firm.

Screw it. What the hell. Why not?

I give in and dance with him. In the middle of the song, Becca, Dimitri, and several other people join us on the patio.

Fisher is a good dancer, and we sync well together. I forget about trying to get away from him and am soon having fun.

The band plays several songs then breaks for a rest and puts on slower music. Fisher draws me closer to him. "You having fun yet?"

I can't deny it. "Yes."

"Are you going to tell me how old you are?"

"Twenty-five. How old are you?"

"Thirty-one," he replies.

Kade's thirty-one.

Stop thinking of Kade.

"Why are you here?"

"Who said I don't live here?" he teases.

"It's a seven-mile island and most places are rentals. I'm on a first-name basis with most residents and *you* are not from here."

"Business."

"What do you do?"

"I own companies."

"Like what?"

He spins me then holds me close again. "I don't mix business and personal. What I do is boring, and you are anything but."

"Funny."

He stops.

Why is he staring at me?

"What?" I nervously say.

"You're gorgeous, sexy, and a bit sassy, which is turning me on. I'm wondering if you've ever been with a real man before?" He arches an eyebrow at me.

My heart races.

Yes. Kade.

You're not anything like Kade.

Stop comparing everyone to Kade.

When I don't respond, he cups my face, dips down, and kisses me.

It's the best kiss I've had since Kade. I lock my hands around his head and return his kiss, feeling some flutters, which is the first time I've felt anything in almost a year. It's not as intense as with Kade, but it's something.

No one will ever make you feel the way Kade did. Stop comparing everyone to him.

Fisher leads me to the bar. He motions to Connor, and another round of shots appear. This time, it's pink.

"What's this?"

He leans into my ear. "It's a pink pussy. All I can think of is what I want to do to yours." His tongue flicks my lobe.

Men have said all kinds of dirty things to me at the bar before, but something about Fisher is different. I can't put my finger on it, but there's something I like about him.

Maybe he's a total stud in bed, and I'll finally be able to get over Kade.

Stop thinking about him!

I clink his glass, and we both finish our shot.

The night evolves into more dancing, drinking, and groping. By the time the bar closes, I hop on the trolly with Fisher and end up at the beach house he's renting.

We have sex all night. I don't remember all of it because we also continue to drink between rounds. The next morning, I wake up to a happy Fisher and a hangover from hell.

The usual escape route I have after my one-night stands doesn't work. Fisher has other plans. After he makes me breakfast with mimosas, he gets me to admit to him I had an awesome birthday then convinces me to shower and fuck him some more.

Morning leads into the afternoon, and, before he drops me off, he insists I give him my number.

"I don't do serious," I tell him.

He twirls a lock of my hair in his fingers. "Not planning to run away and get married. But I'm going to be here a lot for work. I don't see why we can't meet up when I'm in town, do you?"

"It's not my thing."

"So, you only do one-night stands?"

Ouch. Now I sound like a slut.

Have I become one?

"No...but..."

What am I trying to say?

"You didn't have fun?"

"No, I did."

"Then what's the problem? You see whoever you want as will I. When I'm in town, I'll see if you're free. No strings. Everyone stays happy."

My heart is racing. I've not dated or given any of my one-nighters my number.

But you did have fun with him.

He seems harmless. What's the worst that can happen?

You can always block him if he annoys you.

"Okay. You can have my number."

3

Kade
Six Months Later

"Come on," I mutter under my breath. For three days, I've been punching in different numbers, trying to gain access to the Twisted Hearts' list of *business vendors* hidden on the dark web.

What once was a domestic gang has now broadened its horizons internationally. Heroin is no longer the primary driver of the gang's funding. It's still an enormous part of the financial pot, but these days it's a small piece of the pie.

Jimmy "Skates" Cline, the leader of the gang, is educated and comes from money. He isn't the ordinary *thug off the street* gang leader.

Skates is smart and uses his brain to create more evil. He's expanded the Twisted Hearts' financial portfolio to identity theft, stealing millions of dollars a day from unsuspecting parties. But those things aren't the worst of it. His operation on the dark net involves drug, human, and weapon trafficking. The newest disturbance is his interest in chemicals.

Like most narcissistic people, Skates believes he should lead— and not only his gang but the world. The Twisted Hearts organization he's built has laws, rules, and codes of honor. It's a dictatorship where Skates calls the shots, and everyone else follows. And it's been growing faster than any other gang and most terrorist groups ever have.

Interpol hasn't officially labeled the Twisted Hearts as a terrorist group because so far, Skates hasn't taken any terrorist actions. Instead, they are on the watch list. But the plans are in the works. And I'm aware of his overall aspirations because I found it.

While surfing the dark net one day, I hacked into a Twisted Hearts' room. My discoveries made my gut flip, and as I dug further, more and more pieces of the puzzle led to terrorism. I sent the information to my boss at the CIA, and, several days later, I came home from the gym, and two agents from Interpol sat in my family room, waiting to discuss a new career path with them.

For the last two-and-a-half years, I've been all over Europe, Russia, and parts of Africa, working on finishing this job so I can get home. I pray I'm not too late when I finally see Gracie again and will be able to win her back. Not a day goes by I don't think about her or search her social-media feed. Every guy I see her with rips my heart, but I have no right to expect her not to live her life. Unable to help myself, I run background checks on anyone who turns up on her feed more than once.

From what I can see, she hasn't gotten serious with anyone, but several guys have come in and out of the picture, and it always makes me nervous.

I hit a few more numbers, letters, and the enter key one more time. The computer screen flashes, and a sound blares through my speakers.

Yes! Come on. Be what I need.

Bingo!

The list scrolls fast over my screen. I save it to my drive and then print it off to give my eyes a break from the strain they've been under the last three days.

I'm on the second page of the list when I see his name. My gut drops, and the hairs on my neck stand up.

Please tell me it isn't the same guy.

I return to my computer screen and punch the keys.

Sure enough, his face pops up.

Fisher Corbyn.

I tap on the desk then pick up my phone. I go to Gracie's Instagram page, hoping I'm wrong but already know it's pointless.

My pulse races. *I need to be with her, now.*

Too many times to count, I've made the phone call I'm about to make again. I pick up my phone and dial my boss.

"Coral, what do you have for me?"

"I got the list. I need to return home."

"We need you here."

"I'll fly in and out."

"You can't. We've been over this and need you infiltrating."

Think, Kade.

"Then let me pick who I infiltrate."

"Why?"

"It's the person we need to concentrate on the most. He's got the money to fly under the radar." I already ran a detailed analysis on Fisher. My boss isn't aware why I did, nor was it legal, but I figure if they want to fire me, they can. And since I have skills no one else does, I never worry about it. Plus, I already have so much money, I don't need any more. I work because I want my life to have a purpose and do something to help others. So if they did get rid of me, I'd be fine financially.

"You've gone through the entire list?"

"Yeah," I lie. "I'll send through code the names of others you should concentrate on. But I get to pick my guy. Wherever he goes, I'll go."

"Fine. As long as you stay within Europe."

Fuck.

"How am I supposed to nail him if he leaves?"

My boss sighs. "You really think this is who we need to concentrate on?"

"Yeah."

Come on. Give me clearance to go stateside.

"Tell you what, you give me evidence, and I'll give you world clearance."

"Fine. I'll send the list over in the next hour." I hang up and throw my phone down.

Even though my eyes are strained, I stare at the computer screen with Fisher's picture on it some more, figuring out how I'm going to nail his ass.

If he's on the Twisted Hearts' payroll, he's bad news. If he's with Gracie, he's a dead man.

I slam my laptop screen down. Picking up my phone, I scroll through Gracie's text messages I know by heart. I've read them every day since I've been gone.

The last one is mine.

"I'm sorry. I don't want this. I love you."

She never responded, and I don't blame her. What I did to her was unforgivable. It wasn't my choice, but I ripped her heart out.

I'm reading her messages and ... pops up on the screen as if she is going to send me a message. It's not the first time it's happened. I hold my breath, but as usual, the ... disappear, and my heart sinks.

I type a message to her but delete it before sending it. I'm still not sure when I'll be able to step foot in Florida again. Any communication with her isn't fair. I can't give her answers she would want, assuming she would even talk to me.

All night, I stay up. I research everything I can about Fisher

27

then dive further into every piece of information no matter how minute it might seem. By morning, I have a plan on how I'm going to infiltrate him.

I'm a spy and a trained killer. If I find out he's done anything to hurt Gracie, I'll kill him on the spot with or without the shoot-to-kill order.

4

_____

Gracie

Twenty-One Months Later

"Fisher's here and wants to see you," Connor tells me. We're up at Ybor City at a club, and I just got to the bar area.

"What are you, his assistant?" I tease, and he hands me a shot.

We clink glasses and throw them back. The sting of the alcohol burns my throat, and I grab the vodka tonic I'm assuming is mine off the bar to chase it.

"Funny. He's in a VIP room. Let's go."

I don't move.

Connor arches a brow. "Are you coming?"

"No. Fisher can wait. I haven't seen who else is here tonight." I scan the room, but it doesn't seem like anyone interesting is here.

Connor shakes his head. "What's your deal with Fisher?"

"He's okay for a fun time. Not someone to get serious about."

Connor gapes at me. "He's loaded and totally into you even though you've blown him off for the last year."

I snort. "Lots of people are into me. And money doesn't mean I should be with him."

"I've seen who you've been with, and trust me, Fisher is the best one."

No, he isn't. Kade is.

Stop comparing him to everyone, Gracie.

Kade left you. Besides the one "I'm sorry" text, he's never even contacted you in three years.

Plus, he left you to make money.

"Gracie, let's go see Fisher. His VIP room is decked out with top-shelf alcohol, and all the interesting people are going to be in there."

I can't deny Connor's point.

"Fine."

Connor leads the way, and we're soon in Fisher's suite. As we enter, Fisher moves away from several girls who are hanging around him and on top of him and comes over and kisses me.

"Gracie, how've you been?" he asks.

"Dying for a drink."

"Cristal?"

"Sure. Thanks."

I breathe a sigh of relief he's off me for a minute and try not to compare him to Kade.

But once again, I fail.

Fisher is the opposite of Kade. Blond hair, blue eyes, and his killer body make all the girls swoon. But all I miss is Kade's thick, dark hair, eyes to match, and olive skin wrapped around his muscle.

When Fisher kisses me, I wish I could feel what I felt when Kade kissed me, but I don't. Fisher isn't a bad kisser, but with Kade I felt lit up.

The only time I feel lit up kissing anyone is if I've got several shots in me, and even then, I'm still only chasing my memories.

As more time passes, I should have forgotten the way I felt in Kade's arms or the heat he brought to every kiss, but the more I can't find what we had, the stronger my memory of those feelings gets. It's like my memories have to torture me and reinforce I'm never going to find anyone who makes me feel the way Kade did.

Fisher comes over with a glass of champagne.

"Thanks." I take a sip.

He leans into my ear. "I've been dying to see you. I'm glad your sister is home safe now."

"Thanks." Gabriella has only been home a little while. When she was gone, Connor moved into my condo so I wasn't living on my own. We both stopped going out and met up almost nightly with the rest of our family. It stopped me spending time with Fisher or anyone else. Now Gabriella is safe, Connor insisted we come for a celebration night out.

I can't put my finger on it, but something feels different than before she got abducted.

"I've rearranged some business things so I can be here more often."

"Oh?" *Tell me it's not because of me.*

The last few months, Fisher has been calling and texting me all the time. I ignored most of them, but he's been hinting he wants to not only return to how we were before my hiatus, but he also wants us to get serious. And he has been asking me to travel the world with him, which isn't something he ever asked me to do in the past.

"I understand why you aren't ready to come with me yet, so I thought I could be here more for us."

For us? There is no us, and I've told Fisher numerous times.

"I don't do serious, Fisher. I've been clear since day one."

He slides his hand through my hair then cups my cheek before kissing me again. "I'm ready to do serious when you are."

"But I don't—"

He puts his finger over my lips. "I'll wait till you're ready. But I'm hoping it's sooner rather than later."

"You haven't even seen me in about a year."

He shrugs. "So what? I'm not a wishy-washy man. I want you. It isn't going to change."

I should feel happy someone like Fisher wants to get serious with me, but I feel nothing but anxiety over it.

"You shouldn't be making business decisions based on me." I don't have any idea what Fisher does. Whenever I ask, he gives me his standard answer which is he doesn't like to mix business with personal. But I wouldn't want him to mess up any business things because of me.

His typical cocky expression emerges. "It's already been decided. Now, I'm only here for the weekend then I have to leave and arrange a few more things so I can return. But I have a surprise for you."

My stomach twists. I don't like surprises with Fisher. He has a way of getting what he wants, and I'm assuming this is part of his plan to get me to do what he wants. "What?"

"I'll show you tomorrow morning." He winks at me.

"Tomorrow morning?"

"Yeah."

"This is your way of getting me to stay with you tonight, isn't it?"

He wiggles his brows. "I won't confirm nor deny."

I cross my arms.

Fisher wraps his arms around me. "I couldn't control the timing of it. Don't be pouty all night. I really do have a surprise for you."

Don't be nasty to him. He likes you and is trying hard to win you over even though you keep shooting him down.

He's lasted longer than Kade did.

I peck Fisher on the lips. "Okay."

"Are you going to dance with me?"

"Sure."

"Finish your drink, and let's go."

I empty my glass of champagne, and Fisher leads me to the dance floor. We spend the night downing shots, and, as the evening progresses, Fisher and I both have our hands all over each other and are pretty intoxicated.

We return to the VIP room, where Connor has several women fawning over him. He's pretty hammered as well.

"Fisher," he calls out.

Fisher slaps Connor's hand and sits down. The girl between Fisher and Connor refocuses her attention on Fisher.

She tries to kiss Fisher, but he moves his head out of the way. "Sorry, I'm taken. Come here, Gracie." Fisher pats his lap.

I see nothing has changed with Fisher. There's always tons of girls around him.

You keep telling him you don't want to be serious.

The girl gives me an evil eye, so I quickly sit on Fisher's lap and make out with him to piss her off.

"Fisher, don't forget you lost tonight," Connor says.

I retreat from the kiss. "Lost what?"

"A friendly wager. No biggie." Fisher draws me close again.

Connor needs to stop making bets with Fisher. I've talked to him about this.

"You both need to stop making bets."

"But Fisher loses," Connor chides.

Fisher snorts. "Won't always happen." He tries to kiss me again, but I don't let him.

"What did you lose?"

"A hotel room."

"A hotel room?"

Fisher moves his palm to my ass. "Yep. Don't worry though. I still have ours."

The waitress brings another round of shots, and everyone

downs theirs. Fisher hands me a glass of champagne to chase it with, and I'm suddenly feeling the best I've felt all night.

"Speaking of hotel rooms, I think we should go to ours, don't you?" Fisher runs his finger down my spine over my dress.

The combination of the alcohol and his touch sends tingles through my nerves. "Yeah, let's go."

Connor turns to the girl who hit on Fisher but is trying to get with him again. "You stay here. I don't do sloppy seconds." He kisses the girl on the other side of him. "You can come with me."

She sticks her tongue down his throat and presses her breasts against him.

"Connor, you coming?" Fisher asks.

"Mm-hmm," he says, they both rise and follow us.

We spend the night at his hotel room in Ybor, fucking, drinking more, and laughing hard from being intoxicated. The next morning, I wake up in his arms, with a headache and remorse about sleeping with him.

You said you weren't going to lead him on.

This is why you shouldn't drink so much. The hiatus you took while Gabriella was gone was good for you. You don't need to fall into old habits.

I try to slide out of Fisher's grasp, but he stirs. "Morning," he says a little too chipper for my current state.

I groan. "Is it? My head is killing me. I haven't drunk like that in ages."

"Hold on, baby. Let me get something for your head." He hops up, leaves, then reenters the room with some pills and a Bloody Mary.

"Seriously?"

He takes a sip. "Yep. The best thing for a hangover. I don't need to tell you this. Here."

I pop the pills in my mouth and swallow them with a sip of the red concoction.

"There's no celery in it." I smirk.

"Hotel room bars, what can I say." He trails his fingers on my thigh. "But, we won't have to worry about no celery ever again."

What is he talking about?

He teases, "Don't squint, you'll get a wrinkle."

"Oh my God, not a wrinkle!"

He runs his finger down my forehead between my eyes and then nose. "Let's take a shower then you can see your surprise."

"What is it?"

"You'll see."

"You aren't going to tell me?"

"Nope. Finish your drink, and let's go enjoy the shower."

Great. I don't have enough alcohol in me for Fisher morning sex.

I down the Bloody Mary, hoping it gives me a boost of spirits.

Fisher and I screw in the shower, and when we get out, he goes to the closet and sets a box on the bed.

"Is this my surprise?"

"Nope. This is just an add-on."

I tilt my head. "Like an additional way to butter me up?"

He grins. "Yep."

"What is it?"

"Open it."

I remove the lid and a designer sundress, pair of underwear, bra, and new sandals and sunglasses are in it.

"Wow. These are beautiful." I love fashion, and this is something I would have picked out myself.

He wraps his arms around me. "I can't have my woman doing the walk of shame, can I?"

He had it all planned out.

Of course he did. It's Fisher Corbyn and he always gets everything he wants.

"What if I didn't stay with you last night?"

His face falls. "Gracie, can we stop playing games? Tell me what you want from me, and I'll make it happen."

My heart races. "I told you—"

"You don't like me?"

"Of course I like you."

"I embarrass you?"

"Fisher—"

"Then what is it?"

You aren't Kade.

"If I left right now, and you never saw me again, would you be upset?"

"Of course I would."

"Don't we have a good time together?"

I can't deny it. "We do."

"Will you at least think about getting serious with me? I'll do anything for you."

My pulse beats in my neck.

I wish I could understand why I'm fighting him so much. He's right. We have fun together, and I don't doubt he would do anything for me.

He strokes my cheek. "Please. Tell me you'll at least consider it."

"Okay. I'll think about it."

"You will?"

"Yes."

He kisses me. "Thank you. You just made my day. Now, get dressed so I can surprise you."

When we're ready, Fisher leads me out of the hotel to where the valet has his Jaguar at the curb. After about twenty minutes, he parks at the marina.

Yachts of all different sizes are everywhere.

"Are we going boating?"

His eyes light up. "Kind of."

He takes my hand and guides me down the dock to a yacht with *Gracie* written on the stern.

My stomach does somersaults. I turn to him.

His cocky expression is full of confidence. "Well. What do you think?"

"Is this your boat?"

"Yep. I just upgraded."

"You named it after me?"

"Yep."

"Why?"

His face falls. "Because I'm in love with you."

No, no, no.

My hand flies over my mouth. I want to love Fisher, but I can't seem to get past Kade.

Maybe you haven't tried hard enough.

He's not Kade and never will be.

Tears well in my eyes, thinking about when Kade said he loved me.

"I'm aware you don't love me, and for now, it's okay. But I'm never going to give up hope you will someday. I may not have seen you in a year, but I've thought about you every day we were apart."

My tears flow, and Fisher embraces me.

What is wrong with you, Gracie? You have a guy who's crazy about you and making grand gestures, and you can't even appreciate it.

How can I love him when all I think about is Kade?

It's time to forget about Kade and appreciate those who are in your life.

"I'll try harder," I blurt out in Fisher's chest.

He freezes. "You will?"

"Yes. I'll try to get past my issues."

"Do you want to tell me what they are?"

"No."

"Is it another guy?"

"Yes."

"Is he still in your life?"

"No."

Fisher pauses. "Okay. I wish you would tell me what he did to you, but I won't push. And I'll never hurt you."

I want to believe him, but I can't. Instead, I just kiss him, spend the rest of the weekend with him, and vow to try and get past Kade so I can move on with my life and not screw up what is in front of me.

5

Kade

Three Months Later

MEET WITH FISHER THEN GO OVER TO GRACIE'S. IF SHE ISN'T GOING TO take your calls, then it's time for a different approach.

For several months I've been calling Gracie, but she always sends me to voicemail. I've left message after message, but she never returns my calls.

It's driving me crazy.

For years, I didn't call her because I didn't have answers for her. I can't tell her I work for Interpol, I'm a spy, or that I'm working to take down the Twisted Hearts, including Fisher. She stopped seeing him for almost a year, but my stateside contacts who watch him tell me they are spending time together again.

And he named his boat after her. Every time I see it, my stomach flips.

I pray Gracie isn't serious about him.

Part of taking Fisher down is making sure we stay tight.

Keep your friends close and enemies closer.

I have worldwide clearance. Anywhere Fisher goes, I can, too. And I already told Interpol, after this case is over, I'm done. A life with Gracie is what I want, and I can't be with her if I'm a spy.

Assuming she still wants you.

Please want me.

I've been in Florida a few weeks, and the only Brooks I've seen is Connor, who I ran into up in Ybor. I was out with Fisher, who had no problem bringing several women to his yacht, which is parked next to mine.

Piece of shit has a woman like Gracie in front of him and still has eyes for others.

His stupidity alone made me want to kill him, and I had to remind myself to keep my cool.

The restaurant isn't far from the marina. I park my SUV, and when I step inside the open-air bar, my chest tightens.

A waitress sets shots and drinks down at a table full of women. Gracie and Gabriella are both there.

When I last saw and touched her, over three years ago, she was crying, and I had broken her heart.

I wanted to meet her alone and not surprise her with others around since I'm not sure how she'll respond or if she is even aware I'm in town. I debate leaving, but then Fisher struts up to her and sticks his tongue down her throat.

My blood boils, and I remind myself to calm down.

In a few steps, I'm right in front of her. "Gracie."

Gracie is still in Fisher's arms, and her face falls. Her blue eyes widen, and as Gabriella jumps in my arms and hugs me, I watch Gracie's expression change.

She still hates me.

Damn it.

"Kade! Are you here for good or visiting?" Gabriella asks.

Trying to keep my face in spy mode, so I don't give any clues about my feelings, I focus on both Gabriella and Gracie. "I'm here for the long term."

Fisher spins but keeps his arm around Gracie's shoulders. "You all know each other?"

Get your slimy hands off my woman.

"Kade is my brother's best friend." Gabriella beams.

Gracie locks eyes with me, and all I see is pain.

You created her pain.

"Do you want to sit down with us?" Gabriella asks.

"Sure," Fisher says. "Kade and I were meeting up for a beer."

Gracie's eyes narrow.

I grab two chairs. Fisher takes one from me, and we sit on either side of Gracie.

"I need to use the restroom." Gracie quickly rises and hightails it to the bathroom.

"Me, too." A brown-haired girl follows her.

Gabriella introduces the other woman to Fisher and me, but I don't remember a word she says. The brown-haired girl returns after a few minutes, takes her phone out, and dials a number.

"The sports bar on Bridge Street. Hudson, can you get Gracie and me? She's sick."

Gracie's sick?

I stand. "Tell Hudson I'll take her home."

"No. That's okay," the brown-haired girl quickly says. "Your friend Kade. Can you come get us please?"

I need to get to Gracie before anyone else does.

I'm on my feet and moving toward the bathroom, but the brunette follows me. "You can't go in there. It's a women's room."

"I'm sure they won't mind."

Fisher is behind us. "I'll take her home if she's sick."

Hell no, you won't.

"Fisher!" a group of girls from outside the restaurant yell out at him.

He sizes them up then says, "I'll be back in a minute."

"Kade, you can't go in there," the girl repeats.

"I know I haven't met you, and I don't mean to be rude, but

41

you need to stay out here." I open the door, step inside, and shut and lock it while she's still talking.

Gracie turns around, and her eyes widen.

"Gracie, are you sick?"

She puts her hand on her stomach and other hand on the counter then bends over the sink. "Why are you here?"

I quickly embrace her. For a brief moment, the world is perfect. "God, I've missed you."

She sobs in my arms.

I blink hard. "Shh. I'm so sorry. I wish I could redo it all."

"Why are you here?"

"To win you back and protect you," I blurt out.

Think before you talk.

She sarcastically laughs. "I'm not sure which of those sounds more ridiculous."

"It's true. I've never stopped loving you."

She shoves out of my arms. "You gave me a six-hour notice you were moving after you screwed me. You disappeared from the face of the earth for over three years. No calls. No texts besides the day you left. Nothing. And now I'm good enough for you to try and win back?"

"This has never been about me not wanting you or you not being good enough. I've been calling you for a few months. As soon as I got permission to return, I tried contacting you. I couldn't before. I had no answers to give, and you deserved more than a call with a blank timeline."

"Yeah, I deserved a lot more."

"I agree."

She glares at me. "After three years, you expect me to take your calls?"

"I don't expect you to do anything," I admit.

New tears fall. "I didn't even know if I'd ever see you again."

I draw her into my arms. "I'm so sorry. I wish I could tell you everything."

"Why can't you?" she whispers.

I hold her tighter and kiss her head. "I can't. I'm sorry, but I can't."

She forces me away again. "I have to go."

"I'll take you home."

"No. You won't."

"Gracie—"

"Kade, what did you think would happen? You would stroll into town, and we would just pick up where you left me?"

"No. I have to make it up to you. I—"

"Make it up to me? How are you going to make over three years of my life up to me?"

My heart drops. "I'm not sure. But I'm going to spend every day till I drop dead trying. Not a day has gone by I haven't thought about you, or stared at your picture, or re-read our text messages. I've been dying without you. And I'm sorry my shit got in our way...you don't know how sorry I am...but tell me you still feel something for me."

She retreats and steps into the wall, her head bobs in tiny movements, and a fresh river of tears fall.

I step forward so I'm pressed against her. "I've never stopped loving you. I never will."

"If you loved me, you wouldn't have left," she whispers.

"I didn't have a choice. You have to believe me."

"Everyone has a choice."

"I didn't."

"Then tell me why you didn't."

"I can't."

"Then, I can't believe you."

"Gracie—"

"No. You don't know what it's been like for me. Everything that's happened to my family...I...I needed you. My family needed you."

My stomach flips. *What's she talking about?*

"What happened?"

She turns away. "Nothing. I need to go."

"Gracie, what happened? Connor said everyone was doing good when I saw him up in Ybor."

"Everything is fine now. Forget I said anything."

"No. Tell me what happened."

She shakes her head. "I need to go. Fisher is waiting for me."

I grunt. "No, he's not. He's with his posse of girls who showed up."

Hurt passes her eyes, but then she shrugs. "So what? Fisher can do what he wants."

"That's not what you deserve."

She jabs me in my chest. "Don't you tell me what I deserve. Don't you dare judge me."

I cup her cheeks. "I'm not judging you. Be mad at me all you want. Fisher is bad news. You need to stay away from him."

She scowls at me. "Fisher?"

"Yes."

"Why? What has he done?"

This just gets worse and worse.

She's never going to trust you ever again.

"I can't get into it."

Hatred, distrust, and pain swirl on Gracie's face. "Move."

I close my eyes.

"Move." She pushes my chest hard, and I move a foot away from her. "Go back wherever you came from, Kade. You had your chance. You didn't want it."

My stomach drops. "Tell me you don't believe that."

"Three years," she cries out. "You haven't even talked to Hudson. What kind of person disappears for three years? You left us all. Deserted us, and now you want things to return to how they used to be? I'm sorry, but no. You don't get to slide into our lives when we're all trying our hardest to put our lives back together."

Once again, I have no idea what she is talking about.

"Gracie, tell me—"

"No." She goes to the sink, grabs a towel, and wipes at the mascara under her eyes. When she finishes, she studies me in the mirror. "How long are you really here for?"

"For good. I might need to travel for work, but I'm never leaving again. I already gave my notice this is my last project."

"Well, I hope you didn't give your notice for me. As far as I'm concerned, we never happened."

No. This is going worse than I ever imagined.

Fuck it.

She turns to leave, but I spin her into me, lace my fingers through her hair, and crush my lips against hers, parting them with my tongue.

My kiss is urgent.

It's needy.

It's every ounce of longing I've had for her for over three years.

Her knees buckle, and I hold her tight to me. Our hearts pound against the other's. Fireworks explode in all my cells, reminding me I'm alive and not dead, which is how I've felt these years without her.

She whimpers in my mouth, gasping for air as I continue to deepen our kiss and firmly hold her to me.

My body responds, and my erection presses against my zipper, dying to be free.

"Come with me," I murmur.

She takes her lips away from mine, breathing hard. "You don't get to touch me."

"Please. I love you. Let me prove it to you."

"No. You lost your right to me," she cries again. "You don't get to keep ripping my heart out."

"I won't ever hurt you again. I promise you," I beg her.

"I don't believe you." She wipes her face and storms out.

I straighten my clothing and leave the restroom. Fisher is at the bar, buying shots for his posse of women. Gracie sits at the table with her friends. I can't help it and watch her every move as she ignores me.

You're supposed to be here because of Fisher. Now isn't the time to mess up your operation. Get done and out so you can move on with your life.

I gaze at Gracie again.

But you have no life without her.

There's more at stake than your life. Go do your job.

I approach Fisher, and a girl is hanging on his shoulders.

"Hey. Did you take Gracie home?"

"No. She's feeling better and over there." I point to the table.

"Oh good." He turns to the bartender. "Send more shots and drinks to the table, please."

"I think they've had enough," I say.

He snorts. "No. They're just getting started, if they are anything like Gracie."

I utilize every ounce of self-control I have not to punch Fisher.

What does he mean? Gracie and Gabriella both hardly drink.

The waitress takes a round of shots to the table. The drinks sit on the table next to the shots, but no one touches them.

What do you know, douchebag? I turn to Fisher, who is telling his female friends goodbye and pecking them all on the lips.

I can't believe Gracie puts up with this.

She doesn't love him.

Fisher returns to the table and sits next to Gracie, dragging her into his arms.

I return to the table.

Gabriella says, "Are you ready, Gracie?"

"Yep."

"Gracie, you're coming with me, aren't you?" Fisher asks.

"Not tonight. I don't feel well."

"Come to my place, and I'll take care of you."

She stands. "No, not tonight. I'm going with my sister."

Fisher glances over at Gabriella. "I'm glad you're back."

Her head drops toward the table. She quietly replies, "Thanks."

Back? Where did she go?

"Ladies, you need a ride?" I ask them.

Everyone except Gracie politely smiles.

The redhead says, "Gabriella hasn't drank. She's driving."

"Okay, well, if you're going to be no fun tonight, then I guess Kade and I will have to represent." Fisher rises. "St. Pete?"

Gracie blinks hard. "See you all later." She hoofs it out of the bar. The other women get up, say bye, and quickly follow.

My gut sinks, and my heart bleeds. It's not a revelation I hurt Gracie, but it's worse than I thought, and I don't believe she's ever going to forgive me.

6

Gracie

"WHY CAN'T I COME?" FISHER ASKS AGAIN.

"I've told you why."

"Tell me again. If my sister were getting married, I would take you."

He needs to drop this.

"I told you Gabriella and Javier only want our family there."

"Are Mia, Chloe, and Lena going?"

"Yes, of course. They're part of our family," I blurt out, angry he would even question their place in our lives.

"So, everyone gets a date except you?"

"First of all, Mia is my sister-in-law. She's married to Beckett. Chloe and Lena are part of our family. It's not my choice who gets an invite anyway."

Fisher crosses his arms. "Does Gabriella not like me?"

I sigh. "Fisher, she's been through a lot and has only met you a handful of times. It's her day. Can you not read more into it than it is?"

"Is Kade going?"

My pulse increases at his name.

Keep it together, Gracie.

"No. He's always been a part of our family, and he didn't get an invite. So you shouldn't feel bad."

Gabriella came over the day after the bar incident and demanded I tell her what was going on between Kade and me. I ended up spilling my guts and swearing her to secrecy. She took his invite out of her purse and ripped it up. I told her she could still invite him, but she said she wasn't going to want anyone there who made me uncomfortable. I was relieved, as selfish as it was for me not to want him there.

But all I've done since seeing him is replay our kiss nonstop in my head. And I'm dying to see him again. It's as if seeing him took all three years of longing for him and put it on an accelerated track.

Fisher grunts. "I'm not sure how I'm not supposed to feel bad. I thought we were doing serious."

I put my arms around him. "We are. Please don't take this personally. I never do serious. Gabriella assumes I'm single."

"You haven't told her about us?"

Oh jeez. Why did I say that?

"Everything has been about the wedding. I haven't had a chance to talk to her."

His eyes turn into slits. "Are you ever going to tell your family about us?"

"Yes. Of course." I run my hand through his hair. "All weddings are crazy, and Gabriella and my family have been through so much. I didn't want anything to be about me and not Gabriella during her special time."

He sighs. "Okay."

"Thank you. I have to go. I'll see you tonight?"

"Yeah. Text me what time you want me to pick you up."

"Okay." I peck him, and he grips the back of my head so I can't move.

"Is that a way to kiss your man goodbye?"

Ugh. Just let me go.

He gives me a deep kiss, and, once again, I'm thinking about how it doesn't compare to Kade's kiss. And I hate Kade even more.

"I'm going to be late."

He slaps my ass. "Have fun."

"Go back to sleep." It's early in the morning. The sun is barely up.

"Will do." Fisher climbs into bed.

Nice of you to be a gentleman and escort me out.

Stop, Gracie. You just told him to stay and get more sleep.

I leave the bedroom and make my way through the yacht. It's only about a mile to the other marina my family is leaving from, and I decided a morning stroll would be good.

Lost in thought, I focus on the sidewalk. When I get to the end of the street and turn the corner, Kade practically runs into me.

Flutters erupt as they always do, and my heart races.

He's shirtless. His skin glows with sweat. And his arms have gotten bigger since we were together three years ago.

My insides throb.

Why can't I lose my attraction toward him?

He yanks his earplugs out. "Gracie. Where are you going?"

"None of your business."

His eyes narrow. "Why are you by yourself this time of the morning?"

"Last time I checked, I wasn't a child."

He scowls. "You were with Fisher?"

I keep moving.

"Tell me you aren't walking home from here?"

I snort. "It's not far."

"It's barely light out."

"So?"

"Gracie—"

"Stop. You aren't my keeper. And I'm not going home. I'm only going about a mile."

He quiets but stays by my side.

Tell him to go.

"You're extra beautiful this morning. Where are you going?"

My insides do a happy dance—he thinks I'm beautiful—then I scold myself.

Fisher didn't even tell you you looked nice.

I curse myself some more for once again comparing Fisher to Kade.

"I have a family event."

"A family event?"

"Yeah, Gabriella and Javier's wedding."

"Gabriella's getting married?" Hurt is in his voice.

As much as I want him to hurt, I don't. "She was going to invite you. She questioned me about us, and it came out. I'm sorry. She ripped your invitation up."

He lets out a deep breath. "I don't blame her. But I'm sorry I'll miss it."

My pounding heart is bleeding being near him, and when his hand wraps around mine, I don't remove it.

"Gracie." He stops, and I spin into him.

"What?"

Pain, regret, and sadness are all in his eyes. "Tell me what I can do to win you back."

"You can't."

"Please. I love you."

He loves me.

He doesn't, or he wouldn't have left. Don't let him fool you again.

I decide to hurt him. "Guess what I did last night?"

He arches his eyebrow.

I angrily spout, "I fucked Fisher. You still love me?"

His jaw clenches, face hardens, and eyes turn into slits. "Yeah, I do."

I step back, shocked he would claim to love me after my revelation.

How can he love me knowing I'm with another man?

He doesn't love you.

Yes, he does.

Time to make him hate you so you can move on with your life.

"Too many men to count I've fucked since you. Still love me?"

He blinks hard. "Yeah. I do."

"No, you don't."

"Yes, I do."

"For years, I've fucked your friend Fisher. On and off, and men in between."

He exhales hard and quietly says, "I'm aware. It doesn't change how I feel about you," he cries out.

How would he know this?

"What do you mean? You've been somewhere far away. How would you have any knowledge of what I do?"

Silence.

"Tell me."

"I can't."

I shake my head in disgust. Tears and anger combust. "I'm so tired of your *I can't* answer. For years, I've been left wondering what I did, or could have done, and why you left. And you reenter my life and still, all you say is *I can't* whenever I ask you something. If any part of the person I thought you were exists, you'll stop giving me this excuse and hurting me."

"The reason I had to leave had nothing to do with you. You have to believe me. And I'm sorry. I don't want to hurt you." He tries to embrace me.

"Don't touch me," I scream, and a bird on the concrete several feet ahead of us flies off.

"Gracie—"

I jab him in the chest. "No. Can you leave me alone? My sister is getting married. It's supposed to be a happy day. Do you think you could let me be happy for just one day?"

His eyes are wet. "Okay."

Wiping my face, I return to my quick stroll. Kade doesn't come with me, but the entire way, he's behind me, watching and making sure I get to where I'm going. I don't need to turn and see him. I can feel it. I've always been able to feel his presence, and the fact I still can cuts me to the core further. When I get to the marina, I turn, and he's stopped, several hundred yards away. I ignore him, force a smile, and step onto the boat where Gabriella and the other girls are.

When I see Gabriella in her white dress and glowing, tears fall again.

Her face falls. "Gracie, are you okay?"

I wrap my arms around her. "Yes. You're so stunning!"

She tears up, along with everyone else, and we all pass the tissues around.

My heart is in shambles during the entire wedding. I'm happy for Gabriella and Javier. I try to convince myself over time I'll feel everything I need to feel for Fisher, but I ache for Kade.

When the ceremony is over, my family and I go to the new house Javier bought to surprise Gabriella. We've all been working on remodeling it and are going to surprise her tomorrow. I work with Lena, who, besides Gabriella, is the only person who I've told about Kade and my past.

She questions my relationship with Fisher and insinuates I should give Kade another shot, but I can't. Fisher doesn't keep secrets from me or hide information regarding us. He wants to be with me and is doing everything he can to get me to love him.

It's time I let Kade go. I still have no clue how, but I need to. As soon as we're done putting the master bedroom together, I text Fisher to pick me up. He arrives, honks, and texts me. My brothers, except for Connor, go nuts about him not coming to the door, and I hightail it out of there.

The second I get into my seat, Fisher pulls me into a deep kiss. "I missed your hot ass all day."

I force myself to respond. "I missed you."

His grin widens. "I have a surprise for you tonight."

"What kind of surprise?"

"We're hosting a party."

"Hosting a party?"

"Yep. Time to break in the yacht with my woman."

My insides cringe at Fisher calling me his woman.

Stop it. Fisher loves you. You need to give him a fair chance.

"What do I need to do to get ready for it?"

"Try on your new clothes."

"My new clothes?"

"Yep. Your closet is full. We've got time before the party starts. I want a fashion show."

Great. I get to be Fisher's doll to dress up for the next few hours.

He just bought you a closet full of clothes. The least you can do is act appreciative.

"Is that what you want?"

"Yep."

I lean over and kiss his cheek. "Your wish is my command."

7

Kade

MY PULSE HAS NEVER BEATEN SO HARD IN MY THROAT.

No one bothered to tell me about Gabriella.

Why would they have? You ignored them for three years.

How could you not have known?

Hudson and Lena have met up with me for a drink and just told me Triker declared Gabriella, Max Crello declared Lena, and they both were rescued.

And now Kate is living at Hudson's.

And Fisher wants to own Gracie.

The Twisted Hearts are targeting the Brooks.

Why?

Gracie alluded to something happening to the Brooks while I was gone, but I could never have imagined something like this. My gut flips with nausea.

And Gracie went through this all on her own.

For the millionth time, I curse myself for not contacting her over the last three years or any of the Brooks.

I warn both of them over and over to get Kate out of the house and stay far away from her.

"You know things because of your job?" Hudson asks.

"Yes."

Every time I have to go around a question and not tell anyone in the Brooks family the entire truth, it makes me cringe. For three years, I didn't have anyone close to me. Surrounded by enemies, I filled my brain with secrets and told lies. Being home, with my family, I detest myself and the predicament I'm in.

Lena leans into Hudson's chest and intently stares at me. "You're in cybersecurity?"

I take a sip of beer. "Yeah."

Her eyes turn into slits. "So, you hack into data?"

"Suppose so."

Lena twists her hair. "You know, don't you?"

"About what?" I try to reflect.

Lena tilts her head.

Goose bumps pop out on my skin.

Lena was Max Crello's Twisted Hearts' wife. Of course. It's the reason why Kate is here.

Lena has the code.

It makes sense. Under Twisted Hearts law, she was married to Max. Then Triker placed her under his protection. She would have been their emergency weapon. It's the one innocent person, someone who wouldn't go to jail, who could save them from prison and keep things moving without having any clue what they were doing. They would tell Lena who to give the code to so they could push one button and become the head of the Twisted Hearts worldwide.

And Kate Contro has suddenly shown up. The real First Lady of the Twisted Hearts. No one except Interpol is aware, and they aren't sharing the details on her. Leak after leak exists in the FBI and CIA, so until we can find the list of offenders, Interpol is staying close-lipped.

Kate Contro is only spending time with Lena for one reason —she has to believe Lena has the code.

"Can one of you fill me in on what you're talking about?" Hudson growls.

"Who do you work for?" Lena asks.

"I'm a consultant for several companies," I lie and curse myself for doing so.

"What do you do for them?"

"Cybersecurity."

"Can you be more specific and tell us what it means?"

Crap. More lies.

"It means—"

"Kade!" Connor bellows out.

I've never been so happy to see you, Connor.

"Hey, man." I rise and pat him on the back.

"I thought you had to get off the island tonight, Connor?" Hudson.

"Nope. I'm heading out to Fisher's yacht party."

My stomach churns again. "Fisher's yacht?"

"Yeah. Gracie just texted."

I check my phone and see the missed message from Fisher.

"Can you try to watch out for your sister tonight?" Hudson barks.

Connor snorts. "Gracie does not need to be looked after. She isn't Gabriella or Mia."

"Just because she can handle her alcohol doesn't mean—"

"Don't worry. I'll make sure she's okay," I assure him. "Fisher's docked next to me."

"You have a yacht, too?" Hudson asks.

"I guess you can call it that."

"Glad to see you've done so well."

Connor does a victory fist pump. "Great. If I need to crash, I'm coming to your boat."

"Whatever you want to do. When are you headed over?"

"Now. I just got Gracie's text."

"She's already there?"

"Yeah. He picked her up hours ago."

I need to get on Fisher's boat before it leaves the dock.

"Kade—"

"Hudson, let's talk tomorrow in private."

"All right. We're tied up at Gabriella and Javier's house most of the day. Do you want to come over? You can see everyone then."

"Perfect. Where at?"

"Javier bought the Forresters' house. We've remodeled it and will have a surprise party for Gabriella tomorrow. We'll be there from ten on."

"All right. I'll see you tomorrow." I lean down and kiss Lena on the cheek. "It was nice meeting you."

"Nice meeting you, too," she quietly says.

I'll have to talk with her tomorrow about the code.

"Let's go," Connor says.

Hudson and I slap hands.

"Thanks for watching out for Gracie. Try to get that douchebag away from her. And I know she can handle her alcohol, but see if you can sneak some water into her," Hudson tells me.

You don't have to worry about me watching her. She's the only one my eyes will be glued to.

Why is everyone acting like Gracie is a big drinker?

But Hudson just told you she and Connor are partiers.

They've always had an active social life. But Gracie was never a big drinker.

"On it," I promise him and stroll out of the bar with Connor.

We get into my SUV.

"Nice wheels," Connor says.

I turn to him. "I've been meaning to talk to you."

He groans. "Why do I feel like I'm about to get a lecture?"

"No lecture. You're a man. But we're brothers, right?"

Connor scowls at me. "Yeah, and all my brothers do is tell me what to do."

"That's where you're wrong. Brothers watch out for each other. It's all they're trying to do."

"Now you are lecturing me."

He's twenty-four. Think back to when you were twenty-four.

All you thought about was girls.

From what I've seen of Connor out at the bar, all he's thinking about is women.

"Am I interfering with your sex life?"

He furrows his eyebrows. "No."

Make sure he's safe tonight, too.

He needs to stay away from Fisher.

"Tell you what. I've got a spare bedroom on my yacht for you."

His eyes turn into slits. "You're going to give me a bedroom on your yacht? As in, use anytime?"

"Yep. I'll even make sure you never run out of condoms."

"Why? I understand I'm lovable, but why would you do that?"

"I thought we were bros?"

"We are."

"Okay. So I give you a bedroom, and I only ask one thing from you."

His jaw clenches. "I figured there was a catch."

"You don't want the bedroom?"

He gazes out the window.

"All right, no biggie." I start the car.

"Fine. What do you want?"

I turn toward him. "Stop making bets with Fisher."

"Why is everyone so worried about this? I win every time."

"Don't you think never losing is a little odd?"

He snorts. "No. I'm smarter than him."

"Cockiness leads to trouble."

59

"Have you let my brothers influence you? I thought Fisher was your friend?"

Nope.

You need to pretend he is.

I hate lying to Connor, but it's necessary.

"He is. But I'm aware of things you aren't. No one has influenced me. You shouldn't be making bets with Fisher or anyone else."

"You act like I have a gambling problem. It's just a friendly thing we do."

"I didn't say you have a problem. But it's not a good thing to do. I need you to trust me."

Connor sighs.

"Do we have a deal? Bedroom, condoms, and I'll even throw in access to the full bar if you stop making bets."

Connor arches his brow at me. "I can use it anytime?"

"Yes. It's yours. I'll give you keys to the yacht."

"You'll give me keys just for not making bets with Fisher?" he says as if he doesn't believe me.

"Tomorrow. First thing, I'll have another set made. But no more bets with anyone."

"Okay. You have a deal, but I get access tonight."

That's exactly where I want you to stay. I don't want you on Fisher's boat any longer than necessary.

"Done. I'm docked right next to his boat, so after you get tired of his party, bring your private one to mine."

Connor fist-bumps me. "Perfect."

"And don't tell anyone about our deal. Not Fisher or your siblings."

"Gracie will find out I have a place at yours. She'll question me why I'm not with Fisher."

"I don't care if people know you have a place on my boat. But don't tell anyone why. If they ask, it's because we're brothers, end of story."

He shrugs. "Fine. But you better stock up on condoms."

At least he's wrapping his shit.

"Done."

As soon as we arrive at the marina, we go right to Fisher's boat, which is lit up and has music blaring. It's packed with people.

"Where would your sister be?"

"Follow me," Connor says. "But Gracie is going to kill you if you try to babysit her all night. My brothers don't like Fisher, but he's harmless. And he's the best dude she's ever been with."

I cringe inside.

He's not the best dude.

Keep it together and play your part, Kade.

"Knowing Fisher, he's going to be in entertainment mode all night. I'll keep an eye on your sister and make sure she doesn't have any issues with anyone who wants to get grabby."

Connor huffs. "If any of my sisters can handle themselves, it's Gracie. You don't need to babysit her."

"Why do you keep saying that?" I growl at him.

He throws his hands in the air. "Calm down. You're reminding me of my brothers now."

I take a deep breath. "Sorry. But tell me why you keep claiming that."

"One, she can handle her liquor. Two, she can fight guys off. Three, I doubt Fisher will let her out of his sight."

My pulse increases. I growl, "What do you mean she fights guys off? Has someone tried to hurt her?"

"No. I would kill them. But she gets hit on probably a dozen times a night when we're out. But no one gets to Gracie unless she wants them to."

"Gracie drinks a lot now?"

Connor shrugs. "No more than anyone else on the party scene. It's not like she has a problem or anything. She just has the ability to handle it."

"Want to bet?"

"How much do—" Connor freezes.

Got you.

"Was that a test?"

"Yep."

My insides flip letting what he said about Gracie sink in. Connor and I step aboard Fisher's yacht. It takes us a while to get to Gracie, and when we do, the boat moves away from the dock.

Crap. Now we're all stuck here.

Fisher has her on his lap, and they're doing shots.

Anger flares through me that he's okay feeding her alcohol like it's going out of style.

When they finish the shot, he sticks his tongue down her throat. I practice the breathing exercises Interpol taught us during training on how to stay calm, but my insides are raging.

Connor sits on the couch next to Fisher. "You guys should get a room."

Fisher pulls back with a cocky grin. "I have a room. Should we see if you can earn one tonight?"

Connor matches his cocky expression. "Nope. I don't need your skanky room."

"Skanky? Since when are my rooms skanky?"

Connor laughs. "Sorry, but I've got my own place."

"Where?" Gracie asks.

"At my bro Kade's."

The color in Gracie's face drains color at the mention of my name. She slowly turns toward me, and I focus on Connor and Fisher.

"Are you moving in?" Fisher asks sarcastically.

"No. But Kade gave me my own room to use whenever I want."

"What made you become his landlord?" Fisher asks.

"Ha ha," Connor smirks.

"Because—"

"I lost a bet," I quickly tell Fisher.

Fisher snickers. "Connor seems to be on a winning streak."

Gracie rises, pissed. "You're making bets with my brother, too?"

Damn it—another reason for her to be angry with me.

I don't say anything.

"Lay off him, Gracie. It's not a big deal." Connor grabs a beer from the waitress.

Her face reddens. "It is a big deal. I've told you"—she points to Fisher then me—"and I'm telling you, stop making bets."

"Okay," I reply.

"Gracie, calm down," Connor says.

"No. What do I need to do to get it through your thick head?"

"Jesus, Gracie. No one is getting hurt. Calm down," Fisher tells her.

She glares at him. The waitress brings another round of shots. Fisher hands one to her. "Have a shot and relax."

"Seriously, Gracie. When did you get so high strung?" Connor says.

"Hey," I growl. "Don't talk to your sister like that."

The room goes quiet as everyone focuses on me.

Connor holds up his hands. "Sorry."

Gracie downs the shot.

Fisher turns to me. "Have a shot and calm down, Kade."

You piece of shit.

Don't blow your cover. Play the friend.

"Sorry. She's like my little sister," I tell Fisher, grab the shot, and try not to grimace as the alcohol burns my throat.

"No worries."

"I need some space." Gracie storms out of the room.

"Where are you going? I said I'm sorry," Connor calls out.

Fisher rolls his eyes and rises. "Shit. There goes my night."

I put my hand on his shoulder and push him down. "I'll make sure she's okay. You entertain your guests." I motion to the girls and hand him another shot. The drunker I get him the more he'll be into other women besides Gracie for the evening.

He downs it. "Thanks, man."

"No problem."

As I make the way to the door, women are already filling the seats around Fisher.

Why is Gracie putting up with this dickhead?

Besides the fact Fisher is bad news, he's just a player. Anyone can see it. Gracie doesn't deserve to be with anyone who isn't faithful to her. In the past, she wouldn't have ever put up with it, either.

What's happened to my girl?

She doesn't love him.

She hates you.

Gracie's blonde hair catches my eye. She passes a waitress with a tray of shots and downs another one then grabs a glass of champagne from another waiter.

Three shots in under five minutes. Why is she drinking like this?

People thin out, and she gets to the front of the ship where it's dark and quiet. She sits down on a cabana bed and guzzles her champagne.

I double-check no one is around or anywhere near us then sit next to her.

She closes her eyes, sighing. "What do you want, Kade?"

Her flute is half full, and I remove it from her hand and put it on the table. "Don't drink any more tonight."

She scowls. "Don't tell me what to do."

"You don't need to do this."

"Do what?"

"Whatever you're trying to achieve by drinking like this."

She snorts. "Get off your high moral horse, Kade."

Silence.

"Stop making bets with Connor, Mr. Morals. He doesn't need to be encouraged."

64

"I didn't."

"Now you're going to lie?"

"No. I said it for Fisher's benefit."

Her forehead creases. "What was the point?"

"I—" I snap my mouth shut.

She shakes her head in disgust. "You can't tell me."

"I want to."

"Wow. How convenient."

Give her something.

"I told Connor he could have a room on my boat if he stopped making bets with Fisher and everyone else."

Her head turns to me. "You did?"

"Yes. But I don't want anyone to know, and especially not Fisher. If he catches wind of it, he'll challenge Connor harder to bet with him just for the fun of it."

She snorts. "That would be Fisher."

"Yes."

"But there's another reason?"

I neither confirm nor deny.

She sighs. "Thank you. He needs to stop."

"I'll do anything for your family or you. My love hasn't changed and never will."

Her eyes fill with tears. "I wish I still believed you when you spoke about love."

More cracks explode in my heart. "I hope you'll believe me again, someday."

She gets up, goes to the front of the boat, and leans over.

I follow her and hold on to her. "Don't bend over the rail when the boat's moving, and especially not when you've been drinking."

She spins on me, angry again. "You want to see drinking?"

My pulse races. "No."

She steps past me and swaggers down the deck.

Shit, shit, shit.

Instead of returning to where Fisher is, she moves into the room where a DJ is spinning records and lights are flashing.

Gracie goes up to the front of the line at the bar. I shove past people and stand next to her, shielding her from the grumbling guests. I order a bottle of water from a bartender. She orders two shots.

"No more shots," I tell her. I hold out the water. "Drink this."

"Nope."

The bartender puts down two shots, but I grab them both before she can. If looks could kill, I would be dead.

"Give me those."

"No. Drink the water." I drink one of the shots, grimacing, so she can't.

"Aren't you a lightweight."

The crowd gets antsier to get their orders in and people bump into us. I pick up the water and motion for her to move out of the way.

She scowls at me but steps aside.

"Drink the water."

"Give me my shot."

"No. Water first."

She crosses her arms.

"What do I have to do to get you to drink this?" I yell through the music the DJ just turned up.

She points to the shot. "You drink."

I obey, hold the water out, then growl, "Drink."

She rolls her eyes, takes it, and consumes half the bottle. "Happy?"

"No," I tell her. "Finish it."

She snags a shot from the waitress who is passing us, and I quickly take it from her.

"You drink, and I'll finish the water."

I'm going to be buzzed. I'm used to having to drink heavy at times with Fisher, but this is quick intake.

Do it so she drinks her water.

I chug it and tap the water bottle. When she is done, she moves toward the bar, and I freeze when I spot two men with Twisted Heart tattoos bellied up there.

They aren't even bothering to hide their tattoos tonight.

Gracie grabs my arm and ogles the men, paling.

"Come on." I lead her out of the room.

I need to get her and Connor off this boat.

Gracie doesn't argue and stays close to my side. I want to wrap her in my arms, but I'm sure Fisher has cameras all over the boat, so he is aware of what is occurring at all times.

"You okay?" I ask.

"Why wouldn't I be?" she snaps.

She doesn't have any knowledge about my involvement with the Twisted Hearts.

I guide her down the hall, take out my phone, and quickly type in a code to tell Interpol where I am and to have the Coast Guard call the captain of the vessel and tell it to return to the dock.

You only have a short time frame.

Time to make your move for the night.

Let's see how predictable Fisher is.

I lead Gracie into the room where we left Connor and Fisher. Connor is making out with a girl on the couch, and Fisher has a girl on each side of him with their hands on his chest and close to his dick.

He doesn't even realize we are in the room. The waitress sets another round of shots down, and each of the girls feeds him one.

"I need to talk to you," Gracie tells Connor, ignoring Fisher.

"Hey, baby," Fisher says, moving the other girls off him. They purse their lips at her.

She ignores him and tugs on Connor's ear.

"Ow!" Connor pulls out of his kiss. "Stop it."

"Now," Gracie demands.

"Hold on a minute." Connor moves his girl off his lap and rises.

Gracie drags him away to an empty spot along the wall.

"What the hell is up her ass?" Fisher asks.

For the millionth time, I want to punch him.

"No idea. We were in the bar, and she wanted to come back."

His eyes become slits. "Something happen?"

"I made her drink some water, and she got angry."

He laughs. "Gracie and water? In a bar?"

God, I hate this guy.

I can't wait till I get the opportunity to put a bullet in your head.

Connor and Gracie are in a heated discussion when the captain enters the room and approaches Fisher.

"We have to return to the dock."

"Those weren't my instructions," Fisher barks out.

"Coast Guard called. There's an issue, and all boats need to return."

"So, pay them a fee and keep going."

Dumbass.

The captain shifts. "Umm...I'm sorry, sir, but it doesn't work like that."

Fisher steps into his personal space. "Listen, I pay—"

I put both hands on Fisher's shoulders and force him back. "He's right. You can't do anything about it. Don't ruin your party over this. You can get arrested. Everyone can still have a good time at the dock."

"Fine," he grumbles.

"Connor, this isn't the time," Gracie sternly warns Connor behind me.

I spin.

"No. Let's ask Fisher. It's his party."

"Ask me what?"

"Drop it, Connor." Gracie tugs on his arm.

68

Connor shrugs out of it. "Why are Twisted Hearts on your boat?"

"It's not a..." Fisher's mouth snaps shut. He sobers. "Sorry, what did you say?"

"You heard me." Connor steps closer to him.

I push Connor a few feet away. "Easy there."

"How would I know who's here?"

"It's your party."

Fisher reaches for Gracie, but she steps closer to Connor. "Gracie, don't be silly."

"Why are they here?" her voice shakes.

He shrugs. "No idea. Surely you don't think I would invite them?"

Connor scowls at Fisher with his arm around Gracie.

Fisher looks at me to help him, but I stay focused on Gracie and Connor so I have an excuse not to.

"Gracie, I wouldn't be involved with those types of people. You shouldn't even have to ask me about this."

"I shouldn't?"

That's my girl.

Fisher arches an eyebrow at her.

Silence ensues.

"What were they doing?" Fisher asks.

"Drinking at the bar."

He waves his hand in the air. "So, they were having a good time like everyone else?"

Gracie shrugs. "I suppose so."

"They weren't harming anyone?"

"No, but—"

"Okay. So people are on my boat, at my party, minding their own business, but you're going to hold it against me?"

"They're gang members," Connor hisses. "The gang who terrorized my family."

I am sick to my stomach thinking about what Hudson told me

earlier and all the things I still don't have knowledge about and need to find out.

Fisher steps closer to Connor. "And I'm sorry they are here. But no one is causing problems right now. We're heading toward shore. As soon as we dock, I'll have security remove them if you want."

"If we want?" Gracie gapes at him with wet eyes.

"You know what I mean."

"Do I?"

He shakes his head. "I know what you're doing."

"What's that?"

"This is an excuse for you, isn't it?"

"An excuse?"

"Yeah. To keep things casual."

My gut flips.

Stay calm, Kade.

"You're drunk," Gracie tells him.

He snorts. "And you've been playing me."

"Playing you?"

"Yeah. Any excuse you can find you'll use not to have to commit to me."

Because she doesn't love you and never will, dickhead.

Connor goes to grab his shirt, but I intercept. "Let's all calm down. We've all had a lot to drink. Tomorrow will be a better time to talk about this."

"Gracie, I want to talk to you in private."

Oh, hell no.

"No," Connor tells him.

"This doesn't concern you."

Connor steps up.

I step between them again.

"Gracie?" Fisher belts out in anger.

Here we go. Show us your real side.

Her eyes widen.

"Don't you ever talk to my sister in that tone."

I push Connor away.

"Don't you—"

I drag Fisher several feet and stand in front of him. "They've been drinking and are sensitive from their family issues. Let them cool off tonight. Tomorrow we can all work this out."

His eyes turn into slits.

"Hey, man, I have your back."

He exhales. "Okay."

"I'll have them stay on my boat. They don't realize what they're saying right now. You have a fun night." I gaze over at the couch full of girls then. "Tomorrow, everything will be fine."

He peers at the women. "Yeah, okay. Thanks for having my back."

"Anytime, man."

"But I want to talk to Gracie for a minute. Help me get her away from Connor, at least."

My stomach churns.

"Not a good idea. Talk to her tomorrow."

"I need to. Have my back and help me."

Great. Now you're cornered.

I scan the room. "The corner is free. I'll help you."

We approach Gracie and Connor.

Fisher points to the area. "Talk to me for a minute over there, Gracie."

"No," Connor barks.

"Let her go," I insist.

He scowls at me, and she looks surprised.

"Let him say good night."

There. It should be clear enough she's not staying.

Fisher takes her hand. "Please."

She hesitates and I nod for her to go. She finally agrees.

They go to the corner of the room, and Connor growls at me, "Why did you allow her to go?"

"Calm down, I'm on your side. As soon as this boat docks, we're getting off. Your sister is coming with us, so if they return and say otherwise, I need you to insist."

"Won't be an issue."

"Good."

Gracie, don't let Fisher convince you to stay.

This is the part where I'm taking a gamble. I'm going all in Fisher is going to enjoy his night of freedom with the two girls on the couch and Gracie is going to be smart enough to leave with Connor and me.

The yacht glides to a halt.

My stomach is flipping as I wait for Gracie to return.

Connor and I don't take our eyes off the corner where Fisher has her against the wall. I restrain from pulling him away from her. He tries to kiss her, but she turns her head so it lands on her cheek.

That's my girl.

He hesitantly steps away from her.

"Go get your woman," I tell Connor.

He helps the girl from the couch get up and leads her over as Gracie returns.

Tell me you're coming with us.

"Gracie, let's go," Connor says.

"Bye, Fisher," she says.

He cups her face. "Tomorrow morning, we'll talk."

"Fine. Now let me go."

He sighs and releases her.

I motion for all of them to precede me. They step through the door, but Fisher grabs my arm.

What now?

"Tomorrow. Everything will be better tomorrow," I tell him.

"I get the fact you've known them forever, but do you have my back or theirs?"

Not good. You need to get off this boat.

I cross my arms. "Why would you even ask me that?"

"Wondering where your loyalties lie."

Not with you.

"I'm trying to help you out. If you don't want my help—"

"I didn't say that."

"All right. Then don't question our friendship ever again. I'll see you tomorrow."

I catch up with Connor, his girl, and Gracie. I only breathe once we're inside the safety of my yacht.

8

Gracie

"FISHER IS BAD NEWS. YOU NEED TO STAY AWAY FROM HIM." KADE'S words pound in my head along with visions of the men sitting at the bar, sporting Twisted Hearts tattoos.

Connor and the girl he brought with him are several feet ahead of Kade and me. Kade has his hand on my waist, and when we pass the dance club, the men are still sitting there.

Fisher didn't do anything once we told him they were on his boat. Any of my brothers would have had them thrown overboard.

"Gracie, I would never harm you or put you in a bad situation. I love you. Don't mess up all the progress we've made because people are here I didn't invite," Fisher said to me.

If he didn't invite them, why are they still here?

I shudder at the sight of the gang members, and Kade tugs me closer.

"Keep going. We're almost out," his deep voice instructs.

I lean into him, feeling safer in his arms, not thinking about how it's Kade and I shouldn't be.

We leave Fisher's boat and stroll several hundred feet over to Kade's. He unlocks his cabin. As soon as we are all inside, he flips the lock.

Connor goes straight to the bar and mixes drinks. His girl sits on the stool. I take the seat next to her.

"I'm Gracie." I hold out my hand.

She shakes it. "Yes. We've met before."

"We have?"

"Mm-hmm. Several times."

She has to be mistaken. I've never met her. Just humor her.

"When?"

"Over the last few months at the clubs. I rode to the hotel with you and Fisher when Connor won the bet for the hotel room in Ybor."

Heat scorches my face. I must have been too drunk all the times I've met her.

I avoid Kade's eyes but feel him watching me. "I apologize. What's your name?"

She smiles at me. "It's okay. It's Novah."

"You have a pretty name."

"Thanks."

Connor slides a drink to both of us.

Kade joins Connor behind the bar and removes four bottles of water then hands all of us one.

"Thanks, Pops," Connor smirks.

Kade lightly slaps him in the back of the head.

"Ouch."

I open the water and take a sip instead of the drink Connor made.

Kade winks at me, and my flutters erupt. It reminds me when he used to sneak winks at me during family events or when we were on dates with other people.

If only he weren't so damn sexy...

He sits next to me, and I restrain myself from leaning into his chest.

Connor doesn't know about you and Kade, so act normal.

The four of us talk for a while, and Connor says, "I think it's time we see this bedroom I earned." He picks up a giggling Novah off the barstool, and Kade rises.

"Give me a minute," he tells me.

"Not sure where I'd go, so take as much time as you want."

They leave the room.

I remove my shoes, grab the blanket off the top of the couch then curl up in it.

Kade returns and sits on the cushion next to me.

"Don't you think you should give me some space?" I ask.

"I think I've given you enough space, don't you?"

"Your choice."

"Gracie, I didn't—"

"Stop. Please. I don't want to get into this right now."

He puts his hand on the side of my thigh. I should remove it, but I don't.

"Okay. I saw Hudson and Lena tonight."

"Yeah, I'm aware. Lena told me they were meeting up with you."

"Kate's living with Hudson?"

Hatred flares through me. "She's still a witch and needs to get out."

"I told him several times the same thing." Kade's thumb brushes my thigh, and my body pulses. "Gabriella and Lena were declared by the Twisted Hearts?"

Emotions overpower me, and a tear drips down my cheek. He places me on his lap, and I don't fight him when he holds my head against his chest.

"I can't imagine how horrible these last few years have been for you. I'm so sorry I wasn't here."

"I needed you. We needed you."

He kisses the top of my head. "I'm so sorry, Gracie."

Silence besides my sniffles ensues.

Kade finally asks, "How did Gabriella even get on Triker's radar?"

"Gabriella and Connor had a party. He got out of prison shortly after Beckett and showed up."

Kade takes a deep breath. "He met Beckett in prison?"

"It's not like they hung out," I hurl at him.

He holds me tighter. "I didn't say anything of the sort."

Calm down, Gracie. He's just asking questions.

You shouldn't be on his lap.

But it's the only place I want to be.

"I still think it's connected to Skates," I quietly say.

Kade's heart pounds faster. "Skates?"

He's completely clueless.

But he should be. If he hadn't left, he would have known.

Anger I wish I could let go consumes me again.

"He set Beckett up for Clay's murder. Henry was there, too, and on Skates' payroll."

Kade's eyes widen. "Henry?"

More tears fall, and I turn away.

"But I didn't..."

I jerk my head toward him. "You didn't what?"

"Nothing." His eyes have guilt in them.

"No, Kade. Tell me."

His jaw clenches, and he gazes at the ceiling.

"How do you even know Triker's and Skates' name?"

He closes his eyes.

I sit up straighter. "You saw the tattoos tonight before I did."

His head turns toward me. "I never said I saw them."

"I only saw they were there because you froze when you looked at them."

He cringes but catches himself.

He is aware of something regarding the Twisted Hearts.

I quickly spin and straddle him. "Tell me what you're hiding. Enough of the lies."

"I've never lied to you."

"No, you tell me nothing."

He stays silent, which only infuriates me more.

I jump off him and go to the bar and pour myself a shot.

"What are you doing?"

"Having a drink." I quickly drink a clear liquid which I soon discover is rum. I grab my water and take a swig.

"Stop drinking."

"Don't tell me what to do." Just to piss him off, I take another shot.

He grabs the bottle from me, and he barks. "Enough."

I take a few steps, but the alcohol hits me, and I grab onto the side of the bar.

"You hardly drank. What happened?"

I spin with anger and jab his chest. "You. You happened. You destroyed my life. You...you left me and for what? I don't even know. So at least when I drink, I get to drink you out of my system."

His jaw clenches, and he blinks hard. He quietly says, "How's that working out for you?"

I turn, grab a fifth of whiskey, and march down the hall while drinking it but feeling sick.

Kade is on my heels. "Gracie, stop." He grabs the bottle.

I turn and get sick all over him.

"I'm sorry," I sob, then puke some more.

Kade quickly carries me into the bathroom, and when I'm done vomiting, he puts me in the shower, but I can hardly stand up. He gets in with his clothes on and holds me.

"I hate you," I cry into his chest.

He puts his lips on my forehead. "I hate myself for hurting you."

"Three years. All I feel is pain. I wanted to spend my life with you, and you screwed me and left me."

His body shakes with emotion. "I'm so sorry. You don't understand how sorry I am. I want to spend my life with you. We still can. Give me a second chance, please."

"I can't," I sob. "You destroyed me. I'm too far gone."

He holds me tighter. "No, you aren't."

"I am. I've done too much."

"No. Whatever you've done doesn't matter."

"It does."

"No. It doesn't. Whatever you've done or do, I'm always going to love you."

"You can't love me when I don't even love myself anymore," I cry.

More pain fills his face. "Shh. Don't say that."

For a long time I sob in his chest. After we get out and he dries me off, I rinse my mouth and brush my teeth with an extra toothbrush he gives me. Kade throws one of his T-shirts over me then tucks me into his bed.

He puts on a pair of boxers and slides next to me, cradling me into his arms.

"Beckett went to prison so Skates wouldn't kill all of us. Hudson and Ryland were the only ones who Beckett told. No one said anything, and he just rot for ten years."

He kisses my head, and I sink into him.

"Gabriella was abducted, and I kept wondering what he was doing to her. And I'm not sure if it was more painful thinking about how Triker was treating her, wondering if she would ever come home, or watching Javier and the rest of my family implode almost every night."

His arms hold me tighter than they ever have, and his tears mix with mine.

"I'm sorry. I should have been there for you. I'm so sorry."

"She's pregnant. They say it's Javier's, but I saw paperwork I shouldn't have. She's further along than they say, and it's Triker's. The baby has to be his. But I can't even talk to her about it because she hasn't told any of us. And Lena, she's the first person who ever has made Hudson truly happy, but Kate's at their house toying with both of them and I'm so tired of it. I'm so tired of people messing with my family. I just want it to stop. But it doesn't seem to ever end." I sob with shaky breaths into his arms.

He kisses me and then mumbles, "I'm going to make sure it all stops. I promise you."

"You can't. No one can."

"I will. I promise."

I cry myself to sleep in his arms. When I wake up, I feel safe and loved, then realize I'm with Kade.

The events of the night rush to the surface, and there are parts I can remember but some are just blurry. I curse myself and realize I'm in his T-shirt.

Did we have sex?

I panic, and his arm tightens around me.

"Stop freaking out," his deep voice commands.

Slowly, I look up.

The smoldering expression I've seen whenever he has kissed me is in his eyes. His fingers brush over my hip, stroking me, then dip lower until they are tracing the curve of my ass. An erection, hard as steel, butts up against my lower torso.

Every ounce of my body pulses, craving to feel his body all over mine, claiming and owning me how he did one night over three years ago.

I've done so many things trying to recreate how Kade made me feel but have never found it with anyone but him.

Don't give in, you'll regret it.

Do it. Just one time to feel how only he can make you feel.

Kade decides for me. In a quick move, he flips me on my back and pins my arms above my head then dips down. As his dark-brown eyes drill into mine, his breath labors then his lips slowly consume the skin on my neck, chin, and ear.

I shiver from his touch and when his mouth meets mine, a concoction of lust, and need, and years of longing combust like dynamite.

His body, warm and muscular, teases and taunts me. Every contact of flesh to flesh sends sinful needs racing through my veins.

"I promise you. I'm going to make everything bad go away," he murmurs then nibbles on my lobe.

He promises.

No. Wait.

He can't promise that. No one can.

Don't fall for him again. It's a trap.

I shove away from him, breathless, and jump off the bed.

"Gracie."

"Don't promise me something impossible, Kade. You've hurt me enough." I open the door. Connor is there and points to the puke in the hallway. "Tell me you didn't lose the ability to hold your liquor?"

"Shut up, Connor."

"Gracie," Kade yells and comes out in his boxers.

Great. I don't need Connor to think anything is up between Kade and me.

I spin. "Thanks for taking care of me when I was sick."

"Gracie, where are you going?"

"I don't know," I shout in frustration.

Kade puts his hand on my shoulder and turns me. "Sit down and relax. I'll make some coffee and breakfast."

"Yeah, chill out, Gracie. Besides, we have to talk to Fisher and then be presentable for Gabriella's surprise party," Connor says.

Kade arches his brow.

I take a deep breath. "Fine. I'll be on the couch."

The rest of the morning, I spend avoiding Kade when possible. When Fisher comes over, he questions why I'm in Kade's T-shirt, and I explain how I drank too much and got sick.

"Thanks for taking care of her, man," he says and fist-bumps Kade.

Kade acts like he's his best friend, and I wonder why.

He doesn't like Fisher. I can tell. He told me to stay away, and I don't think it's only because he wants me for himself.

Fisher tells us his security team traced the gang members to one of the guests who he won't be inviting anymore. He apologizes for it even though it sounds like it wasn't his fault.

He comes and sits by me and tugs me on his lap. "Are you going to forgive me and return to my yacht?"

I can feel Kade watching me.

My wish is to stay with Kade forever. But there is no forever with Kade. He showed me what his forever looks like three years ago.

"It wasn't your fault. I'm sorry I accused you. Let's go."

Fisher kisses me, and I put everything I have into it, but it lacks all the fireworks Kade and I have. Without saying a word to Kade, I let Fisher lead me off the boat and onto his.

Fisher is safe. It's clear who he is and what I get with him.

Kade is danger. With him, my heart can only get destroyed further. And there isn't a lot left to break.

9

Kade

Watching Gracie kiss Fisher is the equivalent of taking my heart, cutting it into pieces then throwing it in a blender to destroy.

What did you expect?

You would wake up, kiss her, and she would choose you?

Tell her about Fisher.

You can't. You have to take him down, or it could put her in even more danger.

The game I have to play, I hate. My woman is involved. No matter what my current state is with Gracie, she's mine to protect and always will be. And it drives my hatred for the Twisted Hearts even deeper. What Gracie told me last night about what her family—my family—has gone through, terrorizes my soul.

And I didn't have any idea.

I should have seen what was going on. I spend all my hours, every day, on Twisted Hearts issues.

But taking Fisher down and keeping him away from Gracie has consumed my every move. Any time I could get Fisher to stay in Europe, away from Florida, I did. Extra trips to Ibiza, Amsterdam, and Monte Carlo were abundant—especially Monte Carlo.

Fisher and I are similar in age, but he's the equivalent to Connor when it comes to partying. He never grew up.

All it takes is a few hints about what will be at the party I'm attending and a suggestion he should come, and he's there.

He can't help himself and turn it down.

Time after time, he had plans to return to Florida. I would see it online, and as soon as I did, I'd pick a spot, tell Interpol the female spies they needed to fly in, and all the other details required to lure Fisher to my party so he didn't step foot near Gracie.

More often than not, I took him to Monte Carlo. It's how I know he's trying to reel Connor into his world.

Fisher is a gambler. One who wins. Victories at the high-end card tables he earns, but he takes calculated losses away from the table to lure men into his world. If Connor continues to make bets with him, Fisher will someday win, and then he'll own him, too. So I have another reason to work faster and end this for good.

But the Brooks are involved in the Twisted Hearts deeper than I could ever comprehend, and I'm kicking myself harder.

Domestic matters left my radar. I was aware Skates died, and Triker took over, but he wasn't pulling all the strings. Domestically, yes. Internationally, no. Triker was the figurehead, the face of the gang, but he wasn't an Elite.

The Elite are a group of "business men and women" throughout the world who stay hidden, calling the shots and profiting from crimes. Fisher is at the top of the pyramid.

But I had no clue the Brooks were a target of the Twisted Hearts. I figured I had bigger issues to deal with and was laser-focused on Fisher. It was a huge mistake.

I could have helped figure out the Beckett situation so he could get released from prison sooner. If I had knowledge Gabriella had a declaration on her, I would have taken action to find Triker and put a bullet in his head before he got to her.

For the millionth time since leaving Gracie, I kick myself for staying away.

I thought if I avoided the Brooks until I had the ability to permanently return, it would be easier for Gracie. Then she could live and one day, hopefully, she would forgive me, and I could make amends. I stopped communicating with Hudson. He knows me better than anyone, and I was afraid I would ask him too many questions about Gracie, and he would piece together that something happened between us.

And he was cut up over Kate. I didn't trust myself not to spill to him the details about her.

Hudson and Ryland would have been angry enough when they found out about Gracie and me, but eventually, they would have gotten past it. If they ever find out what happened three years ago, that I slept with their sister and then left six hours later, they will hate me for life after attempting to beat me to a pulp.

I'll take their beating. I deserve it.

Since Beckett was released, I haven't seen him, but he was always protective of his sisters before he went to prison. I'm sure he'd want to pummel me and never forgive me, either.

Connor may be the most laid back and okay with a lot of things the other Brooks brothers aren't, but if he ever discovered the truth, he'd hate me as well, and someone would have to drag him off me.

When I told Interpol I wanted to infiltrate Fisher because he was the person we needed to concentrate on the most, I already knew he had the money to fly under the radar and be at the top of the Twisted Hearts food chain. What I've learned about him over the last few years makes my stomach churn.

Fisher has his hand in every pot the Twisted Hearts has. In order to gain his trust, I've done deals with him. As far as Fisher is concerned, I'm another guy who got rich the way he did, and I'm his ally to stay in the gates of greed. And he's let me into all of it, except one thing—the main players in his chemical dealings.

But my time on the outside is about to change. He's been hinting, and I'm doing everything I can to get in on it.

Interpol has enough to take Fisher down, but the chemicals he's been buying are what terrorist organizations use to build nuclear bombs or create germ warfare. Fisher has purchased enough to not only blow up several countries but create a new type of disease to essentially wipe out a majority of the population. And this is his plan. I'm the one who discovered it on the dark net.

Interpol needs the contacts Fisher is buying from as well as any scientists he's working with. We also need the location of where they've stockpiled everything. And while my hacking has gotten me far, there is one code I can't crack.

Last night, it became clear to me. Lena has it.

I need to get the code from Lena.

Fisher doesn't need to be around Lena, either.

How do I get Gracie to break things off and stay away from him?

Gracie stops the kiss with Fisher, says nothing to me, and leaves.

"We need to leave in an hour," Connor calls out to her.

She avoids me, puts her hand in the air, and waves.

"I'll drop you both off. Come over when you're ready," Fisher instructs Connor.

And he's once again in their good graces.

Damn it, Kade. You didn't think past last night. Where was your plan on how to handle today? You let him waltz in here and squirm his way back in.

You had to kiss her and freak her out today. You had to promise her again you'll make all the bad things go away.

I will make them go away or die trying.

You're a spy. Use your skills and shut your mouth.

"I'm going to shower," Connor tells me.

"Where's Novah?"

"She already left."

"How?"

"I ordered her an Uber."

"Did you at least walk her out?" I bark at him.

"Chill out, Kade. Of course I did. I don't treat my women like shit."

I pull out a barstool. "Sit down for a minute."

Connor groans. "Am I going to get lectured every time I stay? If so, you can keep your room."

"A lecture and a man-to-man talk are two different things. You should realize the difference by now."

He plops down on the stool and loudly sighs. "What are we talking about?"

"Fisher."

"What about him?"

"If he tries to get you to work for him, you say no."

His eyes turn to slits. "I thought you were his friend."

I stay quiet.

"This is about Gracie, isn't it?"

"This is about you not getting into what he's into."

"What is he into?"

Silence.

"Why was Gracie in your room all night?"

"She was sick."

Connor arches an eyebrow.

"You saw the puke."

He crosses his arms and tilts his head.

Hudson always said Connor was the smartest out of all of them.

He shakes his head. "I'm not dumb."

"Never said you were."

"From the way you and Gracie are eyeing each other, my guess is something is going on. You're trying to remove Fisher from the picture so she can be yours."

We've been obvious? Shit.

"You have it wrong," I lie and cringe inside, hating every untruthful word that comes out of my mouth and realizing I've told Connor several over the last 24 hours.

"I'm closest to Gracie. I spend the most amount of time with her. She's angry with you and has been since you stepped foot on the island. It's not only from your babysitting efforts."

Think, Kade.

"She's upset I haven't been in touch the last three years."

"Why weren't you?"

"I can't get into it."

"Why not?"

"There are things about my job I can't discuss."

"Your career kept you from picking up the phone or sending a text message? Or responding to the ones we sent, like the one I sent you on your birthday every year?"

So many wrong decisions you've made, Kade.

You thought it would be better for them all.

You were wrong.

"I'm sorry."

"You say we're brothers, but one thing I'm sure about is my brothers would never ignore me for three years. Or skip town without even saying 'goodbye.'"

"Connor, I'm sorry. I hope I can explain it to you one day, but I never meant to hurt anyone. You have to believe me."

"Why are you even in Florida?"

"I've always wanted to be here."

"Why now?"

"My employer allowed me to finally come home."

"What is this job? You reference your work all the time but

don't give any details. What is so important for you to have ignored us for three years?"

How do I even answer him?

Connor waves his hand around the room. "You've done well. You're living large. Congratulations. I hope it's made you happy."

"You think this is about money?"

"All you refer to is your job. What else would it be about?"

I put my hands on the bar and lean closer to him. "Listen to me, Connor. One day, I hope I can tell you everything. Right now, I can't. Your family means everything to me. It may not appear like it from where you're sitting, but it does. You need to not get involved with Fisher. If I'm not around, you keep your eye on your sister. Stop saying she can handle herself. She can't. And stop encouraging her to drink. It's destructive and not helping her."

"She threw up one time."

I slam my hand on the counter and bellow out, "It doesn't matter. It's not good for her."

Connor rises. "I'll watch her closer, but you don't get to reenter the picture and make demands. I'm going to shower and get ready. Keep your key. I don't need it."

"Connor—"

"No. I may be younger than everyone and do my own thing, but I'm not stupid. You want Gracie, and you're willing to sabotage your friendship with Fisher over it. I suggest you watch how you act around my brothers, or they'll be questioning you much harder than I am." Connor spins and stomps out of the room.

Great. This is not how I wanted this to go.

If Connor can tell something is up with you and Gracie, then you need to do a better job hiding your attraction toward her.

I'm still cursing myself when Connor returns.

"I made the bed and hung up the towel. I'm not sure what to do with your laundry."

"It's fine."

"Thanks for a good time. See you later."

"Connor—"

"Leave it, Kade." He waves as he passes me and leaves.

Shit, shit, shit.

My phone vibrates, and a text message from Hudson pops up, reminding me to stop into Gabriella's surprise party.

I get ready, go off the island to buy her and her new husband Javier a wedding gift. It kills me I wasn't at her wedding, but I understand why she ripped my invite up.

She needs a baby gift, too.

Gracie confided in you about the pregnancy and you need to pretend you had no clue when Gabriella finally tells you.

My stomach flips, thinking about what Triker put her through. And the pain it caused all the Brooks and especially Gracie.

I grab a wedding card and write a ten-thousand dollar check and stuff both inside the envelope then tape it to the gift.

After the party has been going for a few hours, I leave to go. I notice Fisher's car parked in the lot, and I'm relieved he won't be there.

Another sign Gracie isn't in love with him. If she were, he'd be at her family events.

As soon as I get to the party, Gracie leaves the room.

Crap. I should have warned her Hudson invited me.

I spend several minutes hugging the Brooks family, and it's like I've finally returned home. My childhood had more hours with them than my parents.

When I finally get to Gabriella, she hugs me, but it isn't as warm as the night I first saw her and Gracie in the bar.

She's upset you hurt Gracie.

I hug her tighter, in the hopes she will forgive me one day, and she succumbs and returns my hug. When she lets me go, she introduces me to her husband, Javier, and I do a double take and remind myself we're supposed to be strangers.

She married Javier Lòpez.

We both shake hands and act like we've never met.

But we have.

When the CIA recruited me out of college, I had several top-secret projects with the Marines and Javier Lòpez. He's one of the best snipers I ever met and became a good friend of mine. During our free time, he taught me how to be a better shooter. The tricks he showed me have given me a 100 percent *aim to kill* record. I plan on adding at least one more person to my record before my time with Interpol is up. The bullet is reserved for Fisher Corbyn.

Lena and I exchange a hello, but she seems uncomfortable around me. Hell, maybe I'm nervous around her, too.

I survey the room. "You've done a great job remodeling this place. It doesn't resemble the same house."

"Let me show you around," Hudson says.

"Actually, we need to talk to you and Lena," Javier tells him.

What's going on?

I need to get in on their conversation. It has to be about Kate.

There is no way right now. Get ahold of Javier later and see what is going on.

Gracie coldly says, "I'll show him. You go."

She's so stunning. Every time I see her, she's more beautiful.

"You look gorgeous," I tell her when we get alone.

She ignores my comment.

I follow her around the house until we get to the master bedroom which is the last one down the hall. We go inside, and I quietly shut and lock the door.

When we get inside the walk-in closet, she spins. "Why are you here?"

"Hudson invited me." I step forward.

She retreats, and I follow until she's against the wall.

"I'm not going anywhere. I want our life back."

"We never had a life. We had secrets and lies."

"Secrets, yes. Lies, no."

She motions between us. "We were a lie."

"We were never a lie. We still aren't."

"You should go back to wherever you came from. I'm with Fisher. You and I have no future."

I press my body against hers, and she shudders. I tilt her chin up. "Listen to me carefully. No matter what you do with Fisher, or how long you stay with him, I'm always going to love you. I'm fully aware you're mad at me and hurt, but he's not good for you. The sooner you cut it off with him, the better."

"The better for who? You?"

"No, Gracie. You. He isn't who you think he is."

"Then tell me what he's done."

"I can't. Stop asking me. You need to trust me."

She scoffs. "Trust you? You want me as yours, so you'll say anything to get your own way."

I put my hands on both sides of her head. "Yes, I want you as mine. But no, I'm not the type of man who will tell you lies to manipulate you. And you don't even love him."

Her eyes water. "What do you know about love?"

"It's what we have."

She shakes her head. "There is no we."

I dip my head lower to her face. "Please stop fighting me. There is an us."

"There isn't," she whispers.

I brush my lips to hers but wait for her to return my kiss. Time stands still, and I stare in her blue eyes, willing her to return my affection.

Her chest rises and falls quicker.

Her perfectly pink lip trembles.

Her warm breath merges into mine.

She caves and leans closer, and I meet her halfway, gliding my tongue into her mouth on contact.

My arms wrap around her, and she laces her fingers through

my hair. All things evil in the world disappear. There's only the beauty of Gracie and my obsession to love and protect her as mine.

"I love you," I murmur to her and ravage her mouth before she can deny it.

Every kiss with Gracie is like a potent drug, flipping an on switch for my senses, masking all the bad things I've ever done or felt, creating an addiction so powerful, I'll never be able to truly live without it.

"I hate you, Kade." She pulls my head closer.

"You do, and you don't," I respond between kisses, trying to make her see we can still be.

"Leave me alone," she says and tugs at my hair while circling my tongue quicker with hers.

I groan, sliding my hand into her pants, through her slit and her wet folds.

She whimpers, grinding into my hand.

"I'm here to love you and protect you and give you everything I should have three years ago," I murmur in her ear while circling faster on her clit.

"You...oh God...can't," she pants out.

"I can, and I will. If you push me away, I'm coming after you, so stop, and let's be together."

"Kade," she cries out louder, and I devour her mouth once again.

Tremors whip through her, and she yanks my hair so hard, I'm sure she's ripped it out. When her moans subside, I move from her clit, into her sex, pumping and curling my fingers before repositioning my thumb on her nub.

My body, pressed against hers, is an inferno, blazing and unable to be contained.

"You're all I've ever wanted, Gracie."

She closes her eyes. Her face is flushed, and she's bucking into my hand, on the edge of climaxing again.

I slow her down. "Tell me you still want me."

"No." She circles her hips faster.

"Please," I beg her.

"No."

My fingers pump faster into her, and her insides clutch around them. "I love you. I'm going to do whatever it takes to give you the life you deserve."

"You...never..." she breathes then flies into another orgasm, so I cover her sounds again with my mouth.

Punishment and reward twist together as the only thing I want to do is take care of Gracie, but my dick is hard, and blood is pulsing in my veins. But this isn't about me.

I remove a thin platinum bracelet from my pocket and slip it around her wrist while her face is buried in my neck, and she's trying to find her breath.

Every ounce of self-control I have is required to move away from her when she is finally able to stand on her own.

I taste her lips one last time and hold her wrist up to eye level. "Don't tell anyone I put this on you."

A new flush fills her face, but this is one of anger.

"I don't want your—"

I put my finger over her lips, and she freezes. "Someday, when you'll allow me, I'll shower you with gifts. Right now, this is so I can track where you're at no matter where in the world you go."

She gapes at me then tries to remove it.

"No matter what you do, it's not going to come off."

"How dare you. Get it off me."

"No. You're playing with fire being with Fisher. This is to protect you."

"Get this off me, or I'll go tell my entire family about us."

I retreat a few steps and cross my arms. "Go ahead. I'm ready to come clean with them about my feelings for you."

Her eyes turn into slits. "No. That's your way of trying to get me in your good graces again."

"You aren't getting this, are you?"

She glares at me.

"Whatever I have to do to win you over, I will. And no matter what your family wants to do or say to me, I'll take it like a man and then keep pursuing you. Nothing and no one is going to stop me fighting for you unless the day comes you really do love someone else. And even then, they better be on the up-and-up."

"Stop talking bad about Fisher unless you're going to tell me why you say this stuff."

"I can't. You have to trust me."

She shoves past me and goes into the bathroom.

I follow.

She fixes her hair, and I wash and dry my hands. She holds her wrist out. "Remove this."

"No. And don't tell anyone what it is, or that I gave it to you." I turn and leave the bathroom.

"Kade," she angrily says.

I spin and draw her into my arms. "On this issue, you have to get past the hurt of what I've done and return to the place where you trust me. I hope I never need to use this, but if you're ever in danger, I will come find you, and don't forget it."

Her eyes widen, but she says nothing. I peck her on the lips and release her then find the others.

Scanning the room, I exchange a glance with Connor and approach him.

He hands me a beer.

"Thanks." I take it and discreetly put a key in his palm.

He looks at it then at me, and the corners of his mouth turn up.

I wink at him, and he nods.

Tracker on Gracie, key to Connor, and a tracker gold chain on his bed for when he goes back to the yacht. Where is Hudson?

Javier and I lock eyes. I grab a beer and he exchanges it for a piece of paper with his phone number on it.

95

"You seen Hudson?" I ask.

"He's outside."

"Thanks." I grab another beer for Hudson then go outside. "There you are."

Hudson scowls at me. "No one else is here. Please don't hide whatever it is you know. And what the hell have you been doing all these years?"

Crap.

"Kade. We've been friends for a long time. Tell me what the hell is going on."

"Why didn't you ever tell me you were aware of who framed Beckett?"

He shifts on his feet. "I couldn't. My family's safety was at stake."

"I could have helped you."

"No one could."

"I thought you thought of me as a brother?"

"I do. But this..."

I cross my arms over my chest.

"Who told you the truth about Beckett being framed?"

Shit. I focus on the sky.

"Kade," he barks out.

"Gracie told me last night. But don't go all apeshit on her."

"I won't. But what have you been doing all these years? And tell me the truth, not the bullshit you told me when you left."

"The only thing I can tell you is I do contract work for the government."

"The government?"

"Yes."

Hudson's eyes become slits. "And it involves the Twisted Hearts?"

Silence.

"Kate is a Twisted Heart?"

I continue not to speak.

"Is Lena, Gabriella, or any other member of my family in danger?"

I close my eyes and take a deep breath. "I'll do everything I can to watch out for you all. But if Kate's here, she's here for a reason. I'm convinced Lena has what she wants."

Hudson pales.

"Let me talk to Lena," I say.

"She isn't going to talk to you. I screwed up big-time. She's upset."

"She needs to talk to me. I think she has a code I need."

His face scrunches. "What kind of code?"

"I can't tell you. But it's important."

He angrily shakes his head. "You're unbelievable."

"Hudson—"

"She won't talk to you. I'll work on her, but she isn't going to tell you anything today."

I scrub my face.

Time is ticking, and I'm getting nowhere fast.

"What's the situation with this Fisher guy?" Hudson asks.

"Don't be pissed, bro, but I can't go into details on him, either."

Hudson scowls at me. "He's bad news, isn't he?"

My gut flips. "He's not who I would choose for your sister."

"Gracie—"

"I'll watch out for her. You have my word."

He pats me on the back. "Thanks. I appreciate it."

"There's something else you need to be aware of."

"What?"

"Connor needs to stay away from him, too."

Hudson's eyes widen. "Connor? What's happened?"

"Nothing yet. But Fisher's trying to drag him into his world. I can see it. It's part of him winning Gracie over."

Hudson's face reddens. "He's trying to earn my sister's affection by harming my brother?"

"I don't put it past him. Gracie doesn't love him. Fisher can see it."

"What's he trying to get my brother involved in?"

A whole lot of nothing good.

"I can't go into it. Connor promised me he would stop making bets with him but reinforce it."

10

Gracie

"Come with me. I need to go tonight, and I don't want to leave you again," Fisher tells me for the hundredth time, in a tone he's never used with me before.

For the last hour, he's been pressuring me to leave, insisting he has to go this evening and not letting up when I tell him no.

"My sister is having a baby. She just got rescued from being abducted. I don't want to be gone for six months."

"You can fly in and out. I'll pay for it. Stop being a child."

"It's not the same thing, and I'm not being a child," I tell him, hurt by his words.

Fisher runs his hands through his blond hair. "I thought we were going to do serious?"

My insides quiver. "We are."

He shakes his head and scowls at me. "I'm not sure how we're supposed to be serious if you're living here, and I'm all over the world."

"So, I'm supposed to leave my family and move?"

"Not permanently. But you are allowed to have a life, aren't you?"

"They are my life," I hurl at him.

He quietly says, "I don't think this is about them. I think it's about me." He leaves the room.

Now you've hurt him again.

Maybe you should go with him.

No. It's too long to be gone.

But he's right. You can't have a life together if you're in different places.

I rise and follow him. He's staring out the window facing Kade's yacht.

Kade. If you left, maybe you could get over him.

I wrap my arms around Fisher from behind. "This isn't about you. My family has been through a lot."

He spins, his face red with anger, something I've only seen the night on his yacht when I left with Connor and Kade. "Do you want me, Gracie?"

My pulse increases.

I want Kade.

Kade is danger. Fisher is safe.

"Yes. Stop questioning it."

He embraces me but aggressively says, "Then come with me."

"I can't—"

From the corner of my eye, I catch Mia running down the dock, and Gabriella trotting along behind her.

Chills run down my spine.

Fisher furrows his brow.

"Something is wrong." I shrug out of his embrace, I run through the yacht, and meet Mia on the deck. "What's going on?"

Fisher is behind me.

Mia blurts, "Kate kidnapped Lena, and they found her."

Goose bumps pop out on my skin. "Kate or Lena?"

Mia replies, "Lena. Kate is dead and Lena is at the hospital."

Fisher steps between us. "Kate is dead?"

"Yes."

"Is Lena okay?" I ask.

Gabriella arrives. "Yes. But we need to go."

It's never going to end.

"Why did Kate kidnap her?" I ask.

"We aren't sure. Beckett said we'd talk when we get there," Gabriella says.

"I'll drive you," Fisher says.

"You don't have to. I'm okay to drive," Mia tells him.

"But—"

"It's okay. You said you have a lot of work to do today. I'll call you once I find out what is going on," I tell him.

"I'll come—"

I peck him on the lips. "Stay. There is nothing you can do. I'll call you as soon as I can with all the details."

Fisher's eyes move from Gabriella to Mia and me.

I step away and glance at Kade's boat. "Call you later."

You should tell Kade.

Why? He has nothing to do with this.

He's part of our family.

No, he isn't.

I step off the boat and follow Gabriella and Mia to the car. When we get inside, I turn to the girls. "Why would Kate kidnap Lena?"

Gabriella's eyes fill with tears. "I told Lena to get away from her. I warned Hudson, too. She has always been bad news but this…"

I hold her hand. "She's okay though?"

"Beckett said she is in shock from killing Kate, but otherwise, okay."

"Lena killed her?"

"Yeah," Mia quietly says.

I sit back in my seat. No one says anything else until we get to the hospital. We find Lena's room and Kade is there.

Why is Kade here?

Gabriella knocks. "Brought you some clothes, Lena."

Lena smiles. "Thank you."

I tear up, happy and relieved she seems okay.

I quickly turn to avoid Kade.

This isn't about you and Kade. It's about Lena.

The doctor comes in, and everyone except Hudson and Lena leaves.

Javier and Chloe escort us to a private area where Beckett and Ryland are seated. Kade follows but stays several feet away from me.

"Why did Kate kidnap Lena?" I ask.

Javier shifts on his feet then tugs Gabriella into him. "Kate was the First Lady of the Twisted Hearts. She wanted information from Lena."

Gabriella gapes at him. "That's not possible."

Javier and Chloe explain how Kate was Skates' Twisted Heart secret wife and how Veronica was just a cover-up one.

"So, I was a cover-up First Lady?" Gabriella asks.

Javier kisses the top of her head. "Yes."

Gabriella focuses on the floor.

"Lena shot Kate?" I ask.

"Yes," Chloe confirms.

"Did you arrest the people who helped Kate kidnap her?" Mia asks.

"They're all dead. The FBI raided the house in Palmetto she was taken to. Then we took down Kate's thug in Longboat."

"Who was Kate's thug?" Gabriella asks Javier.

"Joaquín Pérez."

Her face drains color. "From Mexico?"

"Have you met him?" Kade asks.

I spin toward him and cross my arms.

What does he have to do with this?

"One of the first nights I left the mansion on Casey Key, we went to a dinner party. Lena always came out with us wherever Triker or I went. Joaquín was there. The moment Lena saw him, she grabbed Triker's arm to steady herself. Triker reminded her he had a protection order on her, and nothing would happen, but the entire dinner, Lena's hand was shaking, and anytime Joaquín would address her, she shook harder. When we returned to Casey Key, I asked her what happened, but she wouldn't tell me."

"Gabriella, what was discussed at this dinner party? Do you remember?" Kade asks.

"What business is this of yours?" I seethe.

Kade's eyes are full of guilt, but he quickly focuses on Gabriella.

She looks at Javier for permission.

"It's okay. Tell us if you remember anything."

"There was a lot of talk about property. It needed to be transferred over and they discussed underground storage."

"Where?" Kade asks.

"They didn't say."

"Did they discuss what for?" Javier asks.

Gabriella shakes her head. "I'm sorry. I assumed drugs."

Javier kisses her forehead and tightens his hold on her. "Nothing to be sorry about."

"Gabriella, did they talk about anything else?" Kade asks.

She hesitates. "Why are you so interested in this?"

He shifts.

Connor comes running in. "Is Lena okay?"

Beckett pats him on the back. "Yeah. She's going to be fine."

Connor exhales. "What happened?"

The information Javier and Chloe told us they rehash to Connor. The entire time, I watch Kade.

It hits me. He listens the way Chloe or Javier does. The questions he asks aren't what someone who is only part of our family and concerned would ask. It's enough to make me believe he's some sort of law enforcement personnel, and then Agent Carter, the head of the FBI, enters the room.

After greeting everyone, he takes Chloe, Javier, and Kade aside.

"Why is Kade with them?" Connor asks.

Ryland and Beckett shift.

He's part of the FBI.

Then why has he been overseas?

Did he lie about his whereabouts, too?

"Who shot Joaquín Pérez?" I ask.

Still, no answers from my brothers.

"Kade shot him?" I only need to see the expression on Ryland and Beckett's faces to tell me I'm right.

"So once again, the two of you aren't going to tell us anything?" Connor accuses them.

"Connor—" Ryland starts.

"No. I'm tired of this game. I'm going for a walk."

"Connor—" Beckett jumps in.

"You, too, Beckett?" He shakes his head and more disappointment fills his face.

"I'll go with you, Connor," I tell him.

As we approach Kade, I lock eyes with him, and something in his are different. It's as if he's worried about what I know. And it occurs to me he killed a man today but doesn't seemed fazed.

Javier wasn't affected when he killed Triker.

Totally different. He did it to save Gabriella.

But Kade was part of saving Lena.

If he's in the FBI, then why couldn't he just tell me?

"We need the black book. Without it, we'll never find all these leaks," Carter says as we pass them.

The black book?

"With Kate dead, there's going to be a bigger fight for power," Javier says.

Connor and I go to the cafeteria. We grab a coffee and sit in a booth across from the other.

"What is going on between you and Kade?" Connor asks.

My heart pounds. "Nothing. Why do you ask?"

"Are you going to be just like them and act like I'm stupid."

"You aren't stupid."

Connor arches a brow at me.

My stomach flips.

"Kade wants you. I see it. What's going on between you two?"

I nervously tap my coffee cup. "Nothing. It was a long time ago."

"Gracie, look at me," he growls.

I turn.

"Did he hurt you?"

I don't say anything. I want to deny it, but anything of the sort is just going to insult Connor, and I won't hurt him.

His eyes turn into slits. "What did he do?"

"Connor, I don't want to get into it. Kade is who he is, and I am who I am. Leave it."

"He broke your heart, didn't he? Before he left?"

I close my eyes, and a tear falls. "No."

"Do not lie to me," he says through gritted teeth.

"I'm—"

"Gracie!"

"It doesn't matter," I cry out.

"It does matter," Connor says sternly.

"No."

Connor rises and throws his coffee in the trash.

Oh shit. My gut flips so quick, I think I might get sick.

"Connor, where are you going?"

"To take care of something," he growls.

"Connor," I shout, but he's far ahead of me, practically running down the hall.

I'm about twenty feet away when Connor taps Kade on the

shoulder, and, right in front of Agent Carter, punches him in the face when he turns.

"Connor," I scream, but he pummels him again.

And when Connor is angry, he isn't easy to stop.

"Connor, what the fuck?" Ryland calls out while grabbing one of his arms to restrain him as Beckett grabs his other.

"You piece of shit!" Connor's legs flail.

"Connor, stop!" I yell as tears fall.

"Don't you ever hurt my sister again."

Beckett's head jerks toward me. "He hurt you?"

"Stop," I plead but no one listens.

Beckett and Ryland both let go of Connor's arm and fly at Kade.

Mia, Gabriella, and I are all screaming and crying. Agent Carter, Javier, and Chloe are trying to stop the fight. Kade never takes a swing, letting my brothers repeatedly punch him.

Hospital security comes, and all my brothers, along with Kade, are handcuffed except for Hudson, who isn't aware of what is going on.

Kade's face is a bloody mess and starting to swell when they take him away.

Gabriella and Mia hug me while Agent Carter, Chloe, and Javier talk to security.

Eventually, everyone gets released, and Beckett, Ryland, and Connor get escorted to the door by the security guards, along with Chloe and Javier. Mia and Gabriella give me another hug goodbye. Kade is nowhere to be seen.

"Where's Kade?" I ask.

"He's with Carter," Javier says.

"Come on, Gracie, we're leaving," Ryland asserts.

"No. I'm not going with you. That was disgusting what you just did."

"Gracie—"

"Don't start, Beckett. You all should be ashamed of your

behavior. No matter what happened between Kade and me, it's between us."

"He—"

"Beckett, enough," Mia snarls.

"What did happen?" Ryland seethes. "I want you to tell us—"

"Shut up, Ryland," Chloe snaps, glaring at him.

He gapes at her and closes his mouth.

"Gracie you're coming with us," Connor barks.

"Connor, you need to go." I cross my arms, but he shakes his head.

One of the security guards warns my brothers if they don't want to be arrested, they have to leave.

Chloe gives Ryland another dirty look then hugs me. "Kade should be out soon. Call me if you need a ride or anything."

"Thanks." I return to the sitting area, trying to stop the tears from falling.

When Kade appears with Agent Carter, my hand flies over my mouth. I don't recognize his face due to the swelling.

"I'm sorry. I'm so sorry," I sob.

Agent Carter gives me a sympathetic pat on the shoulder, says, "Goodbye," and leaves.

Kade embraces me. "It's okay."

"No, it's not. Your face," I cry.

"Shh."

"I didn't say anything...Connor just...he figured it out."

Kade strokes my head. "Gracie, it's okay. You didn't do anything wrong."

"I'm—"

"Gracie, what's wrong? And what the hell happened to your face, Kade?" Hudson barks out.

I freeze. *Oh no.*

"Hudson, let's go home," Lena sternly says.

"Someone better start talking," Hudson growls.

I spin in Kade's arms, but he doesn't release me.

"Your brothers got upset."

Hudson's face turns red. "And exactly what were they upset about?"

"A big misunderstanding," I tell him as my insides shake once more.

Lena tugs on Hudson's arm. "Let's go home," she repeats.

"It wasn't a misunderstanding. I'm in love with Gracie, and three years ago, I hurt her when I left."

Lena puts her hand on Hudson's jaw and turns his head. "Let's go home."

He takes a deep breath then scowls at Kade. "You're in love with Gracie?"

"Yes."

"You hurt her?"

"Not intentionally, but yes."

"Hudson, please." Lena tugs on his arm again.

Hudson focuses on me. His expression is a mix of disappointment and anger. "You should have told me."

"Like you told me about Beckett?" I snap.

Hurt crosses his face.

It's not fair for me to throw it in his face. It took me a while to understand why my brothers kept it from us all these years, but I do. "I guess we all have our secrets, don't we, Hudson?"

He shifts to Kade. "You and I are going to talk about this later."

"Yeah. We will."

He shakes his head then turns. "Let's go, Lena."

Lena and I hug. Hudson continues to throw daggers at us but pulls me into him. "Please come with us."

"No."

He sighs and releases me. They leave.

I turn into Kade and wince. His face is such a mess. "You should have fought back. Your face wouldn't be this banged up."

"No. I hurt you. This has been a long time coming, Gracie."

"You didn't deserve this."

"Didn't I?"

"No one deserves this."

"I disagree. I—"

My phone plays music. I remove it from my pocket and close my eyes.

Shit. I forgot to message Fisher.

I turn from Kade. "Hey, sorry, it's been crazy—"

"I had to leave. I'm sorry, but I couldn't wait. We'll talk when I return," Fisher says.

"When will that be?"

"I'm not sure."

"You aren't sure?"

"I asked you to come, and you didn't want to."

"It wasn't—"

"I don't want to fight, Gracie. I'll call you later." Fisher hangs up.

I fixate on the screen.

"He's leaving, isn't he?" Kade quietly asks.

I spin. "Yes."

"I thought he would."

"Why?"

"Did he ask you how Lena was?"

The hair on my arm stands up. "No."

"Was he concerned about Lena or Kate when you learned what happened?"

"Kate is dead?" Fisher asked.

But he never asked about Lena.

How does he even know about Kate? He's never met her, and I've never talked about her to him.

"Kate," I whisper.

Kade's hand cups my cheek.

"Why did he ask about her?"

Kade gives me his usual silent treatment.

Oh my God.

My stomach twists, and my hand flies over my mouth. "Tell me it isn't true."

"I can't."

"He's...no," I say.

"I'm sorry, Gracie."

I pound my fists into Kade's chest. "You let me sleep with a Twisted Heart?"

"Gracie..."

"No. You knew, and you didn't stop me?"

"I warned you. I told you to stay away. I could only tell you—"

"Tell me what? You told me nothing!"

"Let's go talk."

"Now you want to talk?"

"Yes."

"Is your boss, Carter, aware we're going to talk?" I sarcastically throw at him.

"He's not my boss."

I step further away from him. "You're going to lie to me now?"

"I'm not lying. Let's go. I can't talk to you here. This isn't the place to have this conversation."

If he doesn't work for the FBI, then who does he work for?

How does he know all this stuff about the Twisted Hearts and Fisher?

"If it isn't the FBI, then is it the CIA?"

"I did work for the CIA. I don't anymore."

"I don't understand, Kade. If you don't—"

He puts his hand over my lips. "We aren't talking about this here. Let's go." Placing his hand on my arm, he maneuvers me through the hospital, steers me to a black car waiting at the curb, and gets in the back seat.

"St. Pete," Kade tells the driver then rolls the divider window up.

St. Pete. I haven't been there since we were there last.

Panic engulfs me. "Why are we going there?"

"You'll see."

My insides shake. "Kade, I don't know who you are anymore. I'm wondering if I ever did."

He puts his arms around me, and everything feels right when everything is so wrong. "You know me, Gracie. Don't question that."

"I don't. You're full of so many secrets and lies."

"I don't lie to you, Gracie. I lie to others but not you."

"Why? When did you become a liar?"

He kisses the top of my head. "No more questions until we get there." Kade repositions his body. "Put your feet up and rest. It's been a long day."

I'm not sure why I obey him, but I do as he says. I put my feet up and lie against his chest. We say nothing else on the ride to St. Pete. From time to time, he kisses my head, and the entire way he holds me.

As always, I feel safe and loved in his arms. But I tell myself I shouldn't. Kade lies. He kills. He seems to be deep into the secrets of the Twisted Hearts. He doesn't have to tell me he's in an underworld—I can now see it.

11

Kade

THROBBING SENSATIONS MIX WITH NUMBNESS IN MY FACE. THE Brooks brothers didn't show me any mercy, but what's worse than any punch is the knowledge I've inflicted pain on them. And right now, it's too volatile a situation to sit down and have a conversation with them to explain how much I love Gracie.

All morning I was tracking Fisher's plans to leave. My nerves sat on edge, hoping Gracie wasn't persuaded to go with him. At noon, I had a meeting with Javier and Chloe to give them all the info I had on Kate—off the record.

Interpol still doesn't want the FBI involved until we find out who the rats are, but I trust Javier, and he vouched for Chloe.

We were meeting when the call came in about Kate abducting Lena.

When Hudson, Ryland, Beckett, and I got to the house on Longboat before the FBI, I didn't think twice about shooting Joaquín Pérez or anyone else in the way of saving Lena.

Joaquín Pérez was a bonus. He was the scum of the earth, and I don't even want to imagine what he did to scare Lena so badly.

But Joaquín and Kate's death was going to freak Fisher out more, and when Gracie arrived at the hospital, I breathed a sigh of relief she wasn't on his yacht. Fisher wasn't going to stay in town with Kate dead. He was going to need to recoup his loses and formulate a new plan.

Kate Contro was an asset to the Twisted Hearts and Fisher's operations.

And now Gracie is in my arms. I'm guessing she's freaking out about the fact I killed a man. She's never been one for guns and violence, so I assume she's going to need to process the fact I'm a cold-blooded killer, even if it is on the right side.

She put two and two together at the hospital and figured out I'm part of some sort of law enforcement agency. But when I told her it wasn't the FBI or CIA, I saw her once again recoil and lose more trust in me.

I'm not sure how she's going to react when I tell her I'm a spy. The Brooks brothers guessed it, and I neither confirmed nor denied, but I've never before said out loud to anyone the words.

We're only a few minutes into our drive. Gracie sits up, grabs the ice bucket, and a napkin. After she creates a cold compress, she holds it up to my face and leans into me.

I put my hand over hers, and she slowly slides it down and onto my chest. I take my other hand and put it over hers and don't let it go the entire way.

Gracie now understands why I told her Fisher is bad, but it doesn't mean she forgives or trusts me again. Fisher was never the reason we weren't together, and deep down, Gracie knows, too. But once I disclose what I'm going to when we get to St. Pete, I'm not sure if it's going to be enough in Gracie's eyes to put us back together again.

Truth and lies can both bite you in the ass, and I'm hoping

that won't happen with Gracie. But my stomach flips fast. If we can't get past the truth today, I'm afraid I'm going to lose her forever.

The car stops at one of the last smaller beach houses on the island. I bought it with my first patent check, and no one is aware I own it. I used to rent it out, but after I left town, I never rented it again.

It was a notion, a sentimental thought that maybe I could bring Gracie here one day and try to make it up to her for taking our time in St. Pete and dousing it in flames. I didn't stop renting it out, thinking we would live here. Gracie wants and needs to be near her family and I would never ask her to move, but I thought she would love it. In my dreams, Gracie and I come here, and I redeem myself and memories of our time in St. Pete.

Because my night with Gracie was the purest, most potent, pleasurable night of my life, and until I got that text from Interpol, my dreams were just getting started.

Over the years, I had the house remodeled, and a property manager oversees it for me, but it's been vacant. When I flew into Florida, I spent my first few nights here, and about once a week I stay, happy to be off the yacht, and always wishing she was with me.

If I'm going to fill Gracie in on things about me and my career, then I need a place we aren't going to be bothered and where she can't run away.

My guess is she is going to need some time to process, and I'm not sure how long it will take. So I'm going to trust I'm doing the right thing telling her what I'm about to and hope she doesn't demand I take her home.

The driver opens the door, and Gracie sits up, and a line forms between her eyes.

I kiss her hand. "Come inside."

"Where are we?"

"One of my properties."

"This is yours?"

"Yes."

She hesitates.

"If you don't like it and want to leave at any time, I'll have the driver take you home."

"I don't come here anymore."

"I'm aware. Let's change it."

She blinks.

"Come with me." I hold out my hand.

She slowly agrees to go inside, and we sit on the couch facing the water.

"Ask me everything you need answers to. If I feel it won't put you in danger, I'll tell you. If I think it will, I won't answer your question, but I want you to trust I'm not trying to hide anything from you. Everything always has been and always will be about your safety."

She pauses and finally says, "Okay."

"And you can't tell anyone what we discuss. No one. Not even your family members."

"I won't."

My heart races, and I take both her hands in mine. "Ask me whatever you want."

"Who are you?"

"The same guy you fell in love with. The one who fell in love with you and still loves you."

"Kade—"

"I'm a spy."

Her eyes widen, and she gapes at me. Silence ensues.

Several minutes pass.

"Say something."

"I...How does someone become a spy?"

"When I showed up to my dorm room one day, two agents

from the CIA were sitting on my bed, waiting for me. One of my patents had caught their attention. I left college after two months and trained in highly skilled, secret, military operations. I did a lot of things on the dark net—"

"What's that?"

"Where criminals hang out to pass information online."

"Oh."

"I discovered lots of gang-related issues. The CIA moved me to the gang unit and relocated me home, to Florida. Then I discovered things... let's just say on a different level. Several days later, two Interpol agents sat in my house when I came home."

"You're a spy...for Interpol?"

"Yes."

"And you kill people?"

"Sometimes."

"Do you have any remorse?"

"No. They're horrible people who hurt others."

She closes her eyes, and my pulse beats in my neck.

She's going to hate me.

"Gracie, there's an entire world of evil you don't see."

She yanks her hands away. "Do you think I live in a bubble? My sister was kidnapped and is carrying a gangster's child. My brother went to jail for ten years for a murder he didn't commit. My friend was kidnapped today, and it's the second time in her life it's happened to her."

I exhale. "I wish you were in a bubble."

"But I'm not. And I don't understand why you couldn't trust me enough to tell me this."

"Gracie, no one is supposed to know any of this. If Interpol found out—"

"I don't care. You told me you wanted to be real."

"I did. I do. We are."

She rises. "We can't be real with secrets and lies, Kade."

"I've never lied to you."

"Your omission is just as bad as lying to me."

"No, it's not." I try to reach for her, but she retreats.

"Don't touch me," she cries out.

"Gracie—"

"Do you not see what you did?"

"I hurt you. I hate myself for hurting you and—"

"You broke me," she yells, and tears fall down her face.

Tears stream down mine, and I try to find words to make it better.

But I can't.

"Every night, no matter how drunk I was or who I was with, I only thought of you. And when I woke up hungover, or with someone whose name I didn't even recall, all I saw was your face. Every day, I wondered if you were ever coming home, or if I would ever know where I went wrong with you."

"Gracie—"

"No. You don't get to talk right now."

I stay quiet.

"Not a day went by where I didn't wonder if you were happy, or sad, or ever even thought of me. Then night would hit, and my thoughts would go crazy wondering if you were with another woman or if I could have fucked harder, or kissed better, or done a thousand other things differently the night we were together so you wouldn't have left and just disappeared."

I don't know if Gracie or I am crying more, but the pain searing through me is a thousand times worse than her brothers beating me.

"You didn't do anything wrong. All I thought about was you," I tell her.

"Then why didn't you ever contact me?"

"I couldn't tell you when I was coming home. I wasn't supposed to disclose to anyone where I was or what I do for a living. I thought it would be easier for you if you didn't hear from me until I could give you answers."

She shoves me away. "Easier? You thought disappearing was easier for me?"

"I did it all wrong. I see I did everything I shouldn't have. And when I say I'm sorry, I know it doesn't come close to making it right."

"That's the problem, Kade. There's no way to make it right."

1 2

Gracie

"GRACIE, DON'T SAY THAT," KADE BEGS ME THROUGH TEARS. "Please."

Watching the man you love cry will stab you in the heart all over again. Knowing your brothers made his beautiful face into a swollen, black and blue, disfigured mess twists the knife deeper.

I'm so tired of everyone I love being so angry and hurt.

That includes me.

So, stop being angry.

I'm not sure how.

"You need to shower. You have blood all over you." The disgust and horror of how my brothers mangled his beautiful face twists my gut further.

He stays silent.

"Go." I cross my arms and concentrate on the waves.

"Are you going to be gone when I get out?" His voice is full of fear, something I've never heard before from Kade.

I hold my wrist out, the one encircled by the bracelet he put on me that won't come off. "Does it matter? You can track me."

"It's only for your protection. It isn't to keep you in places you don't want to be or take away your choices."

My choices. I hate the decisions I've made. Actions resulting from trying to escape the memory of him.

He stands a foot behind me, and like always, I feel his energy zing through me. Kade puts his hand on my arm. "Gracie."

"Go shower. I should show you what it's like to have someone leave you, but I'm not that cruel."

He hesitantly kisses the top of my head and slowly releases his grasp on me. "I'm sorry. If I could—"

"Go," I sternly tell him, tired of hearing sorry.

What does sorry mean anyway?

It doesn't change the past.

It won't take away my years of pain.

Your future. It's the first step in moving forward.

With Kade? How would it even work?

As the tide rises, the sun sets. When Kade returns from showering, darkness has set in and I'm grappling with trusting him or cutting my losses.

All I keep returning to is how I've tried to forget about him but never could. He's haunted me.

Now you know the truth. Maybe you can move forward and past him.

As soon as the thought enters my mind, I see it for the lie it is. There is no getting past Kade.

Once again, energy radiates off him. He's said nothing to me and quietly entered the room, but I feel him behind me.

"I'm struggling with how to forgive you. And we can't just start up where we left off," I admit.

His heavenly arms, the only ones that ever have felt right and make me feel safe, circle me.

I close my eyes, wanting to stay in his embrace forever, but still full of anger.

"Give me another chance, Gracie. Please. I promise I won't screw up this time."

"What about the next assignment, or mission, or whatever you call it?"

"After I take Fisher down, I'm done. Interpol has already been informed."

Fisher.

I turn into Kade. His face is still swollen and black and blue but better without all the blood on it. "Why can't you be done now?"

"There's too much at stake."

"Money?"

He cups my face and sternly says, "Gracie, this has never been about money. I made mine from patents and investments. What Fisher is involved in is..." He takes a deep breath.

A chill runs through my spine. "What?"

"I'm sorry, but I can't put you in danger, and telling you might."

Anger pops up again. "I was sleeping with him. Don't you think I have the right to the truth?"

He shakes his head. "Not if it puts you in harm's way. I told you this at the start."

"You're going to kill him, aren't you?"

He nervously shifts. "Once I have what we need, and the opportunity arises, yes. I have an order to kill. That's how dangerous he is."

I should feel sad, or some sense of loss, or beg him not to do it. But Fisher's a Twisted Heart. He knew what my family has already been through and still tried to make me his. And it removes all sense of humanity from me. "Good. Kill him."

Kade's eyes widen.

"Oh, you thought I was the same girl? The one who believed in happily ever after and there's still good left in the world?"

"There is good in the world. You're proof of the good."

"No. I don't believe in rainbows anymore. Every time I turn around, my family gets another glimpse of reality. It's like we need all the lessons in suffering to make up for something bad we've done."

"You've not done anything bad. You've been targeted."

Tears fall again. "Why?" I angrily ask.

"I haven't figured it out. But I'm going to find out."

"Stop promising me things you can't deliver, Kade."

"I'm not. I will find out why."

"How? It's been going on for too long."

He cups my face. "I promise you. I will."

"But you won't tell me how?"

"No. It's too dangerous."

His face is such a mess. It has to be painful.

I go toward the kitchen.

"Gracie, where are you going?" he says in a panic.

I open the freezer. A bag of peas is in the door, and I crush it up then wrap a towel around it. I return to the couch and sit at the end. "Lie down."

I pat my lap. When he lays his head there, I place the peas on his face and brush my lips on his. "You should have tried to defend yourself."

"I would have if it was anyone besides your brothers."

I sigh, brushing my hands through his hair. "Why doesn't Fisher have a Twisted Hearts tattoo?"

"The Elite don't."

"The Elite?"

"Fisher...Kate...they were both at the top. The Elite stay hidden, running things behind the scenes."

My insides flip. "They are more dangerous, then?"

"All the Twisted Hearts are vicious, just in different ways."

"If you're a spy, why are you using your real name? Wouldn't you have a fake identity?"

"I usually do. I didn't with Fisher because he was with you."

My hand combing through his hair stops. "Before you came back to Florida you knew I was with him?"

"Yes."

"For how long?"

Kade stays quiet a minute. "Before I found out he was a Twisted Heart."

"How?"

"Every day, I scrolled your Instagram account."

My heart flutters. He really did think about me all these years.

"So when did you find out he was in the gang?"

Kade swallows hard. "Two years ago."

I jerk the peas off his face. "Two years ago? You didn't do anything to get me away from him for over two years?"

He sits up. "I did everything I could. I friended him. Whenever he made plans to come to Florida, I created parties for him to attend elsewhere. Whatever I could do to keep him away from you, I did."

"You should have told me."

"You stopped seeing him for about a year. I thought you were done with him, but then you started again."

"Gabriella was abducted. I wasn't going out partying or dating anyone!"

"If I had any idea Gabriella had a declaration on her or was kidnapped, I would have gotten involved in taking Triker down."

"You should have told me the minute you found out about Fisher," I insist.

"I couldn't. You don't understand what I'm dealing with."

"Tell me." I throw the peas on his lap.

"I can't. And when he contacts you next, you can't tell him you know anything."

My pulse increases. "What do you mean? He left me. He won't return."

Kade puts the peas on the coffee table and turns into me. "Gracie, Fisher isn't going to forget about you."

A chill runs down my spine. "Sure he will. He left without me."

"He wants to own you."

Maybe it's to convince myself, but I deny it. "No, he doesn't."

"He named his boat after you," Kade belts out.

That's when I see it. Hurt in his eyes.

"You did lie to me," I quietly say.

Kade's jaw clenches. "When did I lie to you?"

"I told you things I've done, and you said you already were aware, and it didn't change how you felt about me. But it does."

"It doesn't," he insists.

"I just saw it in your eyes."

Kade shakes his head. "No. How I feel about you has not now and never will change. But I don't have to like the thought of you with Fisher or anyone else."

I put my hands over my face, frustrated with yet another issue between us.

"I'm not judging you, Gracie. I've not been a saint, either," he blurts out.

Jealousy flares through my bones. "What do you mean?"

Silence. His face hardens.

"You say you thought of me every day. Was this while you were screwing other women?" I snap.

"I had to infiltrate. It's my job."

Nausea fills me. "You sleep with people for your job?"

He swallows hard. "A few times I've had to sleep with the enemy, yes."

"I hope you had fun." I get up and storm off down the hall.

"Gracie," Kade calls out and follows me.

I turn into a bathroom, lock the door then slide down it and hug my knees while tears flow.

It's hypocritical of me to get upset at Kade about sleeping with anyone over the last three years, but it stings. And if he can fool the enemy, then is he trying to trick me?

No, you know Kade. He loves you.

I don't know Kade.

I'm not stupid. Kade had to have slept with women while we were apart, but hearing him say it crushes me.

"Gracie." Kade knocks on the door.

"Go away."

The door presses against me, which I can only think is Kade sitting against it on the other side.

"You're the only woman I've ever loved, Gracie. My heart has never changed. We've both done things we wish we could undo over the last three years. Can't we move forward? I want to move forward."

"I'm not sure how," I quietly admit.

"We'll figure it out. We can," Kade insists.

Time passes. Answers on how to move forward seem to be nowhere. I finally rise and unlock the door.

Kade jumps up.

"I'm tired. Where can I sleep?"

"Take my room. I'll sleep on the couch."

"Fine. Ice your face. It looks painful."

13

Kade

ANTI-INFLAMMATORIES AND A BAG OF PEAS ARE MY ONLY FRIENDS *right now.*

This must be what they call hitting rock bottom.

It shouldn't be any different from the last three years. Spy life is lonely. You keep your enemies close and your friends far away. But the entire time, I assumed the day would come when I would eventually return to Anna Maria and have the Brooks' back in my life.

But now you've really screwed it up.

At least she didn't leave.

You keep hurting her.

Why did you have to blurt out you weren't a saint?

If we're moving forward, we can't do it with lies.

She's disgusted by you.

My timer beeps, and I sit up and shove the bag of peas into the freezer again. My phone reads it's three in the morning.

Deciding I'm not going to be able to sleep, I pick up my laptop and go out to the deck. It's pitch black, and I can't see much but hear the soothing ocean sounds.

I need the code from Lena.

Hudson was upset with me at the hospital before Gracie got there. Now that he found out about Gracie and me, I'm pretty sure I just screwed myself from getting any code from Lena.

I'm about to open my computer when I see Gracie's door is open. The white curtain is blowing outside in the wind.

My pulse races, and I jump up and go into her room. She's nowhere.

"Gracie!" I yell in, but there is no answer.

Within seconds I'm down on the beach. "Gracie!"

"Shh. You're going to wake people up," her voice replies, but I can't see much.

"Gracie, where are you?"

"Over here."

I turn, and a faint silhouette is sitting on the beach.

When I get to her, I wrap her in my arms. "What are you doing down here?"

"I couldn't sleep." She's wearing the T-shirt I gave her to sleep in and hugging her knees.

"You should have told me you were coming out."

"Why? You can track me."

I sigh. "Gracie—"

She puts her finger over my lips. "It's okay. I feel safer knowing you can find me."

"You do?"

"Yes."

"I will. If Fisher or anyone ever tries anything, I'll come for you."

"Do I need to worry about this?"

"Don't worry. Be aware."

"What's the difference?"

"I'm tracking him. Every move Fisher makes, I see. If I tell you to do something, there's a reason. So be aware. Don't question it. Trust I'm guiding you in a certain direction for a reason."

Her eyes glisten in the moonlight, and she says nothing.

Trust. She can't trust me anymore.

"Do you ever think about how our biggest issue about being together was my brothers?"

I grunt and point at my face. "I guess it came true today."

She frowns. "You should have fought back."

I drag her onto my lap. "I'm a trained spy. If I fought them, your brothers would be dead."

She shudders, and I tighten my arms around her.

"Your family is my family. They always have been. I thought I was making the right decisions for all of you. I know my disappearance for the past three years didn't make sense to any of you, but..." I try to compose myself.

She turns my head toward her. "Kade."

"Every moment being away from you killed me. I used to see you start to text me, and I'd wait, holding my breath, praying you would send it so I could hear from you. And I wanted to talk to you. I missed our conversations, and your laugh, and everything about you. But I couldn't tell you when I was coming home, or why I was gone, or what I was doing." I blink hard. "And I'm dying inside right now. All I kept telling myself was get back to you before it's too late. But I'm scared I am too late. So tell me it's not true, Gracie. Tell me I'm not too late. That some tiny part of you still wants me and believes in me. Tell me I haven't ruined us forever."

Her lip shakes. Tears stain her cheeks. She straddles me. "There lies the problem, Kade. There's no tiny part of me that wants or believes in you. All of me wants you. Every fiber of my being believes in you. But we've both ruined us. We aren't the same people we were. We can't return to three years ago."

My heart cracks. *I've lost her.*

"So, I'm too late?" The blinking doesn't help, and a tear escapes.

To torture me, the most delicious lips on earth kiss me. "You're too late for that girl. She doesn't exist anymore. And I'm too late for that guy. He left and is never coming back."

I brush her hair off her face. "We still exist, Gracie. I'm not saying we haven't changed, but we're in there."

"Are we?"

"Yes."

"I don't think so. The old me was happy and hopeful. She saw the world with different eyes."

"You mean she saw me with different eyes."

Gracie freezes.

"How did you used to see me?" I ask but am afraid of what she's going to say.

"Smart. Sexy as hell. Honest."

"And now?"

"Smart. Sexy as hell. Full of secrets and lies."

"I don't lie to you, Gracie. I won't. The secrets—"

"Don't try to justify it. You deal in secrets and lies. It is what it is, Kade."

I cup her face. "Listen to me. After I take Fisher down, I'm done. I don't want this life. You're the life I want."

"I'm not the girl you remember anymore."

She is. "You know how I used to see you?"

"No."

"Clueless."

She furrows her brows. "Clueless?"

"Yeah. You had more beauty inside and out than any person I'd ever met, but you weren't even aware of it. Whenever I was around you, I felt alive, but you had no idea how you lit the world up or me. And I saw you as my future. My wife. The mother of my children. The person who I would wake up to every day and thank my lucky stars you were mine because you were way too good for me."

Gracie takes a shaky breath, and I wipe the tears away with my thumbs. "And now?" she murmurs.

"Still clueless. Still the most beautiful person on the planet and the only woman who's ever made me feel alive. Still my future. And I'm desperate to wake up and thank my lucky stars you're mine because you're still too good for me."

"How can you still believe those things?"

I put my hand over her chest. "Easy. Your heart. And no matter what's happened, it hasn't changed."

Waves crash against the shore, time stands still and Gracie caresses the side of my head then quietly says, "There's something we have in common."

"What?"

"You're the only person who's ever made me feel alive." She sobs, "I've felt dead without you, Kade. So dead."

The dam breaks again, and my tears explode everywhere. "I'm sorry. So sorry. Forgive me. Please. I need you to forgive me."

She nods in tiny movements. "I have to. I've tried to hate you, but I can't."

Salty lips from tears, tongues crashing, and chests heaving with emotion all merge together. Hope that almost fizzled out burns bright again.

"Tell me we can try again." I kiss her some more. "Tell me you'll let me be the man I should have been for you."

Her tongue rolls around in my mouth, and she grips her fingers in my hair. "Yes."

"Yes?"

"Yes."

"Just you and me, Gracie. No one else."

"I don't want anyone else."

"Neither do I."

Cold ocean water washes up my calves, but all I feel is the

warmth of Gracie in my arms. The blood in my veins boils from her touch, and the heat of her sex flares through her thin panties. She grinds against my aching cock and frees it from my boxers.

"God, I've missed you," I murmur to her.

"Promise you'll never let me go again."

"Promise," I vow and mean it.

I remove her shirt, needing to feel the warmth of her flesh. My arms quickly circle her. I dote on her breasts, licking and teasing them as she arches her back.

She strokes my shaft, caressing my wet cap and pressing on my vein.

I groan, and then she moves her panties to the side and slides on me.

"Kade...oh..." she whimpers, and nothing has ever sounded sweeter. Hell no longer exists. Evil cannot reign. Heaven is officially on earth, right here, right now with Gracie.

My mouth travels to her neck, lightly sucking on the spot that drove her wild the one night, years ago, when we were together.

"Oh God," she cries out into the night and rocks her hips on me faster.

Sweat breaks out on our skin as our flesh becomes a melting pot of heat.

Everything I've ever wanted is with her. She's my beginning and end and everything in between. And the nights and days I've spent obsessing over her are too many to count.

Her body glistens in the moonlight, majestic, as waves crash against the shore. "You're beautiful. So beautiful."

"Kade...oh God...Kade...oh...oh...oh," she cries out into the dark, her mouth in an O, as her body unravels in my arms, spiraling into euphoria.

Gracie's pussy spasms on my cock, and my groans rival the sound of the waves.

Pools of pleasure and emotion course through my body.

"I won't screw up again, I promise," I pledge and suck on her neck again while she trembles harder in my arms.

My balls shrivel, heat rolls through my bones, and adrenaline surges through me. I pump my seed hard into her, sending her into another orgasm, holding her tight in my arms.

When we find our breath, I kiss her, knowing I'll never get enough, hardening in her again, just like the first time we ever made love.

"I love you. I always have," I murmur.

"You're the only one I've ever loved," she whispers and returns to kissing me.

The dark is fading. "Let's go into the house before the beach walkers come out." Snatching the T-shirt off the sand, I stand her up, rise, then pick her up. Her arms wrap around my neck, and while I carry her to the house, our mouths never leave the other's.

We stand in the outdoor shower, removing the sand, lip locked, and as soon as we get inside, we go straight to the bed. For hours, we make love. When we finally fall asleep, Gracie is in my arms. For the first time in over three years, I feel happy and whole. And I vow never again to make a decision unless it puts her first.

14

Gracie

Seagulls are squawking, the tide is crashing against the shore, and the smell of Kade flares in my nostrils. I scoot deeper into his arms, and they wrap tighter around me. He kisses my head, and I open my eyes and tilt my head up.

The swelling on his face has gone down, and his black-and-blue marks have turned yellow.

He's smiling at me, and flutters of happiness surge through my soul.

Is he really here?

Are we finally going to get to be together?

His face falls. "What's wrong?"

"Nothing. I'm hoping I'm not dreaming, and this is real."

He dips down, and his lips are on mine. The zings I always get with Kade ricochet through me like a boomerang.

"We're real," he murmurs.

I lace my fingers in his hair. "I want to stay like this forever."

"Me, too." He kisses me again.

"But I want to check on Lena and Connor, too. He shouldn't have hurt you but—"

"Gracie, stop. I'm not mad at any of your brothers and especially not Connor. I'll make it right with him...with all of them."

"How?"

"Don't worry. I'll figure it out."

I lightly kiss his bruised cheek. "I think they need to make it right with you."

"No. This is on me. Don't be upset with your brothers."

Not possible. They're going to get an earful from me when I see them next.

I kiss him again then ask, "What time is it?"

"Close to noon."

"Does your face hurt?"

"It's fine. Stop worrying about it."

"It's not fine. My brothers—"

Kade's lips crash into mine, and his tongue swirls in my mouth. The arms I've dreamed of for years slide under me. "I don't want to talk about your brothers," he mumbles and moves his mouth to my chest, licking my areolas until my nipples pucker and harden then sucking on them until I'm like a corked bottle of champagne, fizzing and ready to detonate.

His manhood, warm and pulsing on my thigh, teases and taunts me.

I'm throbbing for him, and his long, dexterous fingers slide into my sex, curling and swiping over my sweet spot.

He's the only man who's ever found it, and I combust, over and over, higher and higher, as he plays my body as if we've been lovers forever.

"Kade," I cry out, shaking under his hard body.

He kisses me, muffling my cries, creating a new turmoil of flutters and heat, making my cells hum on all cylinders.

My only desire is for Kade. He's all I've ever wanted. And the need I have for him only grows. There is no turning back, no future without him, no way to exist if he isn't with me.

"I dreamed of feeling you like this again," he murmurs and swipes his thumb on my clit, keeping me in a constant state of tremors and gliding his tongue into my mouth for one last kiss.

He's still a sex god.

He shimmies down my body, brushing his lips on my glistening skin.

Before his tongue takes the first swipe of my sex, I've lost track of how many times he's made me soar. But he does it again, licking me, sucking me, worshipping every part of my pussy.

I grip his thick hair and shove his head into my quivering body.

"Oh God...Kade!"

Every moment I've spent hurting, missing, and crying for him wasn't a memory exaggerated. Comparing him to others wasn't fair. No one comes close to how he makes me feel.

And it isn't just the high.

Kade only has to be in the same room as me, and my body reacts. When he touches me, I'm like a firefly lighting up.

After his tongue and lips make me spiral so many times, I lose track. I'm drenched in my juices, exhausted, but still needing all of him.

"Kade...I need you," I pant with labored breath.

He sits up, and I flip over, resting on all fours, wanting him to fill me and pound me as hard as he can.

The girth of his steel erection stretches me as I pulse with delight. His length reaches so deep, I see stars at his first thrust.

As he slides in and out, he leans over me. His arms go next to mine, his torso full of muscle grazes the flesh of my back; his lips flutter against my shoulders. "You're my soul, Gracie. I'm going to take care of you forever."

"Yes. Forever. I want you forever," I breathe.

The air in the room is thick with our fornication: slapping balls, the smell of sex, sweat, adrenaline, and cries of promises and pleasure.

Endorphins crash through my system. Kade's warm breath oscillates on my neck and ears. My walls spasm against his hard shaft.

"Gracie," Kade growls as his thick cock pumps hard, sending his seed deep in me.

I climax like never before then collapse on the bed. Kade falls over me, and we stay in child's pose, gasping for air and shaking.

He rolls off and pulls me into his bulging muscles, holding me tight.

The only person I have ever felt safe with is him. When he holds me, I feel like nothing bad could ever happen again.

And I wish it were the truth and Kade alone could stop all the evil in the world and the danger constantly threatening my family.

But it's not. And I sink deeper into his embrace, wrapping my arms tight around him, craving to have a normal life where happiness and love are the only things residing.

It's the life I used to believe we could have.

I tilt my head up.

He pecks me on the lips.

"Can we stay here forever?" I ask him. "Let's just forget anyone else exists."

"You'd get bored with me."

"No, I wouldn't."

"You'd miss your family. I'd miss your family."

I roll into him. "What's it been like for you?"

"What do you mean?"

"By yourself. Did you have friends?"

He shakes his head. "Not real ones. Targets don't count."

"Targets?"

"Bad people I have to pretend to be friends with."

"Like Fisher?"

"Yes."

I run my hand through his hair on the side of his head. "Your life sounds lonely."

He quietly admits, "It is."

My heart drops, and I wonder if he could have possibly been in more pain than I was all these years. "Do you enjoy what you do?"

He takes a deep breath and pauses. "I want there to be less evil in the world. I hate the people I have to associate with."

People like Fisher.

A chill runs up my spine as I think of how mad Fisher was yesterday when I wouldn't go with him. I sink deeper into Kade's warm arms.

You need to protect yourself better.

"Before Gabriella got abducted, Hudson wanted Connor and I to learn to shoot."

"Did you?"

"No. They got into a bad fight. After Gabriella was kidnapped, Connor and all my brothers went out to Hudson's gun range at least once a week. Javier, too."

"You still didn't go?"

"No."

"Why not?"

"I'm not sure. But with everything continuing to happen, I think maybe I should learn how to shoot."

Kade nods. "Okay. Let me teach you."

"Do you think it's a good idea?"

"Yes. It won't hurt you to be confident handling a gun. Did Javier teach Gabriella?"

"Yeah. Before Triker took her. Should we go out to Hudson's?"

He shakes his head. "We can't."

"Why?"

Silence.

"Hudson will be fine with it. He's upset right now, but—"

"Gracie, it doesn't have to do with Hudson."

"Then what—"

"Something was discovered yesterday. I can't tell you what. I just need you to trust me."

My pulse increases. "Is Hudson in trouble?"

"No. He's fine. But we can't go there until further notice. I'll take you to the gun range."

"You're sure Hudson is okay though?"

He caresses the side of my head. "Yes. I promise."

I let out a big breath.

"When Fisher contacts you, I need you to tell me."

"I will but I thought you were tracking him? Won't you already know?"

"He may be extra cautious now Kate is dead."

"Do you really think he's going to expect me to be with him after he left without me?"

"Yes. In Fisher's eyes, you belong to him."

I shudder, and Kade clutches me tighter. "I still don't see Fisher as a Twisted Heart. I've just always viewed him as a rich party boy."

"Looks are deceiving, Gracie."

"That's what Chloe always says."

"She's right, so be aware. If anyone new suddenly appears in your life, or a person who you normally would see with Fisher reenters, you tell me."

"I'll tell you."

"And he can't find out we're together. Whatever we do, it needs to stay private until he's taken down."

I shudder again. "Okay."

He pecks me on my lips. "All right. As much as I want to stay here forever, we can't. I don't want you by yourself until I eliminate Fisher. So if you aren't with me, then I want you with your family."

I groan. "This sounds like Gabriella's situation all over again."

Kade strokes my cheek. "Sorry, but we can't take any chances."

I take a deep breath.

"Let's get moving. I need to go make peace with your brothers."

15

Kade

HAVING GRACIE AS MINE AGAIN IS LIKE BEING A KID AT DISNEY greedily wanting every experience, sugar-filled treat, and souvenir in the park.

We're in the car and almost on Anna Maria Island. The divider window is up, and my hands, lips, and tongue are all over her.

She threw on her dress from the day before but isn't wearing any panties. The moment the car door shuts, I slide my hands up her skirt and cup her ass.

"I think we should have a rule," I say between kisses.

She flicks her tongue in my mouth, and my cock twitches. "What would it be?"

"You shouldn't wear panties around me ever."

She softly laughs. Her hands run through my hair. "Speaking of panties, can we stop at my place before Hudson's? I need to get some fresh clothes."

"No problem." I lick behind her ear. "I already told the driver to go there."

"Connor texted me he's home. He was worried since I wasn't there all night."

"Let me text him we're stopping by and I want to talk to him so he isn't unprepared."

"Okay."

Connor is who I worry about the most. Hudson, Ryland, and Beckett will have cooled off enough for me to talk to by now. Plus, I'm sure Lena, Chloe, and Mia would be helping in that arena. Connor already had a lot of hurt feelings and trust issues regarding my three-year disappearance. My guess is he won't forgive me as easily as his brothers. I'm hoping his car ride home with Gabriella and Javier influenced him to cool off a bit.

I remove my phone from my pocket, and a message pops up. My gut drops.

No, no, no. Not now. This can't be happening.

Gracie tilts her head. "What's wrong?"

How do I even tell her this?

"Kade?"

"Don't freak out," I blurt out.

Her body freezes. "Why would I?"

"Interpol sent orders for me to return to following Fisher."

Her eyes widen. "You're leaving?"

I tighten my arms around her. "Not like that. It's not the same as before."

"Really? What's different?"

"As soon as this is over, I'm done with this life. But I have to finish this. It involves you. Until Fisher is dead, he's a danger to you."

She turns toward the window.

"Gracie, look at me, please."

Her tear-filled eyes drill into mine.

"Fisher won't stay away forever, and whenever he's here, I'll be back. We'll talk on the phone. As soon as this is over, I'm home for good."

"It feels the same as last time."

"Yeah, it sucks. But it's not the same," I reiterate.

She sighs. "When do you have to go?"

"Today. I need to at least talk to Connor and Hudson first. But I should get moving."

"How long are you going to be gone?"

I close my eyes and exhale. I open them and admit, "I'm not sure."

She takes a deep breath.

I quickly say, "Hopefully not long."

The car stops outside her condo, and the driver opens the door. We get out. I stop her and cup her face. I sternly repeat, "This isn't the same as last time. You have to believe me."

"I believe you. I don't have to like it though."

"Fair enough. I don't like it, either." I dip down and kiss her, trying to show her she is my everything. "When this is over, I won't be traveling unless you're with me, okay?"

"All right."

One more peck, and I lead her to the elevator and punch in her number. "Crap. I didn't text Connor a warning I was coming."

"He should be calm by now."

I hope you're right but doubt it.

The elevator opens. We step out and go directly to her door. Gracie taps in her code on the keypad.

"When's the last time you changed your combination?"

She shrugs, opens the door, and we go inside. "Ummm...never?"

"You should get a new code. Does Fisher have it?"

She pauses. "Maybe."

"You should do it today."

"Do what?" Connor stands with his arms folded across his chest.

"Change the key code," I respond.

"So now Fisher is a bad guy?"

"Yeah, he is."

Connor shakes his head and clenches his jaw. "Unbelievable."

Gracie crosses the room. "Connor, Fisher is a Twisted Heart."

Connor scoffs. "Fisher? Wow. This is entertaining. Is that what Kade told you to get back into your good graces?"

"It's true," Gracie insists.

"You're upset with me. I get it. I'm sorry I hurt Gracie, and I'm sorry I hurt you. But Fisher is dangerous, and you and Gracie both need to stay away from him."

Connor bypasses Gracie and steps in front of me. "Why should I believe a word you say? All you've been doing is trying to sabotage Gracie and Fisher's relationship since you've been home." Connor angrily spins. "And why are you with him right now? Kade's a liar. You deserve better than him."

"Connor—"

"Gracie, can you go get changed so I can talk to Connor alone?"

She hesitates, glancing between Connor and me. "Only if you both promise me there won't be any fighting."

"There won't be," I assure her.

Connor's face hardens; his hands fist at his sides.

"Connor?" Gracie arches her eyebrow at him.

"Fine."

"Promise me."

He scowls. "I promise."

"Okay. I'll be out in a few minutes." She leaves the room.

The only way to get Connor to take you seriously is to tell him the truth.

"Can we sit?"

He grunts but plops on the couch, and I do the same on the farthest cushion from him.

"I love Gracie."

He snorts. "You have a funny way of showing things."

"I never wanted to hurt her."

"Doesn't matter, you did, and I don't even have all the details."

"True. I'm not here to argue it or make excuses. But we need to get past this because there are issues regarding her safety and yours, too."

"You'll make up all sorts of bullshit to get Fisher out of the picture, won't you?"

He's so angry. You really hurt him.

"What I'm going to say doesn't leave this room. I'm going to tell you because I trust you—"

"Trust. What an interesting word."

Screw this.

I take my wallet out of my pocket and lay a row of identification cards on the table. They are all of me with different names. Crossing my arms, I wait for his reaction.

Connor furrows his brows. "Why do you have these?"

"I'm a spy."

"A spy?"

"Yes. You can't tell anyone. But I work on Twisted Heart cases, and it's how I know about Fisher."

The color drains from his face. "You're serious about Fisher?"

"Yes. I'm leaving tonight, and I need to make sure you watch out for Gracie while I'm gone."

"You're leaving again?"

"Yes, but once I take Fisher down, I'm done."

"So, Gracie really is in danger?"

"Yes."

"But you're leaving her?"

I sigh. "I have to."

Red flares in his face.

"Connor, I need you to assure me when I'm gone, you're going to watch out for her. It's best if both of you stay away from the club scene until this gets resolved, too."

He groans and scrubs his face. "I only started going out again."

"It's not forever, but while this is going on, it's the best thing for both of you."

"Fine," he grumbles.

"I'm glad Gracie isn't living on her own anymore, but if you aren't going to be here, I want her staying with one of your brothers or Javier."

He scowls again. "Javier is our brother."

"You're right. Point taken."

"Anything else?"

"The code on the door needs to be changed to a number not associated with anything related to you or Gracie. And Gracie told me you learned to shoot?"

"Yeah."

"Javier taught you?"

"Yes."

"Good. I need you to teach your sister while I'm gone. Hudson's place is out of commission, so go to the gun range."

"Why is Hudson's not free?"

"The FBI discovered something yesterday. Until they clear it, you can't go there."

"What did they find?"

"It's classified."

Connor's face hardens.

"If it weren't classified, I'd tell you, so don't take it personally."

Connor crosses his arms and shakes his head.

"There's something I need you to tell me."

He arches his brow.

"What do I need to do for you to forgive me?"

He turns away.

"Connor. I never meant to hurt Gracie or you."

"You lied to me. I asked you about Gracie, and you lied."

"I'm sorry. You're right."

His face grows hotter. "You knew Gracie was dating Fisher and he was a Twisted Heart, and you didn't stop her?"

"It's not as straightforward as you think. There are things you don't—"

Connor rises. "I don't want to hear your excuses. I'll watch out for Gracie, but you and I are done."

"Connor, you don't mean that."

"No, Kade. I do. I'm done with secrets and lies and people hurting my family. If Gracie and everyone else wants to forgive you, that's their choice. But I don't have to. You aren't the same person you used to be. Or maybe I just never knew you to begin with."

"That isn't true. I am the same person. And I'd never intentionally hurt your family. I love all of them and you."

"No, I don't know you. And—"

"Connor, enough," Gracie cries out.

We both spin toward her.

"If I can forgive Kade, you can," she quietly says.

"No. I can't," he says.

My heart sinks. "I'll give you time. Think about what I need to do to make this right between us."

He tries to remove the gold necklace I left on his bed in the yacht with a note saying it was for all his birthdays I missed.

"It's not going to come off."

His hands freeze, and he glowers. "Why not?"

"It has a tracker. Gracie's bracelet is the same. If Fisher or any other Twisted Heart ever abducts you, I'll come find you."

"Abducts me? I can handle myself."

"You're underestimating them."

"Are you kidding me? They've messed with my family."

"Yes. And you were making bets with Fisher and people he associates with."

"Get it off me." Connor yanks at it again.

"No. It's staying put so I can protect you."

"Kade—"

"Connor, I realize you're mad, but once you calm down, you'll see this isn't a bad thing. If Gabriella had one of these—"

"I'm done with this conversation." Connor storms out of the room.

Great. Now he hates me more.

Gracie frowns. "I'm sorry about—"

I put my finger over her lips. "Don't apologize. This is my fault. I'll keep trying to make it right with him."

Her blue eyes are full of worry.

I place my hands on her head and kiss her. "You look beautiful."

A sad expression remains on her face. "Thanks."

As much as I don't want to leave her, I have to. Time is ticking. I've already stayed longer than I should have.

"Let's go. I need to talk to Hudson and then get going."

We leave. I wrack my brain, trying to figure out how I'm going to earn Connor's forgiveness, but nothing is coming to me. My plan to return to his good graces has failed. I'm now further from them than yesterday.

Gracie snuggles into my chest on the quick ride over to Hudson's. He isn't there when we arrive, and she calls him and finds out he and Lena went to stay at his parents'.

When the car stops, and we get out, my gut flips. Hudson and I have been best friends forever. He's the reason I never made a move on Gracie before I did. With Hudson, bro code has been violated, and I hurt him differently than Connor.

Gracie leans into me and takes my hand when we enter the house.

I wink at her and squeeze her hand.

We get in the kitchen and discover Ryland, Beckett, and Mia are also there.

Betrayal, hurt, and anger covers Hudson's face.

"Gracie, you okay?" Ryland's hardened expression matches his brothers'.

Gracie steps closer to me. "I'm fine, and everyone needs to get over this."

"I don't know. I think Kade's face isn't as bad as it should be," Beckett mutters, and Mia elbows him.

"Ouch," he mumbles.

Gracie's face reddens. "Not funny, and you all should be ashamed of yourselves."

I turn to her. "Would you mind letting me talk to your brothers alone?"

"Why?"

"Please?"

She sighs and turns toward them. "No fighting. Promise me."

Silence.

"Hudson," Lena quietly says.

"No fighting. Promise," he agrees.

She kisses him on the cheek and motions to Mia. "Come on." Lena pats my biceps as she passes me, and the girls all leave the room.

The three brothers lean against the kitchen counter with their arms crossed, jaws clenched, and scowls on their faces.

"I love her. I always have," I blurt out.

I'm not sure whose face gets redder with anger.

"Always?" Hudson seethes. "How long were you screwing our sister behind our backs?"

"It wasn't like that."

"No? Why don't you tell us what it was like," he demands.

My pulse races, and I breathe while focusing on the ceiling beam.

"Answer," he barks.

"We used to run into each other and hang out. The night before I left, we got together."

"Then, you left and never talked to her or any of us for three years?" Ryland asks.

I shift on my feet. "I didn't do things right. They didn't prepare me for this, and I can't change things. All I can say is I'm sorry."

"They?" Beckett asks.

"Interpol."

"So, what now? You sleep with my sister then break her heart all over?" Hudson accuses.

Shit. Why do I have to be leaving now?

I sit down on the barstool. "This isn't the same situation and I'll be returning. But Fisher is a Twisted Heart. He wants Gracie. Until I stop him from coming after her, she's in danger."

They all step forward.

"I knew that douchebag was bad news," Ryland mumbles.

"You can all be pissed at me, but I don't have a lot of time. I should have already left. While I'm gone, I need to make sure Gracie and Connor are both protected."

"Connor? What's he done?" Ryland growls.

"He's been in Fisher's world. Neither of them are safe until I can neutralize Fisher."

Hudson scrubs his face. "Fine. We'll talk about this at a different time. Tell us what we need to do."

We spend thirty minutes discussing Gracie and Connor's safety precautions. The Brooks brothers are still not happy with me, but it's better than how Connor and I left things.

"I need to go. Will one of you take Gracie home tonight?"

"I will," Ryland says.

"Thanks."

Hudson says, "Let me talk to Kade alone."

My gut flips.

The others leave and Hudson shakes his head, scowling. "You could have told me."

"Hudson, you would have told me to stay away from her."

"Damn right."

"I couldn't. I love her."

"If you told me you loved her, I would have gotten over it."

I take a deep breath. "I'm sorry."

"If you hurt her again, I'll kill you."

"I won't."

He pauses then says, "I'm going to trust on our friendship you won't."

"I promise I won't. But there's something else important we need to discuss."

"What?"

"Lena has a code. I need it."

"Nothing has changed, Kade. Lena isn't going to talk today, and I don't want you pressuring her. She's been through a lot."

I sigh. "I understand she has, but—"

"No. Leave her alone," Hudson growls.

Great. I need the code.

He's not going to help you right now. Be happy you made some progress today.

I hold my hands in the air. "Okay."

Silence.

"Take care of Gracie while I'm gone."

Hudson's jaw clenches. "We will. Are you going to kill that bastard?"

"Yes."

"Good."

We both go into the family room, and I take Gracie's arm and lead her outside.

Her blue eyes are full of nerves. "What's going on?"

God this sucks.

Everything I felt the first time I left her comes rushing to the surface but even more intense, knowing how much I hurt her three years ago. Instead of talking, I dip down, brush my fingers on her head, and devour her perfect pink lips one last time, parting them quickly and sliding my tongue into her mouth.

She's the only woman who's ever kissed me and left me wanting more. This kiss is no different, highly potent and intoxicating, creating fireworks in my blood.

When I tear myself away, I still hold her close to my thumping heart and we're both breathless. "I have to leave. Ryland will take you home."

"I'll go with you to your boat."

"No. You stay with your family."

"But—"

"Trust me."

Her eyes fill with water. "I don't want you to go."

"I don't want to, but I need to finish this. I'll call you later tonight." I kiss her again until my erection is so hard, I make myself stop.

"Be safe," she whispers and a tear falls down her cheek.

I hug her. "I will. I love you. Don't ever question how much I love you."

"I won't. I love you, too."

I stroke her cheek. "And if Fisher tries to get in touch with you, don't answer. Contact me right away. Tell Connor the same."

"Okay."

I give her one last kiss. "Now, go inside."

Gracie hesitantly turns and disappears inside. All the heartache I feel is like the last time, but this time, I'm clear about what my mission is and there's an end in sight.

Once I get what I need from Fisher, I can put the bullet in his head. Then I can come home to Gracie and never be away from her again.

16

Gracie

DAYS TURN INTO WEEKS. KADE AND I TALK EVERY DAY. SOMETIMES it's quick, sometimes for hours, but every contact makes me happy but miss him even more.

In some ways, it's like we never were apart. Our conversations come as natural and comfortable as they always did. I haven't had any desire to go out or drink, and for the first time in over three years, I laugh all the time when I'm sober.

Fisher hasn't contacted Connor or me, so I hope it means he never will, but Kade keeps insisting he will.

Connor is still angry at him, and my other brothers haven't mentioned Kade. Hudson and Lena are remodeling their new beach house, and my family has all jumped in to help.

It's a Thursday night. Everyone is at the house. Lena and I just finished knocking down bedroom walls, and Connor is grumbling about being on cleanup duty again. Gabriella yells out dinner is ready, and the three of us run down the stairs.

When I get to the bottom, Kade's there, jeans and a form-fitting T-shirt hugging his muscles. His face is no longer bruised and is back to normal. Tears roll down my cheeks as I jump into his arms. He picks me up, and within seconds we're lip locked.

"Why didn't you tell me you were coming home?"

He steals another kiss. "It was better seeing your surprise."

"How long are you here?"

He brushes the hair that escaped from my ponytail off my face. "A week at the longest." He gives me another kiss, leaving me breathless, weak-kneed, and throbbing.

"Gracie, are you—"

Kade wraps his arm around me and turns. "Hudson. Need some help?"

Hudson's jaw clenches. "Sure. Good to see you. Come have dinner with us."

I mouth a thank you to Hudson for being nice.

"Thanks. Sounds good." Kade guides me into the dining area, and my brothers all take deep breaths, except for Connor. He scowls at Kade.

No matter how many conversations I have with Connor, he can't seem to get over his anger toward Kade. I glare at him to behave, but he doesn't change his expression.

Gabriella, Mia, Chloe, and Lena are all happy to see Kade and hug him. He and Javier embrace, and Ryland and Beckett say hello, which isn't overly friendly, but at least it's a start.

Kade and I sit next to each other, and he puts his arm around me and kisses the top of my head.

"What were you working on?" he asks.

"Lena and I were knocking down walls."

Kade's eyebrows arch, and amusement fills his face. "You were knocking down walls?"

"Yep."

"Connor got cleanup duty again so he's being grumpy," I tease, trying to lighten the mood. Connor ignores me and eats his food.

"Kade, how long are you in town?" Ryland asks.

"Week at the longest."

Connor's phone rings, and he reads the screen. "Shit."

"Fisher?" Kade says.

Connor's face hardens. "Yeah." He hits the button for voicemail.

"How did you know it was him?" I ask Kade.

"He's here."

A chill moves down my spine.

Of course he is. That's why Kade can be here.

"Did he call you?" Kade asks.

"My phone is in my purse."

"I'm sure he has."

"He wants us to go to Ybor tonight and for you to call him." Connor relays a text message.

Panic grips me, and heat fills my face. "What should I say to him?"

"Connor, text him you're both busy with family stuff all weekend," Kade instructs him.

"Don't tell me what—"

"Connor," Hudson growls.

"What?"

"This is regarding Gracie's and your safety. Do what Kade says and don't argue."

"Fine," he grumbles and sends a message off.

Kade turns to me. "We should stay in St. Pete."

"Okay."

"What's in St. Pete?" Hudson asks.

"One of my properties. Connor, you shouldn't stay at the condo while Fisher's in town."

"Why?"

"The first place he will go to find you is your condo."

"So? He wants Gracie. She's not there."

"It's not safe for you."

"I'm not scared of Fisher."

"You should be. He's dangerous," Kade barks.

"I can take care of myself."

Ryland throws his hand on the table, and everyone jumps. "Stop being an egotistical idiot. He's a Twisted Heart. You know damn well he isn't someone to mess around with."

Connor rises. "I'm sick of all this. I have no social life since I can't go out. The only thing I get to do these days is have Novah over, and now I can't even do that."

Kade pulls keys out of his pocket. "Catch." He throws them to Connor.

"What's this?"

"My house in St. Armand's. No one knows about it. It's got a hot tub, pool, fireplace, the works. Have at it. Take Novah there."

"No, thanks. I don't need anything from you." He throws the keys at Kade.

Kade's face falls.

"Connor!" Gabriella and I scold him at the same time.

He turns to Gabriella. "You, too?"

She puts her hand on his arm. "Can I talk to you privately? Please?"

He hesitates.

"Please?"

"Fine."

She rises, and they leave the room.

"He needs to grow up," Hudson growls.

Lena puts her hand on his. "Go easy on him. He's hurt. It's only going to make it worse if you yell at him."

"Agree. You shut it, too, Ryland," Chloe scolds.

"And you," Mia says to Beckett.

Ever since the fight at the hospital, Ryland and Beckett have been in the doghouse with Chloe and Mia.

Beckett holds his hands up. "I'm just eating my dinner."

Javier clears his throat. "I'm glad you're here, Kade. Chloe and I need to talk to you about some things after dinner."

155

"Okay."

"Beckett and I closed on the building today for the boutique," Mia announces.

Everyone congratulates them.

"When do I get to try on your inventory?" I ask her.

She laughs. "Depends on how quickly these guys can get the renovations done. But we have to file for permits and things."

"When it comes in, I can take pictures for social media. I've got several influencers who agreed to repost."

"Awesome. Thanks!"

Gabriella and Connor reenter the room. Gabriella holds her hand out to Kade, and he hands her the keys. She sits down next to Connor and puts it in his hand.

Connor's jaw clenches.

I sink into Kade's chest, relieved Connor is going to be somewhere Kade thinks is safe. Gabriella winks at me, and I mouth, "Thank you."

The rest of the meal is spent with our typical banter, and when we get done, Lena, Connor, and I return upstairs. Kade, Chloe, and Javier talk, and everyone else continues to do whatever they were working on. After about thirty minutes, Kade joins me.

There is one wall left. "I think it's time we went on cleanup duty." Lena hands Connor the sledgehammer.

Good idea. Get Connor to work out some of his anger.

I hand Kade mine. "Your turn."

"But I was looking forward to watching you do this." He wiggles his eyebrows.

"Another time."

"All right. Whatever you want."

"Hold on a minute." Lena yells down the stairs, "Hudson."

"Yeah?"

"Can you bring my purse up here?"

"Why do you need your purse?" Connor asks.

"You'll see."

Hudson comes upstairs with it. "What's going on?"

Lena opens her purse and takes out a Sharpie. "I think it's time for a friendly competition." She draws a line down the middle of the wall. "First one to knock their side down wins."

"What do I win?" Connor asks.

"Who says you're winning?" Kade counters.

Connor grunts.

"Loser cleans everything up," Lena says.

"So you and Gracie still get out of trash duty?"

Lena shakes her head. "If you lose, I'll help you."

"I'm not losing," Connor boasts.

"You're pretty cocky," Kade counters.

"It's a given. You might want to get your trash bag ready."

Kade licks his lips. "Bring it."

"Everyone get up here." Hudson stands behind Lena and wraps his arm around her waist.

The rest of my family arrives upstairs. Javier grabs the Sharpie from Lena and draws a line on the floor.

Beckett stands a few feet in front of the wall, with his arms in the air. "Mark, get set, go!"

Kade and Connor both take off and start slinging the sledgehammer against the wall. Their movements are fast and furious, and the pieces of the wall go flying. The air fills with cheers and claps from my family.

It's neck and neck. Both men have eliminated half of their portion of the wall, but then Connor slams his tool into the top corner, and the entire wall collapses.

He tosses the sledgehammer and throws his hands in the air. My family rushes him in victory.

I run over to Kade, who's shaking his head. "Good effort." I kiss him.

His arms I've missed wrap around me, and everything feels

right in the world. When his lips leave mine, he keeps hold of me but says, "Well done, Connor."

Connor cockily grins. "Have fun cleaning."

Kade grunts. "Get out of here. The hot tub code and app you need to download is on the fridge. Tell Novah I said hi."

"You all enjoy your night." Connor waves. When he walks past us, Kade holds his fist out. Connor hesitates but then bumps it.

Relief he is finally going to let go of his hurt shoots through me. Connor holding onto his grudge against Kade has been killing him. He may act like it wasn't, but I know it was. Lena seemed to somehow understand what he needed, and I gratefully smile at her.

Hudson hands Kade a broom and trash bag. "Have fun, man."

Kade snorts. "Will do."

Ryland pats Kade's shoulder on the way out. "Nice try. Don't feel too bad. Connor's never lost to any of us."

"Is that right?" Kade asks.

"Yep. Whoever suggested it set you up."

Kade arches an eyebrow at Lena.

She shrugs. "Hey, it was a fair challenge."

He turns to me. "You didn't tell me about Connor's track record."

I playfully squeeze his biceps. "Maybe I wanted to see what these could do."

He licks his lips.

"Okay, I'm leaving now," Hudson growls, and everyone follows.

Kade and I ignore all of them, never taking our eyes off each other.

I finally grab a trash bag. "Let's get this done so we can get out of here."

Kade spins me in his arms, pressing his body against mine. Lips crash, tongues urgently flick, and energy zings through me like lightning bolts. Kade's erection hardens against my stomach, and I moan into his mouth.

"God, I've missed you," he murmurs, and his hand cups my ass cheek, holding me firmly to him.

"I've—" I can't finish.

His tongue swirls in my mouth, consuming my every breath, instigating a need so zealous, I forget my surroundings and become lost in him.

I release his belt buckle.

He moves one foot forward, and I move mine backward until we're in the corner of the open room, farthest from the staircase but without any shelter should anyone come upstairs.

Our pants drop to the floor. He picks me up, and I wrap my legs tight around him.

He thrusts in me, and a deep, animalistic groan rumbles through his vocal cords so loud, it suffocates my moan.

My back sinks into the studs, and I dig my elbows into his shoulders to give me leverage, lacing my hands through his hair.

Energy from his body infiltrates my cells, setting my body ablaze. His scent, raw and potent, mixes with the smell of sawdust, flaring in my nostrils and stirring the flutters in my stomach.

"Missed you so much," he murmurs again and thrusts deeper in me.

I tremble in his arms, whimpering, clenching his cock that fills me, grinding and circling on him faster, desperate for every sensation only he gives me. "Kade!"

"Shh," he says against my lips then devours me once more.

I gasp for air as adrenaline whips through my body, shattering all things stable, claiming my every atom that ever felt dead or lost without him.

"Gracie," he groans, and his cock detonates in me, pulsing violently against my clenched walls, firing his hot seed deep within me.

I cling to him, panting as hard as he is, not wanting to let go, and suddenly filling with happiness this time, he left and returned. This time we're real and together, and nothing got in the way. And I bury my face deeper into the crook of his neck.

The powerful arms I'll never get enough of hold me tighter. Our hearts beat against each other's.

"I'm so glad to be home," he murmurs, and my heart soars.

I may have never left the island, but I've not had a home since he's been gone. And I know he is talking about me and not any place or material possession.

17

Kade

BLONDE HAIR COVERS MY CHEST, AND GRACIE'S SOFT SKIN LAYS against mine. In a deep sleep, her eyelids are shut, and I kiss the top of her head for the hundredth time.

Happiness is an understatement. Everything I've ever wanted is in my arms right now. The ache of missing her while I was away is now gone, but it's only temporary.

Fisher won't stay here forever. And while he's here, he will try to find her and Connor. He realizes if he gets to Connor, he'll have an avenue to Gracie.

In the last few weeks, a similar pattern has evolved to when Skates was announced dead. The demise of Kate Contro has startled the Elites, and they are increasing supplies of chemicals.

I've had to get closer to Fisher, and my time away from Gracie has been spent mostly with him, expressing my desire to do more business with him and proving to him I'm trustworthy.

More business means I sell chemicals to him and, combined, they create a deadly mix in many different ways.

Every deal I make with him allows the devil to jump up and down, and I feel sick doing it. If he accelerated his plans, whatever they may be, I would have a part in it. Interpol has approved it, and my role is a necessary evil to take him down, but it doesn't help my guilt. If any combination of things occurs, I'll have had a hand in too many deaths to count.

I'm not a Twisted Heart. In Fisher's eyes, it makes me valuable. I'm doing business with him and not other Elites, and the more I express my loyalty to him, the more secrets he shares with me.

Fisher is aware I'm in town. I made it clear I was coming here once I found out about his plans to return stateside. All it took was a text inviting him to a party I told him I was throwing, and he admitted he was already going to be here.

He has no clue I'm following his every move.

Gracie's protection is my top priority, and I'm going to have to be careful Fisher doesn't find out we're together. But I won't have him anywhere near her and not be close to protect her.

I need to end this quickly.

Lena needs to give me the code.

If Lena has the code I think she does, whatever Fisher and the other Elites are planning will fall into my hands. Skates created it before he died. It was to ensure he never went to jail and always had bargaining power. A get-out-of-jail-free card he, Max Crello, or Sid Triker could play should they, as figureheads, ever need to collapse the system.

It's not a secret in the Twisted Hearts underworld the code exists. Kate Contro wanted it for her protection so she could step deeper into her role.

Now she's dead, and it's time for the next Elite to step into their role as the head of the underground organization. That person might be Fisher, but I'm not certain yet.

I fear Fisher will put two and two together and realize Max

would have told Lena the code. Triker put a protection order on her when Max died and it wouldn't take much for him to figure it out.

No matter how many hours I've spent online, trying to hack into the system, I can't get the right combination. Not a bone in my body doubts Lena has it. And I need to get it from her before Fisher does.

Lost in thought, I'm trying to figure out how to get Lena to give it to me when my phone rings.

I grab it off the table as Gracie stirs in my arms.

Fisher. My gut drops just like whenever I see his name appear.

Hitting the button, I send him to voicemail. I immediately get a text.

"Knocking on your door. Where are you?"

I kiss Gracie's head and sigh, carefully pulling my arm out from under her so I can text.

"Not there. I met up with friends and some ladies last night. What's up?"

"You with the Brooks?"

"No."

"You heard from Gracie or Connor?"

"No."

"Can you get ahold of them and get them to meet with me?"

My pulse increases.

"What's going on?" I text him to stall.

"I think they're still pissed I took off when I did, but you understand how business works."

"Yeah."

"So, can you arrange it? I'll owe you one."

I scrub my hands over my face. "I'll see what I can do, but they're both stubborn if they don't want to do something."

"Then set it up and don't tell them I'm coming."

Fuck, fuck, fuck.

"Not really my style, man."

"Thought you had my back?"

My gut drops. Now I'm cornered.

"I do. Let me see what I can do."

"Thanks. When are you returning to the yacht?"

"Not sure."

"Stop over when you get to the marina. I want to talk to you about our deal."

"Will do."

I throw the phone down on the bed next to me and close my eyes.

This isn't good. I need to figure out how to keep Fisher in the trust zone and Gracie and Connor away from him.

My eyes are still closed when Gracie's delicious lips graze mine.

I don't open them but roll her on top of me and grasp her head.

"What's going on?" she murmurs.

I slowly open my eyes. "Nothing."

"Kade, don't lie to me."

"It has to do with work. Everything is—"

She puts her finger over my lips. "Don't say okay. That's a lie."

"It will be okay. I'll figure it out."

Her blue eyes sear into mine. "What does Fisher want?"

"What makes you say it was Fisher?"

She tilts her head. "If it has to do with me, tell me what he wants."

Silence.

"Kade, I need you to tell me. I should know in case I run into him while he's here."

She's right.

"He wants to meet with you and Connor."

"And?"

"And what?"

"What did you tell him?"

"Gracie, don't worry about it." I try to kiss her, but she doesn't let me.

"Tell me."

I stare at the ceiling.

"Kade, don't shut down on me about this."

I sit up and move her onto my lap. "I'm not. You don't need to know all this."

Her eyes turn to slits. "Fisher wants you to trick us, doesn't he?"

My chest tightens. "Why do you say that?"

She raises her brow at me. "I've been around him for years. He gets what he wants by bets and tricks."

My mouth goes dry, listening to her admit she knows Fisher so well. It's not a secret, but she does, but I don't like hearing her say it out loud.

"Maybe we should meet with him."

"Absolutely not."

"Wouldn't it be safer for us to tell him we're done with you there? You could control the environment, and maybe he'll leave us alone after."

"He's not going to leave you alone."

She bites on her lower lip then sighs.

"He's not going to go away from a text message, either. Maybe we should play him."

"Gracie, it's not even open for discussion."

"Kade, hear me out."

"No. Fisher is dangerous. You and Connor need to both stay away from him."

"It could buy us time. Make him think I'm not happy with him but willing to think about giving him another chance. We could hold him off for the week. I'll insist I want space and him to tell me ahead of time before he returns. No surprises if he wants me to trust him ever again. Then he leaves, and we all have more time."

"No. I won't have you in the same room with him."

"You did before."

Blood pounds in my ears. "I didn't have a choice then. Do you think I wanted you with him?"

"No. But you didn't stop me."

"I tried. I did everything I could think of without blowing my cover."

"You didn't tell me he was a Twisted Heart."

"I couldn't. I've explained why."

Gracie turns away.

Every demon I've had over the last few years since finding out Fisher was a Twisted Heart comes crashing to the surface. I turn Gracie's chin toward me. "Every single day, I thought about how I could keep him away from you. It wasn't just about taking him down for the greater good. It was about annihilating him so he could never touch you again. I chose to infiltrate him when I saw his name on the list. I did it because of you. If you think I like knowing all the things I shouldn't about him both personally and criminally, you're wrong. And the hardest thing I've ever done is stay away from you longer by luring him to other places. But I did it because it was the best thing for you."

"Kade—"

"Let me finish. Please."

She slowly nods.

"I'm not sure if I should have told you sooner. It could have put you in more danger. I'm not sure what the right thing would have been, but I did what I thought was best for you, with all the information I had. And the question of what I should have done versus what I did burns in my mind all day, every day. It's something I'll always beat myself up about, so I'm not giving myself a pass."

Gracie cups my face. "Kade, I shouldn't have said that. I'm sorry."

"No, you should have. You're right to be upset with me."

"I'm not."

"Now you're the one lying."

She closes her eyes and takes a deep breath before opening them. "I know in my heart whatever you chose to do, you thought was the best thing for me."

"But it doesn't negate anger about my choices."

"Kade—"

"Don't try to sugarcoat it."

"Okay. I'm still angry you didn't tell me sooner even though I know in my heart there are reasons for your decision."

My insides shake. I'm so angry at myself, and I'll never be able to say I chose the right thing. I hate the fact I let her down with another decision I made.

"I still love you. I still don't want to be without you. I still am never going to get enough of you." Gracie leans in and kisses me, making me feel so wanted, the doubt I've always had over my choices stabs my heart a little more.

All I've ever wanted to do is protect her, and the path to do it hasn't always been clear.

She strokes my cheek. "I've spent a lot of time with Fisher. Different than the time you spend with him."

I stare at the ceiling, take a deep breath, and try to control my jealousy. "Yeah, I know."

Gracie sighs. "I'm not trying to hurt you by talking about this."

I lock eyes with her. "I know."

"My point is this. If he is reaching out to you, he isn't going to leave unless he sees me."

"Let me worry about solving this."

"Kade—"

"Gracie, please. I'll figure this out. I don't want you or Connor around him."

167

"Okay. But if we need to meet to trick him, I can do it."

"Tricking him can be more dangerous. I'll figure this out."

Gracie agrees with me, but the expression on her face tells me she doesn't think I'll be able to. I spend a few more minutes reassuring her, but in the back of my mind, I'm praying she isn't right.

18

Gracie

"THERE'S SOMETHING I NEED TO TELL YOU ABOUT TONIGHT YOU aren't going to like," Kade tells me.

The air in my lungs seems to get thicker. "What is it?"

Kade pulls me onto his lap. "I have to go to a party with Fisher tonight."

I take a deep breath. "Okay."

"Hudson and Lena said they would be at your parents', and you can hang out with them."

I lace my hands through his hair and lock my fingers together. "All right. I'll miss you, but I understand. Come over when you're done."

He swallows hard.

My stomach flips. "What?"

Kade's eyes have guilt in them. "Fisher parties."

I release my hands from his head. "So? What is your point?"

"You do realize the entire time he was with you he was with other women, correct?"

My stomach pitches. "We weren't serious."

"Even when you were."

I close my eyes. Fisher always had girls around him, but I liked to throw the thoughts of what he did when I wasn't around into the back of my mind. He and I were both free to see other people. I was the one who always insisted on it until I finally agreed to try for real with him. So it wouldn't have been fair for me to expect him not to be with other women when I wouldn't commit to him. When I finally did agree to it, I told myself he was faithful since he was the one who wanted to be serious so badly. But deep down, I would have to admit it wouldn't surprise me if he hadn't been. "Why are you telling me this?"

"Hear me out before you freak."

My pulse increases. "Now you're giving me anxiety."

Kade exhales and cups my face. "There's going to be a few women who are spies there tonight."

Heat rises in my cheeks. "And?"

"I'm going to have to play the part."

My voice rises. "What part is that, Kade?"

"Can you stay calm? I'm trying to tell you what's going to happen."

I take a deep breath. "Are you going to fuck other women tonight?"

"No. That's not what I'm saying," he sternly says.

"Then what are you saying?"

"What I'm trying to tell you is I probably have to do something I don't want to do. But I doubt I'll get around it."

My chest tightens with anxiety. "What are you telling me?"

"I'm going to have to make out with at least one of them at the club. If I don't, Fisher will think something is up."

Rage boils in me. The thought of any woman touching Kade makes me feel sick.

"They're agents. It isn't real. But I wanted to tell you so I'm not hiding anything from you."

Blinking hard, I rise and storm into the bedroom then pack the few items Kade bought me when we got to St. Pete.

He comes up behind me and puts his arms around me. "Gracie, I don't like it any more than you do. I'll do everything I can to not get into that situation, but you understand what Fisher is like. The agents are there so I can control who I have to pretend to be into and can end it behind closed doors. Clothes will be on at all times."

I sink into his chest and shut my eyes. My insides are shaking, but everything he says about Fisher is true. And any man who is ever with him has girls on him, or he ends up finding ones for them.

"I'm only doing this to take Fisher down. You have to believe me. I don't want anyone besides you."

I spin into his arms and see all the worry and more guilt in his eyes. And this isn't an ordinary situation. "I hate it, but I trust you."

"I'm sorry. I—"

"Stop. We're in a crappy situation. Do what you need to do, but come home to me as soon as you can."

"It won't be until tomorrow morning. Fisher's parties go all night."

Another fact I can't argue. I sigh again. "Okay."

"Gracie—"

"Kade, let's not talk about it anymore. I trust you. Do what you need to do and just come home to me safe," I tell him again.

He dips down and kisses me, and I try to get rid of the thought some other woman will have her lips on his tonight. I understand why he has to do it, and as much as it's going to bother me all night, I'm glad he disclosed it.

In the past, Kade would have omitted this because it was part of his job. I wanted him to be honest with me about things. So as screwed up as this is, it makes our relationship feel even more real.

"As soon as I take Fisher down, I'm through with this life, Gracie. I only want to be with you and not deal with any of this shit."

"I know." I slide my fingers through his thick hair and kiss him with everything I have, trying to help him melt some of his guilt away.

Music blasts on his phone, and he groans.

"What's that?" I murmur against his lips.

"We have to go. I set the alarm so I could get you to the island on time."

We've been in St. Pete for two days. The beach house is bright and cheerful. It's not too big, and the ocean views from every room are breathtaking. "I like it here."

"I'm glad. I love it here when you're here. It feels complete."

My heart soars. "Yeah?"

"Yep. Oh, I forgot to mention something."

"What?"

He caresses the side of my head. "I want you to pick a beach house out on Anna Maria."

"Pick...what?"

"One you want to live in."

I gape at him. "Sorry?"

"I understand we're in limbo, but I want to keep moving forward. Hudson said there were some places going up for sale around where your family is at. If you don't want to be that close, we can go somewhere else, but if you want to be down by them, talk to Hudson."

In a bit of shock, I ask, "You want me to check out places and choose one?"

"Yes."

"For both of us to live in?"

"Yes. Unless you don't want to live with me when this is all over."

"That's not even a question."

"Okay. Then will you talk to Hudson to see what is available? I'm going to have to leave in a few days."

"You don't want to have any input in where we live?"

He shakes his head. "As long as you come with the house, it'll be the best place I've ever lived."

"You're serious?"

"Yes. Find something you love or something you want to fix up so you love it. Whatever you want."

I'm touched and overwhelmed. I've never cared about money the way some people do, and I'm aware Kade has a lot of it. But he wants me to be near my family because of how much they mean to me. And he loves them and wants to be part of their life, too.

For some reason, I compare Fisher to Kade. Fisher, no matter if he is a Twisted Heart or not, never understood or cared about my relationship with my family. I don't even have to say a word to Kade, and he gets it.

My eyes well with tears. "I love you. Thank you."

"I love you, too." He pecks me. "We need to go."

I wipe under my eye. "All right."

We ride mostly in silence to Anna Maria just enjoying being with each other. Kade holds my hand the entire way, from time to time, kissing it.

When we park in my parent's driveway, Hudson and Lena are returning from a sunset stroll.

"Hey—"

Lena stops mid-sentence, and her eyes widen.

"What's he doing here?" Hudson growls.

We turn, and Kade's body stiffens next to mine. Fisher is in his Jaguar in the driveway. He gets out of the car, and Kade turns his head quickly to Hudson. "Stay calm."

I try to calm my shaking insides.

"Gracie!" Fisher saunters right up to me as always and tries to kiss me, but I step out of it.

"What are you doing?" I accuse him.

"Gracie, don't be pissed. I had business to attend to."

"Fisher, it's over."

"Gracie—"

Hudson shoves through Kade and me. "She said it's over. Take your cue and leave."

Fisher crosses his arms. "This isn't your concern."

"Want to make a bet?"

"Hudson," Lena says and tugs on his arm.

Kade steps toward Fisher. "This isn't a good time."

He raises his brow at Kade. "Why not? Hmm?"

"Fisher, it's over." I turn to leave, and he reaches for my arm.

Hudson steps up to him, and Kade pushes Fisher toward the road. "Time to go, Fisher. Let's talk at the dock."

"Gracie," Fisher yells in a tone so angry, shivers run down my spine.

I spin as Hudson lunges at him, and Kade steps in between them right before Hudson touches him. "Back off," he barks out, and Lena and I both yank on Hudson's arms.

Kade shoves Fisher to his driver's door. "Get in," he growls.

Fisher scowls.

"Let's be smart," Kade tells him.

Fisher points at me. "We're going to talk, Gracie."

"Get in the house," Hudson growls to Lena and me.

"Fisher, let's go. We have plans tonight," Kade says and opens his car door.

"Fine. But this is bullshit."

Kade nods. "I agree. We'll talk at the dock."

Fisher points at me again. "We're talking before I leave." He gets in, reverses out, but waits for Kade.

Kade gets in his car, catches my eye quickly, and they both drive off.

Hudson's face is red, and he spins. "You okay?"

"Yeah. Fisher usually doesn't lose his cool."

"Let's go inside," Hudson says, and the three of us don't leave for the rest of the night.

We talk about other things, but the entire night, I'm worried about Kade. Hearing Fisher is a Twisted Heart is one thing, but seeing how he acted tonight made it more real.

I toss and turn all night, praying nothing happens to him, and he comes home to me safely. When six a.m. hits and Kade still hasn't returned, I pace in my room. At seven, I go downstairs and into the kitchen. Lena and Hudson have put coffee on and are sitting on the patio.

They try to assure me Kade is okay, and he can handle himself, but when Hudson gets a call from him and says he needs to meet him on his own, my heart races.

Hudson makes Lena and I go to Javier and Gabriella's house when he leaves. Everyone tells me not to jump to conclusions about what is going on, but my gut is telling me something is.

I call Ryland and tell him to track Hudson's phone and check on him and Kade. Then I call Beckett and ask him to get ahold of Connor. Until I know where Kade and my entire family is, I'm not going to be able to relax.

Something is going on. I can feel it. Fisher's anger from the night before is etched in my mind. And I kick myself for ever getting involved with him.

19

Kade

As soon as I return to Fisher's yacht, he gets out the liquor. "What were you doing with Gracie?" he barks, his eyes in slits.

"I went to visit Hudson. We're working on a few property deals for my investments. I didn't know she would be there."

"Did you tell her I wanted to see her?"

"I just got there when you showed up."

Fisher pins me with his gaze.

Don't waver. Fisher will think you're guilty.

I turn away from him and move to the bar, pouring three fingers of whiskey in a glass for each of us. I'm not a fan, but Fisher loves it. I hand him a glass, and he drinks it in three chugs, then states, "I need to see her."

"Why? You can have any woman you want. Seems to me like a lot of hassle." I question him, but it's pointless and won't detract him from his obsession with her, but I hope for some miracle.

"Because she's mine," he says.

I let the whiskey burn down my throat, holding in my rage and desire to kill him right then and there.

"Seems to me like it's a headache for nothing."

He grunts. "Thought you were on my side?"

I grab the bottle of whiskey and pour more in both our glasses. "I'm getting tired of you questioning my motives."

He scowls. "You're awfully close to them. What am I supposed to think?"

Unwaveringly, I cross my arms. "So you think I'd put them over all the deals we have going on?"

He hesitates. Fisher will do anything for money. As far as he's concerned, I'm the same. The reminder of what he has at stake with the chemicals I can provide him puts me back in his good graces.

"Gracie's mine, and she won't disrespect me."

I force a snort as my gut flips. "I don't see what the big deal is about her. You can get pussy anywhere. Shit, you have had pussy everywhere."

Disgust fills me talking about Gracie like that, but I have to play the game.

Almost absentmindedly, he replies, "It's not about pussy with her."

Nausea consumes me. His words confirm everything I already know in my gut. In his sick, twisted way, he loves her. He will never stop until she is his.

I try again to get him to reason. "Seems like a headache to me."

Hours pass with us discussing Gracie until two of his men enter the room, and our conversation switches to business and then we go to the bar.

After downing shot after shot all night at the club, Fisher takes the after-party to his yacht.

The debauchery is in full force. I have an agent on my lap all night who pretends to be cozy with me. Normally, we would go into a bedroom, lock the door, and both sleep with our clothes on. But Fisher isn't allowing anyone to move to different rooms. He needs all the attention on him tonight.

His yacht is a smorgasbord of sin. Strippers show up and turn into hookers with sexual acts taking place in front of everyone's eyes. Cocaine is passed around on a silver platter then eventually just spread out on the coffee table for everyone to sniff as they please. And the alcohol never stops.

Around six, Fisher is still up, high from sniffing so much cocaine, he probably will be up till at least noon. He usually keeps his habit hidden, but on rare occasions, he lets it shine, and last night was one of those. I keep hoping he will overdose so I can pretend to attempt to save him but instead let him die.

Luck isn't on my side.

At half past six, I order an Uber for Agent Carmichael, who pretended to be into me all night. Fisher just sniffed another line of blow off a girl's pussy and is now getting a blow job from her.

As soon as I leave his yacht, I breathe a sigh of relief and escort Agent Carmichael to the parking lot, call Hudson then order a second Uber for myself, since I'm still too inebriated to drive.

When I arrive at the restaurant in Bradenton, exhaustion is setting in. Hudson is already waiting there with two coffees.

"Jesus. You look like shit," Hudson tells me.

"Good description of how I feel."

"What's going on?"

"I don't want Gracie to see me like this."

Hudson snorts. "If anyone isn't going to judge you, it's Gracie. And she's freaking out right now."

The ache in my chest grows, thinking of her worrying.

"I can't see her the rest of this trip," I blurt out.

Hudson's eyes turn to slits. "Why? What's happened now?"

I try to collect my thoughts, fighting the tiredness and inebriation. "I convinced Fisher we should leave today."

"You're leaving...today?"

"Yeah. I can't stay here with Gracie. He's obsessed with her, and it's too dangerous with him around her."

"She's going to flip if you don't say bye."

I take a long sip of coffee, letting it burn my throat, which is already raw from the burn of pure alcohol all night. "I'm not happy about it, either. But I can't see her. Fisher questioned me for over two hours about what I was doing and why I didn't bring Gracie to him."

Hudson scrubs his face. "When is this going to end?"

"When Lena gives me the code."

Hudson reddens.

"Don't get pissed. Lena has it. I'm confident she does, and I need it."

"What's it for?"

"I can't tell you."

Hudson sinks further in his booth and scowls at me.

"It's for your safety and Lena's. But as long as she has the code, she's in danger. If she gives it to me, I can remove the danger."

"How?"

"It'll end things."

"End things?"

"That's all I can say."

Hudson drinks his coffee, and the waitress sets two plates of eggs, bacon, potatoes, and toast in front of us. The smell makes my stomach rumble, and I shove a piece of bacon in my mouth, realizing I haven't eaten since lunch yesterday.

"You need to talk to Lena for me."

Hudson sighs. "Okay. I will. But I don't think she'll give it to you."

"Work on her."

"All right."

"Can you keep Gracie at your parents' with you?"

"Sure."

We both take a few bites of food, and Ryland shows up. He slides into the booth next to Hudson. "Good God, what the fuck happened to you?"

I shake my head. "Just another awesome night partying with Fisher."

Ryland raises his eyebrow. "Fisher?"

"Don't ask. What are you doing here?"

"Gracie made me track Hudson's phone. She's going nuts with worry."

"Shit." My heart stings. I'm going to hurt her again when I take off and don't even say goodbye.

"So, why are you here all the way off the island?" Ryland grabs a piece of Hudson's toast.

Hudson elbows him. "Get your own food."

He grunts and shoves half of it in his mouth.

"Fisher is getting antsy. I don't want Gracie anywhere alone."

"Don't worry. We've got it," Ryland assures me.

"There's something else I need you to do," I tell them.

They both arch their brows at me.

"Make sure Gracie knows I love her, and I don't like leaving like this, but it was necessary for her safety. I'm going underground with Fisher. I'm not sure how often I'll be able to call her."

Both their faces harden.

Shit.

"You're still not happy I'm with her?"

"More like not happy you broke her heart, and now she's going to be hurt again." Ryland's voice is laced with anger.

"It's not intentional."

"It never is."

"I wish I could make a different decision and it wouldn't hurt her, but there's no way to get around this."

"I'm okay you're with her," Hudson says.

"You are?" I expected Hudson to be the last of the Brooks brothers to accept my relationship with Gracie.

"Yeah. No matter what's happened, you're still one of the best guys I know. She's happy with you. And I know you love her. I'm not stupid. I see it."

"I do." I remove a card from my wallet and hand it to Hudson.

His forehead creases with a deep wrinkle. "Why are you giving me a bank card?"

"Give it to Gracie. It's an account in her name not connected to me. I was going to give it to her when I dropped her off but couldn't because of Fisher."

"Why does she need a bank card?" Ryland asks.

"So she can buy a beach house or whatever else she wants."

The brothers shift in their seats.

"This account has enough to buy a beach house?" Ryland gapes.

"Yeah."

Ryland whistles.

"Does she know about this?" Hudson asks.

"About the beach house. Not about the account."

Silence ensues until Hudson says, "So you're going to have her buy a beach house and move in together?"

"No. That's just what she thinks."

Ryland and Hudson's faces harden like they want to kill me.

"I'm going to have her buy a beach house and, as soon as this is done, I'm going to ask her to marry me."

Hudson's lips twitch.

Rylands eyes grow wide. "Marry you?"

"Yeah. She's all I've ever wanted."

Hudson's eyes drill into mine. "Tell me how we end this sooner."

"Get me the code."

He sighs. "I can't guarantee anything, but I'll work on Lena."

Gracie

PANIC ENGULFS ME. "WHAT DO YOU MEAN, KADE'S LEAVING AND isn't going to say goodbye?"

"This is for your safety," Ryland says.

I spin and put on my shoes.

"Gracie, what are you doing?"

"I'm going to say bye."

Hudson puts his hand on my shoulder. "You can't."

He didn't even kiss me goodbye when he dropped me off.

Kade left me again.

It's not the same.

It feels the same.

I shrug out of his grasp and head for the door, but Ryland is standing in front of it.

"Move."

"No. You need to trust us."

"I'm so tired of everyone telling me to trust them. This is my life. He's my life."

Ryland's dark eyes soften. "And you're his. He will return when it's safe for you."

My tears fall. Ryland embraces me and strokes my head, which only makes me more emotional. "He'll call you in a few hours, but you have to stay with us."

"Please let me see him before he goes."

Ryland sighs and wraps his arms tighter around me. "You can't. He said it's too dangerous right now."

"Kade said to give this to you," Hudson's voice calmly says.

Ryland releases his arms around me, and I lift my head off his chest. Hudson is holding a piece of paper, and I take it.

It's a bank card with an account number. "I don't understand. What is this?"

"It's an account he set up for you. He said you're supposed to buy a beach house and whatever else you want."

I gape at the card. Kade and I discussed finding a beach house, but I didn't expect him to have an account set up in my name.

I bolt past Hudson into the kitchen to get my phone, but he rips it out of my hand.

"You can't call him right now."

"Why not?"

"He'll call you in a few hours. You need to be patient and do what he asks."

Hollow emptiness turns into fear and consumes me.

"Did something happen to Kade and you aren't telling me?"

"No. He's fine," Ryland claims.

"He'll call you in a few hours," Hudson repeats.

Lena strolls into the kitchen. Her hair is wet from the shower. "Everything okay?"

"Kade's leaving." I tear up again. "They won't let me say goodbye."

My brothers both protest it's for my protection. Lena hugs me then leads me to the outside patio and shuts the door.

"I need to see him before he goes."

"Gracie, you need to trust Kade. If he thinks it's too dangerous, then it is."

"But—"

"No. Kade loves you. He doesn't want to go like this, either, I guarantee you. He's dealing with things you aren't aware of. Do whatever he asks and don't question it."

Does she know something?

"Lena, what aren't you telling me?"

Her face pales, and her eyes leave mine. "Nothing."

"You're lying to me."

She twists her hair around her fingers. "The people Kade deals with are dangerous. You need to trust him and in your relationship. That's all I'm saying."

"Do you know them?"

She shakes her head. "I don't think so."

"But there is something about them you aren't telling me?"

"N...No."

"Is there something Kade should know?"

"No." She twists harder.

She's lying to me.

"Lena—"

She rises. "The best thing you can do right now is stay busy. Let's go work on the house."

Guess I'm not getting anything out of her.

What is she hiding from me?

I follow her inside, and we get ready and go. It's Sunday and, as usual, my entire family is at the house.

For hours I work quietly, looking at my phone every few minutes, double-checking my ringer is on full blast. The morning turns into the afternoon.

Why isn't he calling me?

"Stop checking your phone. He'll call you when he can," Ryland tells me.

"Would you tell me if something happened to Kade?"

"Yes. He's fine. Just be patient. He will call you," Ryland tells me for what seems like the hundredth time today.

It turns dark. Connor brings over a bag of clothes from my condo. My brothers have told me I'm to stay away from it until further notice, and I'm staying at my parents' with Hudson and Lena.

"Where are you staying?" I ask Connor.

"St. Armand's."

"At Kade's?"

"Yep."

"So, you like it?"

He grins. "It's pretty awesome."

"I'm glad you like it." I read my phone again.

"They haven't left yet."

"What? He's still here?"

"When I passed the marina, both Fisher's and Kade's yachts were still docked. It's probably why he hasn't called you yet."

He's on the island.

It's possible to still say goodbye.

I glance around at my family members, who are all focused on their projects.

"No," Connor says.

"What?"

"You aren't going."

Silence.

"You could come with me."

"Don't be—"

My phone rings, and Kade's name and a picture of us pops up.

"Kade!" I step outside for privacy.

"Gracie, what's wrong?"

"Nothing. I've been so worried about you."

"I'm sorry. It's been...let's just say a long day. Hey, can we switch to FaceTime?"

"Yeah."

185

My phone rings again, and I hit the accept button. Kade's face pops up. His eyes are red, and stubble is on his face.

"Have you slept?"

"No."

"Why not?"

"I can't get into it. I'm fine."

"Are you still here?"

"No. We're out on the Gulf now."

Tears blur my sight.

"I'm sorry I didn't get to kiss you goodbye."

I nod, unable to answer due to the heaping emotions filling my chest.

"Did Hudson give you the bank info?"

I sniffle. "Yes."

"Good. I'll work on ending this, and you work on finding somewhere you love."

"Kade, we can live anywhere, and I'll love it."

A tired smile appears. "Me, too. But I want you to have a place you really love."

"Okay. I'll get with Hudson and see what is available."

We say nothing for several moments.

"When will I see you again?" My gut flips because I already know the answer.

"I'm not sure. And..."

"What?"

"I'm not going to be able to call you every day. I may not be able to call you for a long time."

My heart races. "What does a long time mean?"

He swallows hard. "Maybe months."

Tears flow. "Why?"

He says nothing.

"You can't tell me?" I quietly ask.

"No, I'm sorry."

"I hate this," I tell him.

"Me, too."

I take a deep breath, trying to stop my tears.

"Gracie."

"Hmmm?"

"I need a promise from you."

"What?"

"Whatever I have to do, believe I'm doing it to protect you and end this. Don't question it or overthink it."

Cold rolls down my spine. "Why are you telling me this?"

"If your brothers or I tell you to do something, please do it. It's the only time in our life I'll ask you to follow blindly. Please."

"You're scaring me."

"I'm not trying to scare you, but I need your promise."

"Okay. I promise."

"Thank you. I have to go now."

"Am I going to get to talk to you later or no?"

Kade's eyes glisten. "I don't know, baby. I hope so, but if not, trust I'm doing this for us."

"I already trust in you, Kade."

His lips turn up. "Okay. Work on finding us a home. The minute I can call you, I will, but every second of every day, I'll be thinking of you."

I sniffle. "Same here."

"I love you, Gracie."

"I love you, too, Kade," I sob out, and the phone goes dead.

Within minutes, Connor comes into the garage and draws me into his chest. "It'll be okay. He'll be fine and home soon."

"Will he?"

"Yes," Connor tells me, but I don't believe him.

21

Kade

FORTY-TWO DAYS HAVE PASSED SINCE I SPOKE WITH GRACIE AND saw her face. What makes it even more painful is I haven't been too far. Fisher and I have been partying all over the east coast of Florida and the Caribbean. Ft. Lauderdale, Miami, and Key West, along with all the different islands, have been our hotspots. I'm trying to keep Fisher as far away from Gracie as possible, but business contacts have kept us stateside.

My yacht has been parked in Miami. I've been living on Fisher's boat, and it's why I've not been able to risk contacting Gracie.

I'm getting more and more into the web of the Twisted Hearts Elite. Every night, it's one more "businessman" from countries all over the globe. The network is deep. No one would ever suspect the people I meet are criminals, and some are even famous athletes, actors, and lawmakers.

Fisher seems to be running it all. Since Kate Contro died, he's slid into calling the shots. And things are escalating.

Weapons and chemicals are being stockpiled.

Where? I still can't figure out the location. I'm spending any free moment I have trying to crack the code and I'm still confident Lena has it, but like the past, I'm no further ahead.

And Fisher is tight-lipped about the storage locations.

He's been pressuring me to sell him more chemicals, but Interpol doesn't want to issue me any more until we figure out where he's keeping everything.

The ache in my heart to see Gracie, or just hear her voice, throbs harder every day. I wonder if she's happy, or sad, or found us a house yet. She's a constant on my mind.

Night after night, Fisher and I party together. Every sinful deed makes me cringe. The drugs, women, and excessive drinking is enough to make me want to go crazy, but the thing worrying me the most is Fisher won't stop talking about plans to have Gracie with him.

So many conversations have me reminding him about different women he's screwing who would love nothing more than to be his arm candy, but he can't get over his obsession with her.

I'm losing any hope this is ever going to end when I get a text. It's from a blocked number.

"I'm ready. Monday at 3 p.m. Parking lot where we met."

My pulse increases.

Please be who and what I think it is.

Fisher comes into the room with two half-naked women as I'm re-reading the text.

We're in the Florida Keys. I'm not sure when the next flight to Tampa or Ft. Myers is, but if there isn't one, I'll rent a car and drive.

"I'm heading out for a few days," I rise and tell Fisher.

"Oh?" He arches his brow.

"Business bullshit I forgot about."

"Have fun."

I grunt. "I'm sure you'll have much more fun than me."

He fist-bumps me as I pass him.

It's Sunday afternoon. I pack an overnight bag, discover there aren't any flights to accommodate my schedule, and rent a car to drive from the Keys all the way to Anna Maria.

When I get there, it's just past midnight. The island is dark and quiet. I park several blocks from the Brooks' house and stride quickly to their home. Quietly, I punch in the key code, turn off the alarm, and sneak up the stairs, hoping I don't wake Hudson and end up with a bullet in my chest.

Without making a sound, I open and shut Gracie's door and lock it. My heart is pounding at the thought of holding her.

The moonlight shines through the window, and Gracie is sleeping. Her blonde hair fans over her pillow, and she resembles the angel she is. When I sit on the edge of the bed, the scent of her skin flares in my nostrils, making my dick stir.

Carefully, I put my hand over her mouth so she doesn't scream. I kiss her forehead then whisper, "Gracie. Wake up, baby."

Her eyes flutter and then widen in fear.

"It's okay. It's me."

Tears leak down her cheeks, and she sits up. I move my hand off her mouth.

"Kade. Oh, my God. Are you really here?" Hands I've dreamed of over the last six weeks cup my face.

"Yeah. It's me."

"Are you here for good?"

"No. I'll be gone in the morning before anyone wakes up."

"What? Why?"

"Shh. Let's not spend our time talking about it."

Lips and tongues merge into a delicious concoction of want and need and pent-up longing. Desire burns, ripping through the core of my being, potent and intoxicating.

My fingers inch on the silk of Gracie's nightgown, wadding it up to get under it and on her luxurious skin.

"I missed you," I murmur to her.

"I'm dying without you," she whispers.

"I know, baby, me, too."

Clothes quickly come off. Flesh to flesh, our beating hearts and throbbing veins pulse against the other.

A sensual kiss becomes carnal and ravishes my senses, hardening my cock, stirring every dot of blood in my veins.

Her hands slide through my hair, gripping my head and reminding me I'm a man—a man she craves like no other man on earth.

Tearing my lips away from hers is punishment and reward at the same time. I let her whimpers, labored breath, and body writhing under mine guide my lips and teeth and tongue.

"Kade," she moans, arching her back as I pebble her nipples in my mouth. I've played it over and over in my head while I've been away from her, but pre-cum drips out of my dick when the sound hits my ears.

I worship all of her. When I get to her sweet sex, I fuck her with my tongue, splaying my hand on her stomach to hold her firmly, getting harder with every buck of her hips or squeeze of her thighs.

Her breathy ohs, clenching pussy, and white of her eyes rolling make me want to orgasm on the spot. My beautiful Gracie is mine, still mine, even through all the distance and complications.

When I've exhausted her from making her soar multiple times, I shimmy up her body, sliding into her tight wetness.

"Kade," she whimpers again and clenches her hot walls on my cock.

Pink lips, already swollen from our kisses, I devour again. She glides her tongue all over my mouth, and I'm not sure if she's claiming me or I'm claiming her.

The digging of her nails into my shoulders, the wrapping of her legs around my hips, the O of her mouth as she unravels under the weight of my body, lights me up like a match when it strikes and ignites.

She's a gift, and I've needed her even more than I realized. As always, I'm dead without her. Every moment without her in my arms or by my side is a wasted part of my life. And she's everything opposite of the hell I've been living in.

I thrust deeper in her, harder and faster. Her face flushes pink, visible in the moonlight. Nails scrape down my flesh, and her orgasm hits her so intensely when she shatters, her spasms send me into my own climax.

Her warm breath pants on the flesh of my collarbone.

I lift my face off her neck and crush my lips on hers, not satiated and aware I won't be, tonight or ever.

"I love you. Don't ever forget how much," I murmur to her.

"I won't." Tears roll quickly down her face, and her chest becomes shaky. "I miss you so much, Kade."

"Shhh." I taste her lips again and caress her head.

"I love you," she whispers.

I wipe her tears away.

"Tell me it's going to be over soon," she pleads.

I close my eyes. I wish I could. But I can't. "I'm doing everything I can. I promise."

More tears fly. "Hold me, Kade. Please."

My arms wrap around her, holding her close. I kiss the top of her head and caress her back.

"Close your eyes," I tell her.

It's better for both our sakes if she's asleep when I leave.

"You won't be here when I wake up, will you?" she asks.

"No."

Our limbs wrap tighter around one another, and nothing feels more right than Gracie in my arms. It doesn't take her long to fall asleep. When I have to pry my body from hers, pain wrenches through me, squeezing my heart.

I sneak out of the house while it's still dark, getting into the rented SUV a few blocks away. I spend the day in St. Pete, making myself scarce until it's 3 p.m.

Please show up, Lena. I hope she is who I'm meeting.

When I arrive, Lena's standing against the brick wall. Hope that I'm going to be able to take down Fisher and finally live my life with Gracie burns brighter than it has in a long time.

Lena hops into the passenger seat, and I hug then kiss her cheek.

"How have you been?" she asks me.

"Good. Ready for this to be over."

She nods. "I'm sure you are."

"Thank you for doing this."

She hesitates then takes a deep breath. "The code is..."

2 2

Gracie

DREAMS CREATE FEELINGS OF HAPPINESS AND PLEASURE. WHEN I wake up, I wonder if Kade was a dream. I'm debating, and then I roll over and see one long-stemmed red rose and a note.

"I love you."

It's a simple yet complex statement, and, amongst all the chaos, I take comfort in it, relieved he didn't write anything more so I'm not crying all day.

My instant thought is to call or text him, but I remember I can't.

I hold the petals to my nose and inhale, closing my eyes and imagine Kade's arms around me again, but nothing feels like the real thing.

There's a knock on my door. "Come in," I say, and Connor appears.

"Do you always wake up smelling a rose?" he teases.

"No. Kade was here." I place the rose on the nightstand and get out of bed.

Connor arches his brow. "When?"

"Only for a few hours last night."

"Where did he go?"

I shrug. "What's going on?"

"Did you forget about the closing?"

My hand flies to my forehead. "I can't believe I forgot to tell Kade about the house."

Hudson said he learned about a house that is supposed to go on the market. It's two doors down from his and Lena's new home. We viewed it a few weeks ago, and I loved it. It needs some work but nothing too crazy. Hudson helped me figure out what to offer and negotiated everything for me. Since I'm paying cash, things have moved quickly, and I'm closing on it today.

"I'm sure you had other things on your mind." Connor cockily arches his eyebrow.

My cheeks heat. "Funny."

"We have to leave in thirty minutes, so I'll meet you downstairs." He shuts the door.

I shower, dry my hair, throw on a little bit of makeup, and get changed. When I get downstairs, Connor hands me a smoothie.

"What's this?"

"Javier's concoction. It's delicious. You can take it in the car."

"Thanks. Since when did you become the Chef Boyardee smoothie maker?"

"Novah's into smoothies."

I smirk at him.

"What?" he asks.

"What's up with you and Novah?"

He shrugs. "She's cool."

"You've been hanging out a lot."

"Yeah."

"So...?"

"So...what?"

"Are you serious?"

"Just having fun. You ready to go?" Connor goes to the door.

I double-check the bank account card is in my wallet and follow him.

Connor takes me to the bank, and I get a cashier's check as the title company instructed me. We go to their office, and the closing doesn't take too long. The sellers hand me the keys.

I wish Kade was with me.

When we get in the car, Connor asks, "Well, how does it feel?"

"Strange."

"What do you mean? You aren't excited?"

"No, I am. But I wish Kade could have been a part of this with me."

"That house would not have lasted more than a few days on the market."

"True." I force a smile. "Kade will be happy when he sees it."

"Did he have any idea when he's able to come home?"

"No," I quietly say.

Connor studies me then focuses on the road. "Are you doing okay?"

"I miss him. It hurts. Not like before but different. I can't explain it."

Connor opens his mouth to speak when an SUV accelerates and moves in front of us, another one next to us, and a third one behind us.

"What the fuck?" Connor bellows out.

Terror races through my veins.

We're on the causeway, the window of the SUV next to us rolls down, and a man points a gun at us. He waves it, indicating for us to pull over. The vehicle in front of us slows down, and we're blocked, so we can't move anywhere except over.

"Get down," Connor shouts and forces my head to my knees.

"Don't stop," I yell.

"I can't go anywhere, Gracie." I've never before heard the panic laced in his voice.

Within seconds, we're parked on the side of the causeway. The turquoise water is sparkling in front of us. The SUVs surround us, and there is nowhere to go.

My chest tightens and heart pounds. "Connor! What are we going to do?"

He grips the wheel tighter. "I don't know. I don't have my gun on me."

Kade. I need to get ahold of Kade.

I'm about to grab my phone out of my purse when a man tries to open my door.

"Unlock the door," his gruff voice shouts, and he aims his gun at my head.

Stay calm, Gracie.

"Don't!" Connor shouts.

"Now," the man yells again and taps the gun against the windshield.

There is no other option. It's open the door or get shot.

I unlock the door, and the man flings my door open and drags me out by my arm.

I'm screaming. Connor tries to grab me, but two men haul him out, and both punch him.

"Connor," I scream but something is put over my mouth, and I'm thrown into one of the SUV's. Within seconds, everything goes black.

When I wake up, I'm groggy, and everything is black. I'm moving, and a man is singing a rap song I can't put my finger on but I've heard it before. The leather is cold on my skin, and my hands and feet are tied. I lose track of how many times I fall in and out of consciousness.

Hours or maybe days later, I regain consciousness. My mouth is dry. My body aches. Sunlight streams onto my face, and I'm rocking side to side. A woodsy lavender aroma flares in my nostrils, which at first is comforting.

I know that smell.

I'm still too groggy to place it, but it's familiar.

Slowly, I open my eyes. The vast blue horizon of the ocean is in front of me.

I shut my eyes again and snuggle into the pillow then freeze.

Woodsy lavender. Ocean. Rocking.

Fear is like a popcorn kernel that starts small and pops into existence throughout my entire body. A chill runs down my spine, and I shiver.

A blanket is put over me. His voice whispers in my ear and sounds warm and nonthreatening, but it's nothing but. "Sleep, Gracie. We'll talk when you wake up."

I don't need to open my eyes. Fisher has me. I'm on his yacht, heading God knows where.

My chest becomes tighter, and I tell myself to stay calm and breathe.

Under the pillow, my fingers grasp my wrist, and I trace the platinum bracelet Kade gave me.

If you're ever in danger, I will come find you and don't forget that, Kade's voice rings in my ears.

A serene feeling washes over me.

He will come find me. I just need to be smart until he does.

I tell myself to stay asleep, even if it's pretending, for as long as possible, to buy more time for Kade to find me. I keep my eyes closed and almost fall back to sleep.

I pop up in the bed. "Connor!"

Fisher sits down on the bed.

Fear fills me.

He cups my cheek. "I've missed you, Gracie."

23

Kade

"Connor," I answer, happy Lena gave me the code.

There's no response, just dead air. The phone shows the call is still connected.

"Connor?"

"Gr..." Connor's muffled voice comes through the line and then heavy breathing.

Chills soar through my bones, and I veer to the side of the road.

"Connor!" I bark out.

"Grace...they...gr..."

I snatch the computer bag in my back seat and unzip it. "Connor, are you with Gracie?"

"No...they..."

They have her.

I put it on speakerphone, open the laptop, and start a search to locate where Connor and Gracie both are. Connor is about fifteen miles from me. Gracie is almost to Key West.

No doubt, heading toward Fisher's boat.

Fuck.

"Connor, stay on the line. I'm coming. It's going to sound like I'm hanging up, but I'm not. Just hold on for a minute."

I create a second line and call Javier.

"Kade."

"Something has happened. I'm sending you details where Connor is. I need you to meet me."

"What's happened?"

"I don't have all the details. They have Gracie."

"No."

"Yes. She's almost to Key West. Connor's on the other line, but he sounds hurt. I'll text you the location."

"On our way."

Fuck!" I scream before switching the line over to Connor and text Javier the location.

"Connor, are you there?"

He moans.

"I'm on my way. Stay on the line with me."

The entire way, he tries to say Gracie's name but can't.

What did those thugs do to him?

They better not touch Gracie.

Anger like I've never felt rages through me. I keep talking to Connor and try to maintain a calm demeanor.

I park in the lot to an abandoned building in Bradenton just as Javier and Chloe arrive.

We're coming in, Connor. Don't die on us.

The three of us have our guns out and safeties off. The door is chained and locked.

"You're sure he's in there?" Chloe asks.

"Yes."

"Stand back," she instructs, and as soon as Javier and I take a few steps away, she shoots the lock.

The three of us run inside.

"Connor," we're all shouting and split up.

"He's over here," Javier shouts. Chloe and I both run over, and she calls an ambulance.

Connor is lying in a pool of blood, his face unrecognizable, a beat-up mess. I'm guessing he might have a few ribs broken, and I worry he may have internal bleeding.

Bile rises, and I swallow it down as anger flares through my bones.

Whoever did this to Connor I will find and kill.

Tears mix with blood as he moans and keeps trying to say, "Gracie."

Javier, Chloe, and I all try to hold it together, but we aren't sure what his injuries are.

"You did good, Connor," I tell him as the paramedics come in.

He grabs my hand. "Grace..."

"I'm going to get her. You did good," I repeat.

Tears roll down his face.

Chloe goes in the ambulance with him. Javier shoots a text to let the family know to go to the hospital.

"Where's Gracie?" Javier asks.

I pick up my laptop and open it. I point at the screen.

"Why Key West?" Javier asks.

"Fisher is docked there."

"I'm assuming he won't hurt her?"

He better not.

"In his warped mind, he loves her. My assumption is he'll give her a bit of time before he attempts to force her into anything." As I say it, my gut churns.

Javier scowls.

"Shit," I mumble as the dot moves on the water. "They have her on the yacht already."

"Where's your boat?"

"Miami."

Silence.

"I'm going to kill him."

"You able to stay calm enough to go take him out?"

I release a big breath. "Yeah. I have to in order to get Gracie out of this."

"You could have the Coast Guard pull him over."

"I don't have the information I need. There's too much at stake not to get it. What he's planning…" I slam my hand on the roof of the car. "I can't believe he got Gracie."

"Kade, are you sure you're able to do this? I can call Carter."

"No. I'm going to finish this."

"Okay. Where do you think he's headed?"

I rub my hands over my face. "We were supposed to go to Monte Carlo next. He wanted to leave tonight."

"Why weren't you on your boat?"

"Dock space was limited, and he needed me in meetings."

"Is it limited in Monte Carlo?"

"No. But if Gracie is on his boat, I need to get on it."

"Call him and tell him you're running late. Make him admit he left, and you can tell him you'll helicopter over. I'll call Carter."

I call Fisher and remind myself to stay calm.

"Kade. I was about to call you," he answers.

"I've got good news about our supply," I say in a chipper voice, so he can't give me a reason to not return on the boat.

"Oh?"

He's so greedy, he can't help himself.

"Triple supply."

"No way."

"Yep. Anyways, it took me a bit longer to secure the deal. I'm going to be a little late."

"That's what I was going to call you about. We needed to take off."

"You left me? Thought your supplier was important," I say in a joking tone.

"Sorry, man. Can we meet up?"

"How far out are you?"

"Just left."

"Tell you what. My buddy has a copter. Why don't I have him fly me out? The captain of my boat called. I've got an issue with an engine they're fixing right now. And we can't miss meeting with Amaro."

He's quiet for a moment.

"Fisher, you there?"

Javier gives me a thumbs-up on the helicopter then motions for me to get in the car. I grab my laptop and jump into the passenger seat.

"Yeah. Listen, Coral. I need to ask you something," Fisher says.

My gut drops. "What?"

"You know how I asked you where your loyalties lie?"

I pretend to get mad and insulted. "I just told you I'm tripling the supply and going to throw more money in our pockets than God himself possesses, and you're questioning my loyalty? Fisher, I'm getting sick of this bullshit."

"Kade—"

"No. Maybe I need to ask you where your loyalties lie. There are other people I can do business with."

"Kade, we're cool. I'm sorry, man. Something just...something came up, and I need to make sure you're going to be cool with it."

"Fisher, whatever is going on, I don't give a shit, as long as my pocket gets lined as we discussed. Just tell me if you're in or out. I don't have time for this game. I just spent several hours kissing ass to get three times what we assumed we could get."

"I'm in. Have your friend copter you in. Text me when you're on the way, and he can talk with the captain for coordinates."

On purpose, I stay silent.

"Kade, you there?"

"I'm putting you on warning, Fisher."

"What are you talking about?"

"Any more questioning about where my loyalties lie, and I'm walking. I need to have confidence we're in this together. I don't have time to make the wrong move for my bank account."

"We're good, Kade. I won't question it again."

"All right, then. Let's get this shit done."

"See you soon." I hang up.

"He fall for it?" Javier asks.

"Yeah."

"You have some backup?"

"I've already got several female agents on the boat."

Javier arches his eyebrows. "Gracie have any idea about the girls?"

My stomach flips. "Yeah. She is aware of how it works. Monica will take her aside and reiterate it as well, I'm sure."

"Monica?"

"My girlfriend in Fisher's eyes."

"Understanding how it works and watching it are two different things."

I sigh. "I don't like it, but I don't have a choice."

"Do me a favor, bro," Javier says.

"What?"

"Remember everything I taught you when you finally put the bullet in Fisher's brain."

"You don't have to worry about my shooting skills."

"Good."

We drive for several hours to get to the helicopter pad.

"Text me what you need," Javier says.

"Can you call Andre? Tell him I'm going to need his help and I'll send a message for him?"

"Sure."

"Notify me when you find out the extent of Connor's injuries."

"You bet. Stay safe."

The helicopter lands, and Javier pats my back. I get on, and we get to Miami where the helicopter stops to refuel. I'm tracking Fisher's boat, but I text him to give me the captain's number for coordinates.

We get into the air, and all I can think about is how he's a dead man.

24

Gracie

"WHAT DID YOU DO TO CONNOR?"

Fisher's expression is the same as every other day, but now it seems sinister.

How did I not see it?

"Connor's tough. He'll be fine."

I sit up then hold my head and cry out as pain shoots through it.

"Whoa. Slow down. You don't want to move too fast." Fisher puts his hand on my cheek, and I want to vomit.

"Don't touch me," I tell him through clenched teeth as another shot of pain slaps my brain.

He moves his hand away. "There's no need to be nasty, Gracie."

Speechless, I glare at him.

His fingers trail over my shoulder and down my arm before I slap it away.

"Don't touch me," I repeat.

He's about to say something when his phone rings. Holding one finger up, he steps out of the room but doesn't shut the door.

"Kade, I was about to call you," he answers.

Kade. He'll come for me. I touch the platinum bracelet again as hope detonates in all my cells.

I don't hear anything else, and a few minutes later, Fisher reappears. He sits on the edge of the bed again.

I wait for him to speak, not sure what I should say, but confident Kade will come get me.

"I've missed you," Fisher says again.

"So, you have my brother beaten up and kidnap me?"

He sternly says, "Connor will be fine. And you left me with no choice."

"Excuse me?"

"We need to talk."

My head is on fire, and every word I speak or try to interpret of Fisher's makes it worse.

I hug my knees to my chest and lay my chin on them, still tired.

"Talk, then," I manage to get out.

He strokes my hair.

"Don't touch me," I repeat and get rewarded with another blow to my brain. Wincing, I take both hands and squeeze them against my head. "Why do I feel like I've been beaten?"

He shrugs. "It's just the drug they gave you. It'll wear off soon."

I glare at him.

"You should rest. You'll feel better in a few hours."

"What did you drug me with?"

"Nothing you need to worry about. There won't be any long-term issues."

"I hate you," I blurt out.

"No, you don't," he tells me and pats the pillow. "Sleep. When you wake up, you'll feel better, and then we can talk."

"No," I tell him even though my eyelids feel like bricks. "Where are you taking me?"

"We're going to Monte Carlo."

"Monte Carlo?"

"Yes. It'll be fun. You'll love it."

"You think I'm going to have fun with you after you had my brother harmed and kidnapped me?"

His face reddens. The scowl he gave me in my parents' driveway appears, sending shivers down my spine. "Enough, Gracie!"

I sink back against the headboard, surprised by his angry tone.

"Games. I'm tired of the games. All you've ever done is play games with me. We said we were doing serious. I had to go away for business. I'm sorry I left you, but there's no reason to hold a grudge."

I stay silent, not wanting to anger him further, but my lips and hands are shaking.

His eyes travel to my trembling body parts, and he sighs. "I'm sorry. I didn't mean to scare you."

When his hand comes toward my face, I cower.

His hand pauses midair. "Are you afraid of me?"

"I..." Tears well in my eyes, and my brain sloshes against my skull. When I close my eyes, my cheeks become wet.

He slides closer to me and drags me into his arms.

I want to shove him away, but I don't have the strength and am fearful of what he will do. "Please don't touch me," I whisper against my pounding head.

Fisher's lips press against my forehead, and his arms tighten around me. "Shh."

"Why are you doing this?" I ask, swallowing the thick knot in my throat.

He pulls away, and his eyes drill into mine. "I love you, Gracie. We're meant to be together."

I huff and shake my head. "You kidnapped me."

"I'm sorry, but it was necessary. Your family has too much power over you."

"What?" I say in disgust.

"It's true. It's stopped us from being together."

"You left me," I hurl at him, not sure why I'm even trying to rationalize anything to him.

"I'm sorry. I told you I had to go." He caresses the side of my head.

I try to move out of his hold, but there is nowhere to go.

"I can give you everything, and I'll prove it to you. You'll see. We're going to have a great time in Monte Carlo."

He's crazy. Seriously crazy.

You need to play him until Kade gets here. Think about how to do that, Gracie.

His lips come toward mine, and I turn my head.

"Gracie—"

I jab him in the chest. "No. You've had time to figure all this out. I've not. Several times, I've told you not to touch me. If you want me to ever truly desire you again, you need to give me some space."

He freezes. Silence for what feels like forever ensues.

My insides are shaking. I'm not sure if I made the right move or not.

Fisher finally nods. "That's fair." He stands. "You need to sleep. Rest, and when you wake up, your headache will be gone. We can talk again."

Go to sleep, and maybe Kade will be here when you awake.

You have the power right now. He just gave it to you. He's never been able to handle anyone not liking or wanting him.

"Shut the door. I'll come find you when I'm ready to talk," I demand.

Fisher crosses his arms. "I'll agree to your terms, but your attitude needs to be gone by the time we get to Monte Carlo."

Sinking into the pillow, I turn away from him and don't respond.

"It's not a request, Gracie." He puts the blanket over me then kisses my head. The door creaks, and I peek around the room to verify he's gone.

My tears turn to sobs as I worry about Connor and wonder what has happened to him.

If Fisher or anyone ever tries anything, I'll come for you. Kade's words are the only things comforting me as I drift off to sleep.

———

WHEN I WAKE UP, THE SUN IS SETTING ON THE WATER AND SO bright, I instantly turn away from it.

Why am I in Fisher's room?

Panic seizes me, and I remember what occurred and my conversation with Fisher.

Is Kade here yet?

Slowly, I get out of bed, go to the bathroom then assess myself in the mirror.

What does Fisher want?

He wants you to love him.

I'm going to have to play the part. Kade's voice once again rings loud in my head.

Play the part, Gracie.

I fix myself up and go into the closet. It still holds all the clothes Fisher bought for me, months ago. Shelves and hangers display one designer item after another.

Choosing a pink silk top with a silver zipper in the front and a pair of white capris, I change and slide into a pair of Gucci sandals, knowing Fisher will approve and be more likely to agree to what I want.

What do I want?

Buy time.

Don't let him touch you.

The thought of sleeping with Fisher makes my gut churn. He's never forced himself on me, but this isn't the past.

Kade will come get you.

Taking a deep breath, I open the door and amble down the hallway of the yacht. Room after room is empty, and Fisher's typical spot in the living area is vacant.

Where is he?

I leave the cabin, and as soon as I open the doors, loud rumbling makes me cover my ears.

When I turn the corner, Fisher is standing on the deck at the very tip of the vessel. There are other men and women I've never met. A helicopter hovers over the yacht, and the door opens.

My heart almost stops, and tears flood my eyes when Kade gets lowered onto the boat by a harness and rope. He releases the harness as soon as he lands, and the helicopter flies away.

I head toward the crowd but halt when a beautiful, exotic woman runs up to Kade. He embraces her and kisses her like she's his everything.

My insides quiver.

I'm going to have to play the part.

It's not real. It can't be. But my stomach twists and turns in jealousy.

Fisher turns and sees me.

"Gracie," he yells with a smile as if nothing in the world is wrong and comes toward me.

My gaze drifts from Kade to Fisher then back to Kade. I momentarily lock eyes with him before he says to Fisher. "How'd Gracie get here?"

Fisher possessively holds me and says, "She called and finally agreed to come with me. Didn't you?" He arches his brow at me.

Something about Fisher's expression tells me I don't want to do anything but agree with him right now.

"Yes." I force myself to smile.

Fisher pecks me on the cheek, happy I'm doing what he wants.

"We still need to talk," I murmur to him, not wanting him to think everything is how it was and expect me to sleep with him.

He winks. "We will."

Kade struts over and hugs me, and it's never felt better to be wrapped into his arms. But it doesn't last long. "Good to see you, Gracie. How's the family?"

I clear the thick knot in my throat. "Fine."

"Good." He only makes eye contact with me for a brief moment then focuses on Fisher. "Ready for me to fill you in on my meeting?"

Happiness radiates off Fisher. "Yes." He turns to me. "Go hang out with the ladies. I'll meet up with you later."

"Okay." I join the women, my insides quivering, my body missing the heat and safety of Kade, but reminding myself I need to play the game.

25

Kade

MONICA, THE AGENT WHO HAS BEEN POSING AS MY GIRLFRIEND FOR the last several months, runs up to me, and I kiss her.

Fisher calls out, "Gracie."

My stomach twists, and although Monica and I are both playing roles and I've told Gracie what part of my job entails, it kills me she had to watch it. And I see the hurt in her eyes.

It's all to get you out of here alive, baby.

When I hold Gracie in my arms, it takes every ounce of willpower to tear myself away quickly so nothing appears out of the ordinary to Fisher. I want to tell her to play the part and remind her to do whatever I ask of her, but I say nothing as Fisher is watching us.

Keep it business.

"Ready for me to fill you in on my meeting?" I ask him.

Greed fills Fisher's face. It's an expression I've gotten used to over the last few years. "Yes." He instructs Gracie to go with the women, and, ignoring her, I leave the deck with him.

"I told you she'd come back to me," Fisher boasts when we get inside.

Vengeance stirs in my gut, and I swallow hard.

Do your job. Find out what you need, kill him, and get Gracie to safety.

I force a smile. "That was good timing. Any later, and we'd have been in Monte Carlo."

"Yep."

"Are we all set for Amaro?" I ask him.

"He confirmed today."

"Good."

Amaro is another Elite. He's an Italian with ties to the mob and contacts all over the world. Fisher set the meeting for us to discuss how to deliver chemicals to different parts of Europe, where Fisher wants to stockpile them.

Fisher has never told me where he's stockpiling the chemicals. In the past, the chemicals I sold him were always transferred to his ships in the mid-Atlantic international waters.

The only hint he's ever given me is everything is in one location, and now it's time to spread it out. And that means trouble.

In the last few months, I've gained enough trust with Fisher to be part of these meetings. My shoot-to-kill order is authorized once I receive information on the locations.

Since Lena gave me the code, I need to get on my computer and hack into the system. I would have already done it had Connor not called me.

There is no guarantee the code will give me all the information Interpol needs, but I'm betting on it.

And now, my mission is no longer only about what Interpol wants. Gracie is here, and I need to figure out how to get her off this ship safely. Every ounce of restraint I have is stopping me from putting a bullet in Fisher's head right now. There are too many of his men on this ship, and I can't guarantee Gracie's safety if I shot him, so I need to wait until we are on land.

Fisher and I go through more semantics. He hands me a drink, and we eventually make our way to the pool area where Gracie is sitting by Monica at a table under the umbrella.

Fisher sits next to Gracie and takes her hand in his and kisses it. She removes it and puts both her hands between her crossed legs.

Fisher's face falls, and I scrape my chair on the floor. Gracie turns and sees me. Our eyes catch, but she turns away.

I put my arm around Monica, and she leans into me, playing the part.

"I told Gracie she'll love Monte Carlo," Fisher says and also puts his arm around Gracie.

She squirms, but he holds her firm to him.

"I'm sure Connor would like it more," I say nonchalantly, wanting to dive across the table and rip her away from him, but instead, I try to send her a message he is alive.

Gracie's blue eyes meet mine, and I see her worry as she blinks hard. "Why would he?"

I take a sip of my drink. "Lots of games to play, and Connor always wins."

"He does, doesn't he?" Fisher says.

Gracie's eyes brighten, and I wink at her when Fisher turns. She blinks harder, holding her emotions.

That's my girl. Play the game.

Fisher brushes her cheek.

Her face hardens, and she moves her head to the side, away from his touch.

Watching him touch her and seeing her distaste for it has my insides cringing. I try to breathe steadily, and Monica digs her nails into my twitching thigh, reminding me to stay calm.

Fisher's phone rings, and he answers it and strolls to the bow.

Monica squeezes my thigh and gets up and dives into the pool.

"Are you hurt at all?" I ask her.

"No. Connor—"

"We got him. He's going to be okay."

She closes her eyes, and I want to hold her so badly, but I can't. "There are cameras everywhere. Remember at all times you're being watched."

Her eyes fly open. "Okay."

"Play the part, Gracie."

"I know. I keep hearing your voice."

"When we dock in Monte Carlo, we'll make our move. There are too many of his men on the boat."

She shivers and her eyes fill with tears again.

"You can't cry right now. I need you to be strong and outsmart him at his own game."

She inhales sharply and puts her sunglasses on.

"Good decision, baby. Keep them on if you need to. I'm going to drug Fisher tonight so he'll pass out. Remember when he does, your every move is still being recorded."

"I will."

"Monica is an agent."

Her eyes meet mine through her sunglasses.

"Whatever I do is not real."

"I know."

"He's coming back now, so play the part."

Monica gets out of the pool and comes over and picks up the towel, wrapping it around her body. I playfully slap her ass as Fisher would expect me to, and she giggles, then I tug her on my lap.

"Gracie, let's go inside," Fisher says.

"I'm happy here."

Fisher leans down and says something in her ear.

"I'm not ready yet."

"Gracie—"

"We're not in Monte Carlo yet. The deal was by the time we get to Monte Carlo."

What deal?

Fisher puts both hands on the armrests of her chair, and growls, "Inside. Now."

I stop myself from punching him.

Go inside. Play the game, baby.

She shoves her chair back and rises. "Fine."

As I watch her leave me, my insides are on fire.

"Stay cool, Kade," Monica mutters.

Five days. We have to get through five days.

Somehow, between Gracie, Monica, and me, we need to figure out how to keep Fisher off her.

After fifteen minutes pass, I rise.

"Don't go in there yet," Monica says.

"I have to."

"You need to wait."

"I can't. Come with me."

She follows but mutters, "This is a bad idea."

When we enter the living area, Gracie is sitting next to Fisher with her arms crossed.

"You asked me once what I wanted from you, and you'd make it happen. Is it still true?" she asks.

"Yes. Anything. You know—" Fisher squints at Monica and me.

"Oh, hey. Are we interrupting? I can't find my bag. Have you seen it?" Monica asks, and I pour another drink.

"You want one?" I ask Fisher.

"Yeah."

"Gracie?" I ask out of politeness, hoping she'll pass.

"Not right now."

Good girl.

"Have a drink," Fisher demands.

"No. I don't want one right now."

"Kade, fix her a drink."

"All right." I peck Monica on the lips. "What do you want?"

"Whatever you're having."

I take my time making drinks and hand Monica hers first. I hand Gracie hers but don't put any alcohol in it, and she sets it on the table. When I hand Fisher his, he tips his head toward the door.

Monica grabs my hand. "I think it's time for us to have some private time." She giggles and rubs up against me.

"Get going." I leave the room and call out, "See you later."

In all my dealings as a spy, I've never been tested like this. It's going to take everything I have not to blow my cover and to get Gracie to safety.

As soon as we get to our room, I open my laptop, ready to enter the code Lena gave me and finish this.

But the Internet is blocked.

I try to connect the internet Wi-Fi on my phone, but nothing is working. Monica's isn't connecting, either.

Uneasiness ripples through me. The only way Monica's and my devices wouldn't be working is if someone was intentionally blocking it. On this boat, only one person would do that.

Fisher.

Is he blocking it to stop Gracie from contacting her family, or does he suspect something?

26

Gracie

"TELL ME WHAT YOU WANT," FISHER DEMANDS WHEN KADE AND Monica leave. Against my wishes he yanks me onto his lap.

"I've asked you not to touch me."

"Enough of this game, Gracie."

I try to stand, but he pins me down. "Fisher, let go."

"No. Tell me what you want, and let's return to the way things were."

Play the game.

I stop squirming and take a deep breath.

He turns my chin to him. "I'm sorry I hurt you. We need to get past this. Tell me what you want." His blue eyes fill with sincerity and remorse.

Don't fall for it. He's a monster.

My heart races.

He waits for me to answer him.

"We can't pretend nothing has happened, Fisher."

"We can."

"No. We can move forward maybe but not go backward," I say, trying to manipulate him and buy more time.

His face hardens, and he lets out a big breath. "What do you want? Tell me so we can move forward."

"I want to talk to Connor."

"No."

Tears fill my eyes. Kade told me Connor would be okay but couldn't tell me the details, and I want to hear Connor's voice.

"Then I'll never want you again, much less love you."

His eyes turn into slits. "I told you he's fine. Pick something else."

"No. You promised me anything. I'm telling you what I want."

Red anger crosses his face. "Stop telling me no. You don't hold the cards, Gracie."

I've only seen this new side of Fisher a handful of times. It makes my insides quiver. I try to get off his lap again, but he holds me firm.

"You don't get up until I say you get up," he growls.

My pulse beats faster.

I'm in a game I'm not sure how to play.

"What do you want from me?" I quietly ask.

"You. All of you. I've been clear about my wishes, and they haven't changed since I've been away."

I stare out the glass.

He moves my hair to one side, traces his finger down my neck, and then his lips press against my flesh.

I cringe, squirming in his hold. "Stop."

"Damn it, Gracie," he yells and shoves me off his lap. I jump up and try to leave, but he grabs me by the throat and shoves me against the window.

My entire body shakes, and his eyes burn with rage. "Stop playing games."

"I'm not," I barely get out.

"You are. You always have. I'm tired of it."

"Let go," I choke out.

His body presses against mine, and his erection grows against my stomach.

Leaning into my ear, squeezing harder, he quietly says, "I hold the cards, Gracie. You will do what I want, when I want it. This isn't up for debate. And you'll like every minute of it."

My airway is getting cut off, and I get dizzy.

He releases my neck then slides his hands into my hair and crushes his lips to mine, roughly shoving his tongue in my mouth.

I gag and try to shove him off me, which only makes him squish his body against mine harder.

"Stop fighting me," he commands through clenched teeth, holding my neck so I'm facing him but not squeezing this time.

The only thing I can do is cry.

His eyes morph from enraged to sympathetic, and he embraces me, wrapping his arms tight around me. "I'm sorry. But you're making me crazy. Stop fighting me, please," he murmurs in my ear.

The waterworks won't stop, and my sobs become louder, which make him tighten his hold.

I don't want any part of him. I want to run down to Kade's room and into his arms, but I can't.

I will myself to stop crying so he will release me, but all he does is use my pain for his gain.

His lips flutter on my forehead, cheek, and ear. He's touching me the way he has in the past, but all I feel is fear and loathing. I want him to stop but am unsure how to get him to.

One of his men comes into the room and tells him he's needed in his office. He releases me. "Go get ready for dinner. We'll eat outside tonight."

Wiping my face, I leave his side, still feeling the grip of his hands on my neck.

On the way to his bedroom, Kade steps out into the hall, and his eyes widen. "Gracie, what happened?"

I turn away and pass him, full of shame. I'm not sure why, but it bubbles and overflows.

Kade follows me, reaches for my arm, and spins me. "What did he do?" he seethes through clenched teeth.

"Kade," Monica calls out and quickly is by our side, tugging on his arm.

"Cameras," she mutters.

"I'm fine," I lie. "I have to get ready for dinner."

His eyes become fixed on my neck, and Kade's face hardens and becomes red. He holds me in his arms, and I try not to but sob.

"Shh," he tries to soothe me.

When my crying subsides, he murmurs, "Where is he?"

"His office. But you can't do anything."

Kade's eyes turn to slits. "Go get ready for dinner. Monica, go with her."

"Kade, no," I cry out.

He turns to Monica. "Go with her."

"Kade—"

"Monica, go with her."

She nods and puts her arm around me. "Come on."

Kade is already halfway down the hall.

"Kade," I yell out, but he only increases his speed.

Either Fisher or Kade is going to end up dead.

"Monica, you have to stop him."

"There's no stopping him. Come on. He said to get changed, so that's what we need to do."

"Monica—"

She puts her finger over my lips. "Shh. Don't question, just do what he says."

If your brothers or I tell you to do something, please do it. It's the only time in our life I'll ask you to follow blindly. Please. Kade's voice replays in my head from our phone call.

"Okay," I tell Monica, and we go into Fisher's room. She helps me get ready, and I sit on pins and needles, worrying about what's happening.

"He'll be okay," Monica says in a hushed voice.

When eight o'clock hits, Monica makes me leave the room. "Let's go. Fisher said dinner was at eight tonight."

With my insides shaking and emotions all over the place, Monica and I go outside on the deck. A dinner table is set up, and soft music is playing. The swimming pool is lit up with pink light, and there's a breeze coming off the ocean. Oversized portable heater lamps are lit around the table.

"Why aren't they here?" I ask in a panic.

"They will be," she assures me.

"How can you be sure nothing has happened?"

"It's Kade. He's smart."

A waiter brings us a glass of champagne, and I'm about to pass, but Monica picks it up and hands it to me. "Have a sip to calm your nerves."

I have a few sips, and we sit down at the table.

"Kade said you're smart, too, and can play the game."

"I don't know how to play this game. I thought I could, but I can't," I admit to her.

She puts her hand on mine. "You've been around Fisher just as much as we have but in a more intimate way. Use it to your advantage."

"How?"

"Give him enough to be pleased without going past your limit."

"My limit?"

"Yes. What don't you want to do with him?"

"Anything."

"Not possible, so what is the absolute no-no."

"I don't want to sleep with him."

"Okay. So you draw the line there but sit on his lap. Kiss him. Make him feel like you're coming around. At night, Kade or I will drug him. In the morning, make sure you leave the room before he does. I'll keep you busy during the daytime. If you get into any situation, fake being sick."

The thought of kissing Fisher and pretending to like him makes my stomach flip.

"I'm with Kade. He isn't going to—"

"It's not real. Kade isn't going to hold anything you do against you. We're doing what we need to do to all come out of this alive and finish taking him down."

"This isn't my world. I'm not used to secrets and lies."

Monica squeezes my hand. "I understand, but you have to think about what it takes to save your life right now. So figure out where your line is and get clear on what you can stomach and can't. Fisher isn't going to allow you to ignore him for five days. When we get to Monte Carlo, you're his eye candy, so he's going to want you to act the part in front of the other Elites."

I shiver. "The other Elites?"

"Yes. The escape route is going to involve that meeting, so Fisher needs to have confidence he can take you. Otherwise, you're not going to be allowed off this ship."

I take another sip of my champagne, letting what Monica said sink in.

"Here they come. Play the game," Monica says and downs the rest of her champagne.

I turn. Kade and Fisher strut side by side as if they are best buddies. My nerves calm slightly at the evidence Kade is all right.

He avoids my gaze and pecks Monica on the lips. "You hungry?"

"Mm-hmm. I'm starving."

"Fisher, what's for dinner?" Kade asks.

"Lobster. It's Gracie's favorite."

Everyone waits for my reaction. Kade's wink gets me back in the game.

I force a smile aimed at Fisher. "That was sweet of you."

He puts his arm around me, and my body freezes. Fisher notices, and a frown forms on his face. "Can I talk to you?"

I swallow the spiked knot in my throat, not wanting to be alone.

"Gracie, go talk to Fisher." Kade points to a cabana a few feet away from us.

I hesitate.

It's the only time in our life I'll ask you to follow blindly. Kade's voice fills my head as I stare into his eyes.

"Go," he commands again.

I turn to Fisher. "Okay."

He takes my hand and leads me over to the lounger. We sit down, and I try to quiet my shaking insides.

"I'm sorry. It won't ever happen again," Fisher claims.

"It's fine," I say and stand up.

He tugs me down on his lap. "No, it's not. I really am sorry."

Fisher seems so sincere, but I don't believe if he got angry he wouldn't hurt me and maybe even take it a step further.

Play the game.

I nod. "Apology accepted."

The smile that first charmed me erupts on his face. "Can I kiss you?"

No, you arrogant a-hole.

You need to get off this ship when it docks.

"I need to take this slow, Fisher. This has been a lot for me today."

He closes his eyes and breathes deep. "All right. I can handle that. But can I please have a kiss?"

I hesitate but then cup his face and kiss him. It's not a deep kiss, and when I go to pull away, Fisher clutches my head and kisses me as if his life depended on it.

He finally releases me. "Thank you, Gracie. I've missed you."

"I've missed you, too," I lie.

"You have?"

"Yeah."

He beams. "Let's go eat lobster." He helps me off the cabana, and, from the corner of my eye, I see Kade watching me with his jaw clenched.

The game has restarted. I'm just not sure if Fisher or Kade and I are the real pawns.

27

Kade

THOUGHTS OF BEATING FISHER TO A PULP ECHO IN MY MIND. MY fists clench at my sides, itching to pummel his face.

He hurt Gracie. I'm going to kill him.

There are too many men of his on this boat. Be smart.

I trot down the hall. The door to his office is open, and Neil is talking with Fisher.

"Out, now," I growl at Neil.

Neil scrunches his forehead. "Who do you think—"

"Go, Neil," Fisher says then sits in his chair and downs the rest of his drink.

As soon as he's through the door, I slam it shut.

"Easy there, Killer," Fisher teases, but there is also nervousness in his eyes.

One thing I've always done is made sure Fisher understands I'm not to be messed with. Deep down, he wouldn't want to go fist to fist with me. He's always got his posse of men around to protect him, and it allows him to make decisions he wouldn't if they weren't there.

I bark, "Did you put your hands on Gracie's neck?"

"She told you?"

I throw my hands on his desk. "No. I saw the marks."

His eyes widen at my rage, and he rubs his hands over his face. "I didn't mean to."

"You didn't mean to?" I growl.

He gets up and pours another three fingers of whiskey then chugs half of it.

I should squeeze his neck and the life out of him.

Gracie would be in danger with his men if you do something stupid.

Be smart.

He spins. "She's not totally into me right now."

Of course she isn't, you dickhead.

"What do you mean?"

He hesitates. "She's upset with me about a few things."

"So you attempt to strangle her?"

"I didn't mean to," he claims. "She just..." He finishes the rest of the alcohol. He grips his hair. "I'm over my head here and need to win her over. She's stubborn."

Let's see how much he trusts me.

"How did you get her on the boat if you haven't won her back?"

He leans against the wall. "We said we would work on things."

Liar.

"How is what you just did working on things?"

He scrubs his hair. "Look, Kade, I'm frustrated, all right? She wants to take things slow and hold on to a grudge."

I sit and point to his chair.

He takes the seat.

"She's like my little sister. Don't lay a hand on her again."

"I won't. I didn't mean to, but you know how she is."

Time to buy time.

I force myself to chuckle. "Yep."

"I want things back to the way they were."

"It isn't going to happen overnight if Gracie is upset with you."

"I'm sick of waiting."

"She just stepped on the boat today. Give her some time."

He takes a deep breath. "She's had enough time."

"If you try to force her, she'll end up hating you. You don't want that, right?"

"No. I love her."

My gut twists at his admission.

You love her, but you just hurt her. You sick son of a bitch.

"You'll get a lot further if you let her call the shots. In fact, by the time we get to Monte Carlo, everything could be like you never split if you let her think she has the power."

Fisher scrubs his face and groans. "She hates me right now."

Because you're a piece of shit.

"No, she doesn't, but now she's scared of you, so you've gotta cool it and give her some space. One thing you don't want is your woman scared of you, unless you want blue balls all the time."

Fisher snorts. "Good point."

I wait for him to ask me what I want him to.

"Will you talk to her for me?"

"Give me your word you won't hurt her again, and you're going to ease off while we're on the yacht. One thing I don't want is any woman on this ship unhappy. All our lives are going to be miserable if any of them are."

Fisher grunts. "True. All right. You've got my word."

"I'll handle her, then. Give her space while on the yacht to do things her way then surprise her with a hotel room or something in Monte Carlo. You'll be in her good graces again if you just give her the upper hand until we get there."

"Good idea. I'll book a suite in Monte Carlo."

"Perfect. Just cool it until then." I don't trust Fisher as far as I can throw him, but he isn't typically stupid. Hopefully, he'll follow my directions.

We have a drink then head out to the front of the ship for dinner. Gracie is sitting with Monica. Her blonde hair is blowing in the wind, and her blue eyes are full of fear and worry.

Get back in the game, baby.

I tear my eyes away from my beautiful woman and focus my attention on Monica.

When Fisher asks to talk with Gracie, I tell her to go and make sure I direct her to only a few feet in front of me.

I don't want her anywhere near Fisher, but it's necessary if we're all going to get through this and eliminate him from ever coming after Gracie again.

Watching her kiss Fisher is a mix of pride and pain. She's playing the game, and, after what he just did to her, I'm sure her skin is crawling. The same reasons cause me pain.

When the four of us sit down for dinner, I sit across from Gracie, with my leg against hers, trying to give her some sort of comfort.

From time to time, our eyes meet, and I remind myself to tear them away from her.

After Fisher has enough drinks, and is buzzed, I drop a small, tasteless pellet into his glass. It instantly melts into the liquid.

He passes out in the main room, and Monica pretends to as well so I can get Gracie alone.

"Walk?" I ask her.

"Sure." We go to the one place without any cameras. It also is completely covered and is a cabana at the stern, facing the water.

It's pitch black outside. There's a soft glow from the moon and no one is around. If Fisher questions it, I'll tell him I was having my talk with her which I promised him I would have.

We lie down in the cabana, and I hold her in my arms and kiss her deeply. "You okay?"

She's shaking both from the cold and what I assume happened

today. She snuggles deeper into my arms. "Yeah. What did they do to Connor?"

"They beat him, but Javier texted he's okay. They're keeping him overnight at the hospital, but he should be able to go home tomorrow."

She puts her hand over her mouth and tears fall.

I caress her head and back.

"He's a monster," she whispers.

"Yes."

"I didn't want to kiss him. I—"

I put my finger over her mouth. "We're playing the game, baby. Necessary evil. When we get to Monte Carlo, just do what I tell you, and this will all be over."

"What are you going to do?"

"I can't tell you. But you trust me, right?"

"Yes."

I kiss her again, feeling like I'm in heaven even though we're in the middle of hell.

"No matter how strange something sounds, if I tell you to do something, don't think about it. I need you to promise me."

"I promise."

"Even if it means leaving me behind."

Her body stiffens, and she cups my face. "Kade, what are you talking about?"

"Just promise me."

"Kade—"

"Trust me and promise me. And I need you to stick to it."

Her lip shakes. "I promise."

I stroke her head. "Good. And no matter what I do here, don't ever forget I love you."

"I won't. I love you, too," she whispers.

I kiss her and restrain myself from taking it any further, but my cock is hard as a rock and pressing against my zipper.

"Tell me what you've been doing while I've been gone."

She lifts her head off my chest, and the light in her eyes ignites. "I bought us a house today. Well, you bought us a house."

"Yeah?"

"Two doors down from Hudson and Lena."

"The two-story, circle driveway?"

"Yes."

"I've always loved the outside of that house. What's it like inside?"

We talk all night about our future, and when the darkness begins to turn into light, I make us go inside and into our bedrooms. Before we leave the cabana, I give Gracie one last kiss.

It's a kiss of hope and promises and all the love I feel for her. It's a kiss for our future. That is what she is...my future.

And I vow to make sure when this is over, Fisher and no one else ever touches my woman again.

2 8

Gracie

FOUR DAYS IN, AND I'VE MANAGED TO STAY IN FISHER'S GOOD graces.

It's strange. Kade and Monica act like a couple. They kiss. They touch each other. They whisper and laugh together.

I do the same with Fisher, avoiding Kade's gaze whenever I can.

After the first night, Fisher snorted cocaine so he wouldn't fall asleep. He didn't even hide it from me. As I gaped at him, Monica mumbled, "Here we go," and Kade muttered, "Fuck."

"When did you start doing coke?" I asked him.

"Don't be a prude, Gracie. Take a hit. You'll love it."

"No, thanks."

How did I hang out and sleep with him all these years and not know he was a cokehead?

The alcohol continued, and all night we had to party with him. As usual, he tried to feed me as many shots as possible, but Kade and Monica usually ran some interference.

Last night was a repeat. Tonight, he's out of coke, thank God. But he isn't out of alcohol.

Fisher reaches into a drawer and takes out a deck of cards. "Let's have some fun tonight."

I'm sitting on his lap and tilt my head. "We've not been having fun?"

Since arriving on the yacht, there is a side to Fisher I've never seen. He was always a big drinker, but it becomes apparent he was hiding his other party habits from me, and I'm now seeing the true side of him.

I can only imagine what Kade has been a part of, but I push it out of my mind, acknowledging he doesn't want any of this and only wants to be home with me.

Over the last few days, I've played the game. Monica was right. I give Fisher a little bit and also pump up his ego, and he's been happy. Every day, I give him a little more. When he tried to go a bit further this morning, I thanked him for giving me time and not pressuring me to do more before I'm ready. He surprised me and told me to take as much time as I need.

I'm not sure what Kade said to him, but whatever it was, it seemed to have a good effect. He's been nothing but nice and sweet like he used to be with me.

He arches his brow. "I think it's time for poker."

"Where are the chips?" I ask.

He snaps the spaghetti strap of my dress and leans into my ear. "Strip poker."

I elbow him, thinking he's joking. He's not. And there is no getting around it.

The four of us are soon in a game, and, one by one, articles of clothing come off.

Monica and I are both down to our undergarments. Kade is in his boxers. Fisher chose to remove his underwear but kept on his shirt. His dick is hard, and he proudly sits with it in full view.

I'm trying not to ogle Kade's glowing torso of muscle, across from me. From time to time, I catch the heat in his eyes as he peeks at me. My body is throbbing for his, and I'm scared if I have to take my panties off. They're wet from the longing I feel for Kade. He's so close but since the first night, I haven't been able to touch him. The last thing I want to do is have to throw my damp panties on the table.

Monica loses, and her top comes off. Fisher, who's very drunk, fixates on her breasts.

She has nice ones, I'll admit it, but Fisher is licking his lips like I'm not even here.

My gaze catches Kade's, and he rises. "Drink?"

"Hit me!" Fisher yells.

Kade slides a drink at Fisher and then makes one for the rest of us. Within minutes of drinking it, Fisher passes out on the poker table.

Monica goes to the closet and grabs robes for all of us.

"Walk?" Kade asks.

"Yes."

We are careful not to touch as we make our way around the ship but soon end up in the cabana.

The second we lie down, he rolls me on top of him and glides his hands under my robe. "Stay quiet, Gracie," he murmurs, and my loins burn from his kiss so powerful, I'm breathless and trembling in his arms.

We don't wait. His cock is hard and dripping with pre-cum. I dip down and suck on his cap then lick his salty shaft before taking it all the way to the back of my throat.

He groans then grabs me and shifts me into the sixty-nine position.

My pussy sinks on his face, and he holds me tight and steady, flicking his tongue through my wet folds and sliding it into my sex.

I gasp with his dick in my mouth, as he rolls my clit with his finger and fucks me with his tongue while sucking on my hole.

I climax almost instantly, shaking violently on him, which causes me to suck him harder while deep-throating his cock.

The ocean wind is cold, but our bodies are infernos of lust and longing. Pellets of sweat pop out on our skin.

After I have several orgasms, I think he's going to release in my mouth, but Kade repositions me. "Ride me, Gracie," he murmurs, and I take all of him in one movement.

"Oh God, Kade," I moan, and he tugs at my nipples, rolling them in his fingers.

The boat sways from the rough sea, and I topple forward.

Kade holds me tight, pulling my bottom lip in his teeth.

My sex clenches on him as I grip his hair, arching my back from the roll of endorphins bursting through me.

He scrapes his teeth on my neck then sucks on my collarbone.

His hands grab my hips and thrust me faster as he bucks up in my downward movements.

"Kade...oh...oh...ohhhhhh," I breathe into his lips as his cock pounds into my G-spot, and I shatter on him,

"Shh," he reminds me and devours my mouth as if I was the most delicious food on earth.

His fingers inch so they're cupping my ass, and I change the movement and circle my hips faster on him.

He groans. A deep, delicious, throaty groan that stirs new flutters in my stomach.

I circle faster. Our warm breath merges as one, and Kade pants harder.

When his cock shoots his hot, thick stream in me, stretching my walls, I convulse in his arms once more.

I collapse on top of him, trying to catch my breath before he kisses me like there's no tomorrow.

Footsteps approach and men's voices are muffled, and Kade puts his hand over my mouth and holds me tight with his other arm.

Our hearts beat against one another as our eyes widen and lock into the other's.

"Nicky, something isn't right about Coral. I can't figure it out, but it's nagging me."

"You're paranoid. Fisher would never let anyone on this boat without a full background check on them."

"I've seen him before. I'm sure of it," the gruff voice insists.

My insides quiver, and Kade's arm tightens around me.

"He's not to be trusted. I'm going to talk to Fisher tomorrow."

"Jack, I think you're paranoid," Nicky repeats.

"No. The more I'm around him, the clearer it gets. I'm so close to remembering where I've seen him."

There is silence.

"How long have you known me?" Jack growls in a low voice.

"Forever."

"Have I ever been wrong?"

"No. You haven't," Nicky says, and my stomach drops.

"Tomorrow then. First thing tomorrow, we go to Fisher."

"All right."

The sounds of footsteps shuffling away echo in my ears, and an extra minute passes before Kade removes his hand from my mouth.

"Kade—"

"Shh." He ties my robe around me then kisses me deeply. "I'm going to escort you to your bedroom, and you're going to bed."

"Why? What are you going to do?" My voice shakes.

"Go to bed, Gracie. Don't come out until the sun is shining, and Fisher comes into the bedroom."

"Kade?" I question. My stomach flips and a sharp knot forms in my throat.

"We have to go. You get up first and remember not to touch me once we leave the cabana."

"Kade, you're scaring me."

"Don't be. Remember your promise to do what I say and

follow me blindly. Even if you're scared or it doesn't make sense. If Fisher asks, we were here, and I was encouraging you to be with him...to get over your anger toward him for leaving you. If he questions what they said, Jack and Nicky discussed Fisher getting arrested in Monte Carlo. Say you didn't understand it all."

"What—"

He puts his finger over my mouth. "Bedtime."

One last kiss leaves me breathless. I tighten my arms around him, not wanting to let him go and scared of what might happen.

We stroll around the deck once, and when he murmurs, "Go to your bedroom," I blink hard, willing myself not to shed a tear.

"Good night. I love you," I whisper.

"I love you. I'll see you in the morning."

I do as Kade asks, forcing myself not to look back, remembering the cameras in the hallway, watching us. I don't sleep, and when the sun rises, Fisher isn't in bed.

I get dressed and wait for him, pretending to read a book, but it's almost noon when he finally arrives.

His eyes are bloodshot. Tiredness looms over his face, and traces of blood are on his hands.

"Fisher," I cry out, and run to him, my heart beating in my chest and praying the blood isn't Kade's. "What happened?"

His eyes turn to slits. "Come with me."

My pulse increases, and I thickly swallow. "Where are we going?"

"Stop asking questions." He grips my arm tightly and leads me out of the bedroom.

Every bad feeling I could ever have permeates all my cells, and all I can think is, "Please let Kade be unharmed and alive."

29

Kade

My cover is about to be blown. The time I have is limited, and as soon as I drop Gracie off, I go into my bedroom and rub lotion on my hands.

Monica sees me, and her face pales.

It's a lotion for emergencies. All I have to do is wave it under Fisher's nose, and he'll wake up.

"Stay in here. Jack and Nicky are suspicious about me. They are going to blow my cover. I'll be in later."

Her eyes widen, but she doesn't question or stop me.

I grab my gun and leave. As soon as I enter the main room, I pat Fisher on the back and put my hands close enough to his nose so he can smell but not so much any cameras would think I'm doing anything except trying to wake him up naturally.

When his eyes open, they're groggy, but I quickly show him my gun, and they widen.

"What the fuck, Kade," he barks.

"Do you not background check your men?" I snarl.

His forehead creases in a deep line. "What are you talking about?"

"Gracie and I were on the deck, talking. I was trying to convince her to let her anger toward you for leaving her go. Nicky and Jack crept up on us. They didn't know we were there."

"And?"

"They're law enforcement."

His face drains of color, but he only stares at me. Part of it is him coming out of deep sleep, and part of it is his shock. Nicky and Jack are two of his top guys.

I slam my hand on the table and yell, "Wake up."

Fisher jumps and rises. "You're sure?"

"Yes," I say through clenched teeth. "I heard them talking about the chemicals and arresting us once we get to Monte Carlo, and they can notify their boss."

The Internet is still down. I've been itching to get on it and enter the code Lena gave me, but I am grateful to use this to my advantage.

"Which agency are they working for?"

"Not sure."

Fisher and I trot through the halls and into his office. He hits a button on his phone.

"Boss," a voice answers.

"Take Nicky and Jack into the pit."

"The pit?" the voice says with surprise and dread.

"Yes, now," Fisher barks.

"Y...yes, boss."

"Those motherfuckers," Fisher mutters under his breath, anger burning red on his face.

The pit is below the deck of the ship. It's a small room boasting black walls, entirely made of concrete. Plastic covers almost every inch of the room, waiting for its next victim. Some men survive it, as it's used to maintain order as the Twisted Hearts do. Others breathe their last breath in it.

When we get there, Nicky and Jack are already in the room, standing with their arms crossed over their chests. Normally the ones to "maintain order," they don't see anything coming.

"Boss, come to watch?" they say, thinking they are going to be the givers of the punishment.

Fisher says nothing, and when they see me enter the room behind them, both their eyes turn into slits.

"Coral," Jack's menacing tone mumbles under his breath.

Four more men enter the room.

"Who's the offender?" Nicky says, but his question doesn't come out sounding confident. Instead, there's a hint of uneasiness.

Fisher turns to his men. "Tie them up."

"Boss?" Jack cries out, and Nicky's eyes widen.

Chairs in the middle of the room are no longer bare, as Fisher's thugs shove Jack and Nicky both into one then tie them with ropes as they protest.

"Take it like a man," Fisher yells out, his eyes red with rage, and they immediately shut their mouths the way Twisted Hearts are trained to do. "Who do you work for?" Fisher demands.

"You, boss," Jack and Nicky say in unison.

I would feel bad for the miserable pricks—their loyalty is after all to Fisher and they've done nothing but their job—but they're just as evil and dangerous as Fisher. Their time on earth has been spent terrorizing innocent people, so I have no mercy or guilt for their blood being shed.

The next few minutes are chaotic and desperate as they try to convince Fisher I'm the traitor and not them.

I stay calm, acting as if I have nothing to worry about or defend myself from, but as they get tortured over the next few hours and don't change their story, the atmosphere shifts.

"He was with your woman, why is that? Think, boss!" Jack blurts out with blood dripping all over, his face a mangled mess.

Fisher stops and turns toward me.

For the first time, I feel a panic in my gut.

He assesses me.

"You asked me to talk with her and have your back. I already told you what we were doing out there."

In the next few hours, Fisher goes between Jack and Nicky and me. Their argument is compelling. Physical harm doesn't make them change their story. The longer it goes without them giving Fisher a different story, the more Fisher questions me.

The sun rises. I can't see it, but the hours have passed undoubtedly created morning light. Fisher suddenly does what I hoped it wouldn't come to.

"No one leaves."

A thick ball forms in my throat, and my pulse throbs in my neck as I wait for what feels like hours.

Fisher finally reenters the room, dragging Gracie behind him.

When she sees the scene, she puts her hand over her mouth. Plastic, bloody men—both Nicky and Jack tied to chairs and Fisher's thugs—are a scene I never would have wanted her to witness. My stomach knots, and my heart aches watching her tremble in horror, but Fisher holds her firmly, not letting her leave. Then she sees me against the wall, and I do everything I can to keep my face hardened and show no emotion.

Gracie's eyes fill with tears. I restrain myself from reaching out to her. Her face turns green, and I think she might throw up.

"What happened on the deck?" Fisher asks her.

She says nothing.

"Answer me," he screams right in her face, and I clench my fists then quickly relax them before anyone can notice.

"Wh...what do you mean?"

"What were you doing there?" Fisher seethes through clenched teeth.

Come on, baby. You can do it.

"T...talking to Kade."

"About what?"

"You."

He steps closer, and his tone softens. "What about me?"

Her eyes never leave his. "Kade told me to forgive you."

Fisher takes a deep breath. "What did you hear or see when you were out there?" He puts his hand on her cheek.

"I...I..."

"Tell me," he quietly says.

Her bottom lip shakes.

Fisher turns slightly to Nicky and Jack. "Did you see them?"

"No," Gracie whispers.

His eyes turn to slits.

"I only heard them," she quickly adds.

He calms. "Okay. What did you hear?"

"I...I didn't understand it all. They said something about you being arrested when we got to Monte Carlo."

His face hardens. "Why didn't you come for me?"

She trembles. "K-Kade told me he would handle it with you. He said you would want me to stay in the bedroom, so I did."

Fisher strokes her cheek then steps forward and kisses her.

The number of times I've watched him kiss Gracie over the last four days hasn't numbed the jealousy or distaste residing in the pit of my stomach. Gracie is playing the game, something we have to do, but watching him kiss her and seeing how frightened she is requires every morsel of my restraint not to kill him with my bare hands.

Tears stain her cheeks as he releases her. "Go back to the bedroom."

She turns, briefly catching my eye, but I don't allow myself to dwell on her terror filled, blue eyes.

A knife rips through my heart and twists slowly. For the rest of my life, those eyes will haunt me.

Visibly shaken up, she leaves the room and the metal door slams.

Fisher turns to me. "You discovered the traitors. You kill them."

Without hesitating, I remove my gun from my pocket and shoot a bullet in both Nicky and Jack's heads.

Fisher spits on them and motions to his men. "Clean it up." He turns to me. "Let's get some sleep."

30

Gracie

FEAR DRIVES ME TO IGNORE MONICA WHEN I PASS HER IN THE hallway. In a trance, I go directly to the bedroom, as Fisher instructed, trying not to look at the cameras. If I say one word to her, I'm going to break down.

Tremors roll through my body, and I sit on the end of the bed with my hands clasped together so tight my knuckles are white.

It's only a few minutes before Fisher comes in. I avoid his eyes, scared of what I might reveal in my own. He goes into the bathroom, showers then comes out in a towel and sits next to me.

"You're shaking," he states in a gentle voice.

I can't respond or stop trembling even though I tell myself to, in fear it may anger him.

He draws me into his chest, and only then do the tears fall.

"Shh. Everything will be fine."

I don't want his comfort or to be in this game any longer. More than ever, I want out. But I can't.

"Gracie, look at me," Fisher demands.

I slowly obey.

"I'm sorry you had to be a witness to traitors."

I only nod.

"Have you slept?"

"No," I whisper.

"You need to sleep. You'll feel better when you wake up. Take your clothes off and come to bed with me."

I don't argue with him. The only vision in my head is of blood, and doing anything that isn't what he wants frightens me.

All I want is to see Kade and make sure he is okay, but I'm scared to ask Fisher without raising any suspicions about us.

I strip down to my undergarments and crawl into bed. Fisher removes his towel and climbs in next to me naked. I turn so I don't have to look at him. He embraces me tightly, and I cringe inside.

There's a knock on the door. Fisher groans. "Come in."

Kade steps in, and I blink fresh tears, relieved he's alive and safe.

He focuses on Fisher. "Is your phone working?"

"No."

"Amaro left a message, but it's cut up. Something about changing the time of our meeting tonight."

Fisher sighs and gets out of bed. He crosses the room naked, grabs a piece of paper off the desk, then hands it to Kade. "Put this code into the firewall. You should be able to get around anything blocking your access."

Kade reads it. "I'll confirm with Amaro, and then I'm getting some sleep before we dock." He starts to shut the door, but Fisher stops him.

"You want the bullets?"

"The bullets?" Kade asks.

"The ones you put in their heads."

Kade killed them.

I should feel some sense of horror, but I don't.

"No. I don't need trophies of traitors."

"Suit yourself."

"I'll see you when we get to Monte Carlo."

"See you in Monte Carlo."

The door shuts, and Fisher climbs into bed. I pretend to fall asleep within minutes, but the feel of Fisher's body pressed against mine is like plastic suffocating me. After several hours, I slide out of his grasp and sneak out to the outside deck. Wrapping myself in several towels, I curl up in the cabana Kade and I were in the night before, wishing I could feel his arms around me. It doesn't take long before I fall asleep.

I don't wake up when we dock. It's only when Monica gently shakes me, I wake up.

"Everyone is searching for you. Fisher and Kade are panicking."

I sit up and rise to my feet quickly, filled with anxiety. "I'm sorry," I whisper, scared of what Fisher may do.

"It's okay. Don't freak out."

I take a deep breath.

"Are you doing all right?"

"Yes," I lie.

"Did Fisher try anything?"

"No. I snuck out while he was asleep."

"Good. We have to leave in an hour, so focus on getting ready. Hopefully, everything will be over tonight."

"I hope."

"Kade told me to remind you that whatever he tells you to do, don't hesitate or question it, no matter his request."

Even if it means leaving me behind. Kade's voice echoes in my ears, and my heart drops.

"Don't let him stay behind on his own, please," I beg her.

She wraps her arms around me and hugs me. "Trust him, Gracie. Whatever he says, no matter what you think, do without question."

I pull out of her embrace. "Okay." We amble toward the bedrooms.

"When I say I need to go to the restroom, say you need to go as well and come with me."

"Why? What will happen?"

"Can't discuss anything."

I sigh. *So many secrets and lies.*

"Let's go get ready. Dress to impress tonight, and whatever you do, don't get into a situation where you're left alone."

Panic fills me. "What do you mean?"

"Amaro and his men think women are disposable. There are no boundaries and they are extremely dangerous. Stay close to Fisher, Kade, or me."

My insides quiver. "Okay."

We pass one of Fisher's thugs in the hallway. "Everyone is looking for you."

"She was getting some air. Leave her be," Monica states.

He grunts, and we pass him.

When we get to Fisher's bedroom, she cheerfully says, "I'll meet you in the main room. Tonight is going to be so much fun! You'll love Monte Carlo."

I force myself to appear excited. "See you in a bit."

Fisher comes around the corner. "Where have you been? I've been worried sick."

I step into the bedroom and say, "I fell asleep in the cabana."

"Why were you outside? Were you trying to get away from me?"

I spin into him and put my hands on his cheeks. "No. I needed air. I...I just kept smelling blood." My gaze drifts to the floor, and I blink hard. It's not a lie.

He sighs and cups my cheeks. "Are you feeling better now?"

"Yes."

"Are you going to ask me?"

Ask him what? I tilt my head in question. "About?"

"Why it happened?"

I bite my lip and focus on his chest.

He tilts my chin up. "Bad men got through my security. They wanted to set Kade and I up and harm us."

"Okay. Thank you for telling me," I quietly respond.

He kisses me. "Get ready. We can't be late. You're going to love Monte Carlo."

"I'm sure I will. Monica told me a lot about it. I'm excited."

"You are?"

"Yes."

"Good. I have a surprise for you tonight."

Great.

"You do? What it is?"

"You'll see. Go get ready."

I peck him and go into the bathroom. As hot water cascades over my skin, I scrub it hard. I didn't have any blood on me, but I feel dirty.

I go through the motions and get ready. My dress is a long-sleeved black cocktail dress with a boat-neck collar. I wear a garter belt and stockings since Fisher had it sitting on the bed when I got into the room.

When I step out of the closet, Fisher whistles in approval then comes over and kisses my collarbone. "There's my sexy girl."

"Thanks. You look nice, too." He's wearing a tux.

We don't stay in the room long, and when we get to the area of the boat to leave, Kade and Monica are there.

My heart flutters when I see Kade. He's wearing a black tux. I've never seen him in one. His eyes scan my body, but he's careful not to linger.

The game continues. Monica is on Kade's arm, and I'm on Fisher's. We leave the dock and get into a black car.

Fisher and Kade talk business in the vehicle. If I didn't know any better, it would sound legitimate, but I do. I spend most of the ride facing the window, taking in Monte Carlo. It's a beautiful coastal city. I wish I could be here only with Kade and not have to deal with whatever we're involved in.

I still don't have details about what Fisher is involved in, but my stomach is flipping with anxiety over what may happen tonight.

We arrive at the casino. Both Fisher and Kade seem to be familiar where they're going. It's elaborate, smokey, and loud from all the gamblers until we get to the private room in a restaurant.

Two men and two women are sitting at a table. Two guards stand against the wall.

A man in a designer tux, with salt-and-pepper hair, and cold, almost black eyes rises. When he's introduced to me as Amaro, he checks me out and leans in to kiss my cheek.

I shudder slightly, and Fisher pulls me closer. "Cold?"

"I'll be all right."

Kade glances at me, and we lock eyes for a brief moment.

We finish introductions and take our seats. I sit between Fisher and Kade, feeling slightly less anxious with Kade close to me.

"I need to go to the ladies' room," Monica says.

Play the game.

"I need to go, too."

Fisher is in an intense conversation with Amaro about storage. "I don't have any idea what it means…" He pauses when I get up. "Where are you going?"

I lean down and kiss him. "Bathroom with Monica."

He hesitates.

Kade rises. "I'll show them where it is."

Fisher gives his approval and returns to his conversation with Amaro.

We leave the room. Kade stands between Monica and me. He leans into me. "You're stunning."

Little flutters erupt.

"Whatever the man says to do, don't question it," he says.

"What do you mean? What man?"

"No questions, Gracie."

We turn the corner, and the elevator opens. A man with a striking resemblance to Javier, but maybe a little older, is inside. He's wearing all black.

I look at Kade in question, and he nods to the man. "Get in."

As soon as I step in, the man pushes a button, and the doors slide together. I turn and see Kade's face on the other side. "I love you," he says, and the doors snap shut.

"Kade," I cry out and lunge for the doors, but the man grabs my waist, holding me tight.

"You have to come with me," the man says.

"No! We can't leave him!" The elevator moves up.

"We have to. He will be fine."

"No," I sob in fear he'll die, and I'll never see him again.

We don't stop on any floors, and the lift opens up on the roof.

A helicopter sits on a landing pad, loud and with the blades circling fast.

The man continues holding my waist tight and maneuvers us into the helicopter. The door shuts, and my tears fall, as we fly away from the building, Monte Carlo, and Kade.

Several hours pass in the air. I sit next to the man, gazing out the window and down at the ocean, praying Kade will be okay. I'm so distraught about leaving Kade, I don't even ask the man any questions about who he is or where we are going.

He finally says, "I'm Andre."

"I'm Gracie," I sniffle.

He smiles. "Yes. It's nice to meet you."

Andre...

"Are you...you're Javier's brother?"

"Yes, ma'am."

"What is Kade doing?" My tears fall again.

"He'll be okay, I promise."

In the middle of nowhere, a vessel appears, and Andre dons a harness and hands one to me. "I need to help you put this on, ma'am."

"I...I don't understand."

He gestures to the ship. "We need to get down there."

I gape at him. "From the air?"

He grins, and once again, I'm reminded of Javier. "You'll be attached to my harness, ma'am. I won't let anything happen to you."

While my heart pounds, he wraps the harness around me and secures it then attaches it to his.

"It's going to get a bit windy. Hold onto me," he instructs, reaches for a rope dangling from the ceiling, and grabs my waist. "Wrap your arms around my neck, ma'am. You can close your eyes or bury your face in my neck if you wish. It's best if you don't look down."

Whatever the man says to do, don't question it, Kade's voice echoes.

I do everything I'm told, and the door opens. With my head crushed into Andre's neck, we are lowered over the ocean. My pulse is racing, but I feel safe with him. When our feet land, he unlocks my harness, and he says, "Ma'am, I need you to let go now."

Slowly, I lift my head but not before yelling, "Thank you."

"You did great, ma'am." He lets go of me, and I'm instantly dragged back as Javier comes into my view. The men quickly embrace, and then Javier retreats, and the man gets raised into the helicopter.

In a trance, I watch. When the copter flies away, I turn and realize Ryland is holding me. Chloe, Javier, and Connor are standing several feet away. Connor's face is bruised from the attack. I run over and cry as I hug him. He groans and informs me he has several broken ribs, so I release my tight grip on him.

I suddenly realize I'm on Kade's yacht.

But where is Kade?

31

Kade

GRACIE CRIES OUT MY NAME, AND IT RINGS IN MY EARS AS THE elevator door shuts, tugging at my heart.

She'll be safe now.

Javier Lòpez's brother, Andre, is another former Marine sniper and now on the rescue team for Interpol. He was the only man I trusted to be able to safely remove Gracie from this situation.

And now I need to end it. Fisher will never again set eyes on, much less touch Gracie.

I motion to Monica, and we head into the room and take our seats.

"Where's Gracie?" Fisher asks.

"Restroom," I say like it isn't a big deal.

"You left her there?"

"Didn't realize there was a problem with her being in the bathroom by herself? This is a safe place, or is it not?" I ask him.

His face turns white.

That's the problem with kidnapping people. They don't want to stay with you, dickhead.

"She's fine," I say, craving to put the bullet in his head before I get my cue.

Patience, Kade. You need to get the info off him first.

The code Lena gave me isn't what I thought it would be. Once Fisher gave me Internet access, I spent hours entering it into the dark web. I tried it in every possible spot, and nothing worked.

The code is for something, but I'm not sure what and I'm no further ahead.

So we haven't found out where the Twisted Heart Elites are storing the chemicals, and until I get the information, my job isn't done.

But I also only have so much time. Once Fisher realizes Gracie is gone, I'll be out of it to get the information Interpol needs. And that can't happen because one thing I did hack into once I got Internet access today was another chat room I discovered.

All the plans for what the Elite want to do with the chemicals opened before my eyes, and as I read them, my stomach twisted so fast, I thought I might get sick.

There's a new drug in town, and it has the potential to be more profitable than any street drug could ever be. And it would be legal.

Over the years, the scientists they employ have been working to create a drug that doesn't cure but extends people's lives. The people who would need to take these drugs would have been exposed to the chemicals the Twisted Hearts have been buying and storing.

The reason we had to meet Amaro is to spread out the stockpile of chemicals Fisher has been buying so they can release it in the air and create a chemical warfare similar to a pandemic. The second an individual breathes the contaminated air, it'll penetrate deep into their muscle tissue, causing the most horrid of symptoms.

The new drug will cover up symptoms and extend lives. It's proven to work and is in production. It's a drug you would have to be on for life, creating a never-ending supply of money to the manufacturer.

Fisher is the owner of the company. He's already filed and owns the patent. My guess is it will make him one of the richest men in the world.

And I was part of getting more chemicals in their hands from my undercover duties.

Since finding out the real reason Fisher has been stockpiling the chemicals, my guilt has shot even higher. That's the thing about being a spy. If you're one of the good guys, the sin of what you have to do to get the job done grows with time. And the guilt of what you've done eats at you like a caged animal that hasn't had any food, clawing and growling to devour its prey.

I sit casually in my chair, listening to the conversation between Amaro and Fisher, watching Fisher nervously take in Gracie's empty seat, getting more and more agitated by her absence.

"Five destinations have been secured with underground tanks —Russia, South Africa, southern Germany, China, and Brazil," Amaro informs us.

"We've always done an exchange in international waters. We need to maintain the ability," Fisher replies.

Amaro shrugs. "We will. Ships are already set up for the exchange."

My pulse increases. "Good. The new supply I secured will be available in two months. Fisher said we need to move the existing supply. Where are we transporting it from?"

"The U.S.," Fisher responds and looks at Gracie's seat again.

He hid it in the U.S.?

I try to hide my surprise. I assumed it was in South Africa or

Russia, maybe somewhere in South America. "What port in the States would I be picking it up from?"

"Florida," Fisher mumbles and turns toward the door.

Florida? It's been in my own backyard the entire time?

"What port?"

Fisher rises. "I'm going to check on Gracie."

Monica stands. "I'll go get her."

Fisher stops, and his eyes form slits.

A chill runs down my spine. *Shit. It's too early for this.*

Monica puts her hand on his arm. "Stay in your meeting. I'll go."

"Why are you so eager?"

Her eyes widen. "I'm just trying to help."

"Fisher, sit down. Let the women be women," I tell him.

Amaro laughs.

Fisher takes a deep breath and nods to Monica. "Fine."

"Maybe you should get a leash," Amaro taunts.

Fisher's face reddens, and he scowls at Amaro but sits.

"I'll see you in two minutes," Monica tells Fisher.

So close to this being over.

Fisher is jittery, Amaro keeps discussing plans with me, and the manager comes in to do a customary check, along with a server refilling water and two servers with trays of salads.

"So what port in Florida?" I ask again.

Fisher cocks his head. "It's on a need-to-know basis. I'll tell you once you need to know."

"How am I supposed to make plans?"

"I'll send coordinates a week out prior. You'll have plenty of time."

As planned, Monica reenters the room in not two minutes but four. As soon as the door opens, I cringe. I still don't have the exact location, and the only option is to end this show now, or we're going to end up dead once Fisher registers Gracie is gone.

In a swift move, the manager pulls out a gun and shoots the

man next to Amaro. The waiters grab theirs and shoot the body-guards. Monica shoots Amaro point-blank in the head, and the fake waiters turn on the screaming women and escort them out of the room.

Silencers are on all the guns. The only person left alive is Fisher, and my gun is aimed right at his head.

His eyes are wide, and he holds his hands in the air.

"Where in Florida," I bark out.

"You fucking traitor," he says through gritted teeth, his face almost purple with anger.

"Where?" I yell.

A calm goes over his face. "What did you do with her?"

I smack the butt of the gun in his face, and blood spurts everywhere. He coughs, and I hold it again to his head. "Where in Florida?" I repeat.

"What did you do with Gracie?"

Rage from hearing her name on his tongue and everything he's put her through takes over. I punch his face so hard, I hear his eye socket crack. "Don't you speak her name."

Fisher wails in pain.

I wait for him to quiet because I need him to tell me the location but also so he can feel more pain.

He composes himself. "Ah. I see it now." A sinister grunt rico-chets in his vocal cords. "She's your whore, too?"

Smack. My fist pummels his face, and one of my hits breaks his nose.

He only seethes, "You know when she comes, she screams out my name, right?"

Bam. Another blow further damages his eye socket.

"Where in Florida?" Monica asks, reminding me we still haven't discovered the exact location.

"Her nails dig in my—"

Boom. My bullet goes directly between his eyes, and he falls forward on the table.

"Piece of shit," I mutter and watch his blood soak the tablecloth.

"Hold your hand out," Monica says and brings me out of my trance.

I hold it out as she pours water on it then uses a napkin to wipe as much blood off of it as possible.

We make our way through the casino quickly and get into a black car waiting at the curb. We ride to a private airport where a helicopter is waiting. We only speak once we get inside.

"Where in Florida do you think he has it?" Monica asks.

I rub my hands on my face. "Could be anywhere, but we can rule out the swamps."

"Do you think anyone else is aware of the location and can release the chemicals?"

My stomach twists. "God, I hope not."

My phone beeps. I read the text message. "Interpol raided Fisher's boat. They are going to send his computer and our stuff."

"Good."

"How bad was it when I wasn't there?"

Monica's eyes turn emotionless.

My gut drops. "What did Fisher do to you?"

"I just had to play the game like all the other women."

I sigh. "You okay?"

She gazes out the window. "Yeah. It's what we do, right?"

More guilt crashes through me, just imagining what she had to do to keep Fisher happy. She was supposed to be my girlfriend, but it wouldn't have stopped him from trying to have her when I was gone. "I'm sorry I had to leave you."

"Nothing to feel guilty over. We did our job and now he's dead. Another person who shouldn't be on earth isn't. End of story."

I stay quiet. It's never the end of the story. The secrets and lies don't just vanish. I worry about how Gracie is going to be affected by everything she saw and had to do to play the game and survive. And I hate myself for not being able to protect her from it.

"Are you really done now?" Monica quietly asks.

"I won't infiltrate anymore. I'll still be a part of Interpol but only to work on cyber issues and I'm not traveling. I'm never leaving Gracie again."

"Gracie's a really great girl. I wish you lots of happiness."

"Thank you. What about you? Are you tired of this life yet?"

She sighs then shakes her head. "I'm not done until I find the storage location and the black book. And there's still a handful of people I need to take out."

"Who?"

"Someone in the Twisted Hearts who needs to pay for their sins."

I grunt. "Isn't that all of them?"

"Some of them deserve it more than others."

Gracie

"Connor." I hug him, and he winces again but returns my affection.

"I'm so sorry I didn't stop them," he says and guilt riddles his face.

"Stop. There was nothing either of us could have done."

"I should have stopped them."

"How? It wasn't possible. Stop blaming yourself."

"Did he hurt you?" Ryland asks.

The memory of Fisher's hands makes me hold my throat. "I'm fine."

"You didn't answer my question," Ryland growls.

"Kade was there."

Ryland is about to say something else, but Chloe puts her hand on his arm.

"I'll have the captain send the coordinates over," Javier says on his phone and hangs up.

"Is that Kade?" I ask, hope filling my chest.

"No. But Interpol is sending things from Fisher's boat over, so my guess is he will be here eventually."

Please, Kade. Come home to me in one piece.

Javier meets my gaze. "He'll be fine."

I release a nervous breath. "Your brother seems nice. He resembles you."

Javier nods. "You should see my other brother. We look like twins. Andre is the oldest."

"He seemed sweet."

Javier grunts. "Not sure he'd want you to call him sweet."

"He kept calling me ma'am."

"That would be Andre. He was in the Marines for years."

"And now?"

"Same organization as Kade but on the rescue mission side."

The noise of a helicopter makes us turn, and a box hooked to a line is lowered. Ryland and Javier release it, and the helicopter flies away.

I ask Chloe, "Why aren't the helicopters landing?"

"They have to record it if they land."

"And landing is bad?"

"Sometimes," she quietly confirms.

The darkness of the night grows, and everyone goes inside except Connor and me. I don't have any proof Kade will be here or even come tonight, but I can't seem to go inside. So I take a seat at one of the tables.

"I really am sorry," Connor repeats for the millionth time since I landed on the ship.

I grab his hand. "Connor, there is nothing to feel guilty about."

He swallows hard and briefly closes his eyes. His face looks painful, and bruises are all over it.

"There..." He stops and takes a drink of his beer. "I found something out about Novah."

My chest tightens, and my pulse increases. "What?"

"She was with Fisher."

My gut drops. "What do you mean?"

"She slept with him. And she worked for him."

Blood pounds in my ears. "What kind of work?"

"Fisher hired her to sleep with me."

"What? Why?"

"It's how they followed me. She told them."

"No. Oh God, Connor, I'm so sorry." I squeeze his hand tighter.

His jaw clenches, and he taps his fingers against his beer bottle while studying the night sky. "We were only having fun, but I can't believe how stupid I was."

"Connor, you can't blame yourself. I was with Fisher for years and was blind to his association with the Twisted Hearts. And Kade met Novah and never put it together."

He takes a sip of beer.

"How did you find out?" I ask.

"I saw her text messages. She pretended to be concerned for me when I returned from the hospital. When Hudson dropped me off at my place, I forgot the bag of creams and bandages in his truck. She went to get it and left her phone. It beeped right when she left, and I grabbed it to run out to her, but the message from Fisher was on the screen."

My heart sinks. "I'm sorry. If anyone understands how it feels to be tricked, it's me."

"I don't know. I think Fisher loved you in his own fucked-up way. It's not an excuse, but I was just a pawn to Novah."

"Did you love her?"

He shakes his head and quietly says, "No. There's only one girl I ever wanted to get serious with, and it wasn't Novah."

"Who?" I wrack my brain, trying to figure it out.

"No one you ever met."

"Connor—"

"Let's drop it," he says and takes another swig.

The sound of a helicopter fills my ears, and I jump out of my seat. A light shines on the deck, swirling around until it stops on the same area I landed in. A faint silhouette appears and two bodies wrapped around each other are lowered.

Connor makes me wait with him until the harnesses get released. The light leaves along with the helicopter.

Within seconds, I'm in Kade's arms, and nothing has ever made me happier. When he sets me on the ground, he kisses me, and every atom in my body lights up.

"Gracie, you're okay?" he asks.

"Yes. You?"

"Fine, baby."

"Is it over?"

"He's dead."

Once again, I surprise myself by feeling no remorse or sympathy for Fisher. "Good. So it's over?"

"Not totally but enough I'm done infiltrating."

"You are?" I ask him with an overwhelming feeling of relief soaring through my bones.

His lips create another heat wave in my loins. "Yeah. Time for us."

When he releases me, I realize Monica is next to him. "Sorry. Glad you're safe, too." I hug her.

We turn, and Connor is frozen.

Monica gasps.

"Gia," Connor mumbles as if she's a ghost.

"This is Monica," I say.

"Oh shit," she whispers so quietly, I almost don't hear her.

Connor's eyes move into slits. "Monica?"

"Connor—"

He tears his eyes away from her and embraces Kade. "Good to see you."

"You doing all right?" Kade quickly glances between Monica and Connor.

"I'm fine. Thanks for finding me."

Kade winks. "Thanks for calling me."

Connor hardens his expression, turns in the opposite direction from where Monica is standing, and takes off.

"Connor," Monica calls out.

"Not interested," he growls.

She follows him.

Speechless, I watch them, wondering how they know each other, and why did he call her Gia? And anger mixes with my confusion. She's hurt Connor somehow. I can tell. I turn. "Kade—"

He holds his hands in the air. "Gracie, I don't know anything. I swear. But it's between them."

He's right. I let out a deep breath. "Okay."

The heaven of his arms hold me. "Let's have one night we don't worry about anyone else."

I kiss him. "I think that is a great idea."

He wiggles his brows. "I think we have a cabana to break in."

EPILOGUE

Kade
Two Months Later

FIRE BLAZES FROM MY TOES THROUGH ALL MY VEINS AS IT DOES every time I kiss Gracie. I hold her in my arms and hardly hear the clapping and celebratory shouts.

My wife.

I should pry myself away from her since everyone is watching, but it's nearly impossible. When I finally do, her blue eyes are shining, and her face is glowing.

"Still clueless," I murmur against her lips, and she softly laughs.

"Still sexy as hell."

Fuck it. I devour her lips once more, holding her body so close to mine, I'm going to have to try and hide my erection when I finally release her.

When I do tear myself away, I wrap my arm around her waist, and the perma-grin I've been wearing all day hurts my cheeks.

Everyone I love is here. It's only my parents and the Brooks family. My family. And now it's official.

I guide Gracie off the beach and through the small crowd of people into our house.

When I set the bank account up for her, I didn't doubt she would find the perfect place. After all, anywhere with her would be. But from the moment she told me about it, I imagined how we would make it ours.

There wasn't a lot to do to the house, and the few things that did need to be updated the Brooks family quickly helped us do to get ready for the wedding.

We stayed on the yacht until things were ready and moved in a few weeks ago.

As I swore to Gracie, my days of infiltrating are over. I'm still working on cyber issues and trying to locate Fisher's underground supply, but, so far, nothing has come up. And there is still one promise I made to Gracie I haven't figured out yet—why was the Brooks family ever targeted by the Twisted Hearts?

Our family follows us into the house, set up for our reception. Gracie, like Gabriella, didn't want anything over the top. So food and music playing from our surround sound are what we have. And it's perfect, just like my bride.

As the afternoon turns into night, I've lost track of how many times I've kissed, or winked, or got caught ogling Gracie.

Everything I've ever wanted, I now have.

It's getting late. Both our parents have left. Gabriella and Javier took their new baby girl Taytum upstairs to sleep, and everyone else is cleaning up.

The doorbell rings, and the hair on my neck stands up.

Who would be here this late?

"I'll get it." Connor goes to the door, but I follow him.

"What are you doing here?" he asks.

I put my hand on the side of the door and open it wider.

Monica. Or Gia.

She still hasn't told any of us her real name, so I call her Monica. It's what I've always called her and until she reveals more, it's what I'll continue to call her. It bothers Gracie, but I'm okay with it. I understand the spy game. Connor, on the other hand, always calls her Gia.

I still haven't learned what happened between them or how they even crossed paths. Connor refuses to discuss it, and she won't, either.

"Kade, I'm sorry, but I have to talk to you," she says in a voice I've never heard from her before. Usually, her voice stays in control unless she's playing the game. Right now, she sounds rattled and terrified.

"It's okay, come in."

At the same time Connor steps forward and pulls her into his arms while blurting out, "What's wrong? You're shaking."

She sobs into his chest, and he tightens his hold and kisses her head. "Tell me what's wrong, Gia," he quietly says.

"I...I..."

"It's okay. Tell me."

She tries to shrug out of his grasp. "I need to talk to Kade. Alone."

He hesitantly releases her but guides her inside.

When we're alone in the study, with the doors shut, I ask her, "What's going on?"

Her hand flies over her mouth in horror. "Oh God. I'm sorry. It's your wedding day, isn't it?"

"It's okay. Just tell me."

"I'll come back another day."

I reach for her arm. "Monica. Stop. Tell me what's going on."

Tears stream down her face. "I...I stepped over my limit."

A thick knot forms in my throat, and I swallow hard. Limits are set to make sure you don't do anything irreversible you can't get out of or would hate yourself for. I had a limit once. I crossed it when I sold Fisher chemicals so I could get into his world, but I felt like I had become Satan himself when I did it. "What did you do?"

"I...I..." She covers her face with her hands.

I embrace her and stroke her hair. "Shh. It'll be okay. Tell me what happened."

"I wanted to find out where the underground storage was. And...and I did."

"That's good."

"It's...it's a part of you."

"Part of me?"

She swallows. "The black book..."

She's not making a lot of sense, but the hairs on my arm stand up. "Okay."

"But..." she sobs.

"Tell me what limit you stepped over."

A river runs down her face, and she steps away from me. She turns and with shaking hands, tugs a small portion of her pants lower, exposing the part of her body where her lower back meets the top of her ass.

A fresh Twisted Hearts tattoo, vibrant with color, glistens against her skin. "I...I had to take the vow."

Ready for Connor Brooks's story? Read ROOTS OF VENGEANCE, book six of the TOGETHER WE STAND series - click here.

ROOTS OF VENGEANCE BLURB

TOGETHER WE STAND SERIES - BOOK SIX

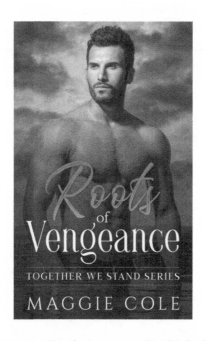

Nothing about Connor Brooks is average. Not his looks, or kisses, or touches.

He's my target. Falling in love isn't part of the assignment.

My job is to determine if he's a Twisted Heart, the vicious gang who killed my family.

He's innocent, but discovers my secret.

My cover is blown. My heart shattered.

But I annihilated his.

Going forward, I tell my boss to only give me the most dangerous men.

Until they cease to exist, I won't stop.

Three years later, Connor reappears in my life.

My actions are unforgivable. I've crossed the line of no return.

But the fire is hotter than before...

And Connor claims he'll pull me out no matter how deep I've fallen. But I don't know how.

(**Roots of Vengeance is the sixth installment of the *Together We Stand* series. It's an epic journey of one family's struggle of forgiveness, hope, and new beginnings amidst dangerous situations. Each story intertwines and focuses on a new sibling trying to find their Happily Ever After.**)

Read ROOTS OF VENGEANCE, book six of the TOGETHER WE STAND series - click here.

ROOTS OF VENGEANCE SNEAK PEEK

PROLOGUE

Connor Brooks

Deception camouflages reality. When women are involved, the mask can be so alluring, you never see it coming.

Soft hair in your hands, the scent of skin flaring in your nostrils, the curve of a waist, trace of a finger, and lips, tongues, and teeth are so vigorous, Satan himself would be blinded.

The worst lie is the one you tell yourself.

It's just for fun and doesn't mean anything.

Whoever said karma is a bitch was right. Twice I've lied to myself. Twice I've been bitten. Twice I've fallen hard...in so many different ways.

The pain I felt when the Twisted Hearts ran Gracie and I off the road then beat me and left me to die... I prefer over the emotional anguish of discovering the woman you're sleeping with double-crossed you.

When I found out Novah was sleeping with me because Fisher paid her, it crushed me. My sister was abducted because I wasn't able to protect her. My body was battered and bruised. My ego was beaten. Novah was instrumental in it all. But the real stinger was it wasn't the first time I slept with someone who tricked me.

The only good thing about the Novah situation was the pain of my broken body, mixed with my hurt heart, didn't feel as gut-wrenching as when Gia did it.

Or whatever her real name is.

Gia. The thought of her to this day sends my blood reeling. That blood is toxic. It has anger, love, lust, and pain swirling in it. And time hasn't done one thing to make it any less potent.

I've accepted the fact she is never coming back. Hell, I don't know who she really is, and I'm better off without her.

Gracie asks me if I'm in love with Novah, and I tell the truth. The answer is no. There's only one girl I've ever wanted to get serious with, but she's gone.

And then in the dark of the night, it's as if the devil himself is listening and has to stoke the fire in hell where my heart currently resides. Gia falls from the air, clinging to Kade.

Long, black hair flies in the wind.

Skin golden and glistening with diamond dust shimmers.

Red, pouty lips haunt me, and all I want to do is lick and suck them.

And dark eyes burn into my soul.

I must be seeing things.

The toxic blood returns, pounding in every shred left of my heart. It's like a hurricane spiraling violently, and when Gracie calls her Monica, the anger and pain wins.

I need to get out of here.

"Connor," Gia calls out.

"Not interested," I growl.

Blood pounds in my ears, and when I get to the stern, I crouch, screaming, "Fuck," forgetting my ribs are broken and then wincing in pain on my way up.

Grasping my side, I lean against the railing, and, when I spin, Gia is in front of me.

"Connor," she quietly says, her eyes wet, and hesitantly reaches to my bruised and still slightly swollen cheek. "What did they do to you?"

Don't fall for her again.

I clench my jaw and close my eyes, trying to regulate my breathing. When I open my eyes, I see hers full of worry and regret. It almost shatters me all over again.

I stay silent. Afraid of what I might say.

Her hands worshipped my body like no one else's and when they cup my face, the intoxicating power of her scent makes my body ache.

She swallows hard then licks her plump, juicy lips. Her warm breath merges into mine. "I'm lost without you."

Heaviness grows in my chest, stealing the air from my lungs, making it hard to breathe. I lash out, "Would that be Gia, Lexi, or Ana? Or maybe Monica?"

Pain crosses her face. I've hurt her. It should make me feel better, but it doesn't.

Not as bad as she's hurt you.

Like the temptress she is, she composes herself and presses her body against mine.

Anger, betrayal, and lust mix in with her deception, and when she pulls my face to hers, I don't stop her. Instead, I roughly slide my hand through her hair, firmly gripping the back of her head and shoving my tongue in her mouth the moment our lips make contact.

She moans and trembles in my arms, and any sense of control I have is gone.

I spin her to face the railing. Her ass is against my groin, and I move her hair aside and suck on the curve of her neck. "Is this what you want?"

"Yes. Oh God...yes," she cries out.

I kick her feet wider and splay my hand on her spine, holding her down against the rail then rubbing my erection against the split of her ass. "You miss this?"

A cold breeze blows off the ocean, and she shivers hard, her body reacting to mine the way it used to.

I tug at her hair, pulling her head so I can see her face. "Answer me."

"Yes," she cries out. "I miss you so much."

I release her and step away, chest heaving and pain shooting through my broken ribs, my cock harder than ever. "You'll never have it again."

As I stomp across the yacht, her voice, calling out my name, reverberates in the air.

And that's all it's ever going to be. An echo of what we once were. A faint memory of what could have been but never really was.

Nothing involving deception is real.

And I hardly survived her the first time. So I'll be damned if I go back for round two.

Read ROOTS OF VENGEANCE, book six of the TOGETHER WE STAND series - click here.

MORE BY MAGGIE COLE

Behind Closed Doors (Series Four - Former Military Now International Rescue Alpha Studs)
Depths of Destruction - Book One
Marks of Rebellion - Book Two
Haze of Obedience - Book Three
Cavern of Silence - Book Four
Stains of Desire - Book Five
Risks of Temptation - Book Six

Together We Stand Series (Series Three - Family Saga)
Kiss of Redemption- Book One
Sins of Justice - Book Two
Acts of Manipulation - Book Three
Web of Betrayal - Book Four
Masks of Devotion - Book Five
Roots of Vengeance - Book Six

It's Complicated Series (Series Two - Chicago Billionaires)
Crossing the Line - Book One
Don't Forget Me - Book Two

ACKNOWLEDGMENTS

To my friends who read several drafts and kept pushing me to make this novel better, I thank you!

To my editors, cover artists, beta team, launch team, and author friends who shared so much wisdom with me, I thank you!

To my readers; from the bottom of my heart, I thank you! I sincerely hope you loved this novel. I can't wait to share all the new stories and characters I've been creating for you!

ABOUT THE AUTHOR

Maggie Cole is the pen name of a multi-faceted woman. She's an entrepreneur at heart and loves writing contemporary steamy romance novels that help her readers feel lots of different emotions. Sometimes you'll laugh, sometimes you'll cry, sometimes you'll have little flutters racing through your veins...and that's Maggie's biggest wish for you when you read her novels.

Maggie loves to interact with her readers in her Facebook Romance Addicts group so click the icon below and join!

She's a wife, mother, and lives in the sunshine, where she can often be found staring off into space while creating new scenes in her mind.

Made in the USA
Coppell, TX
07 March 2022